AF508476
OTEL

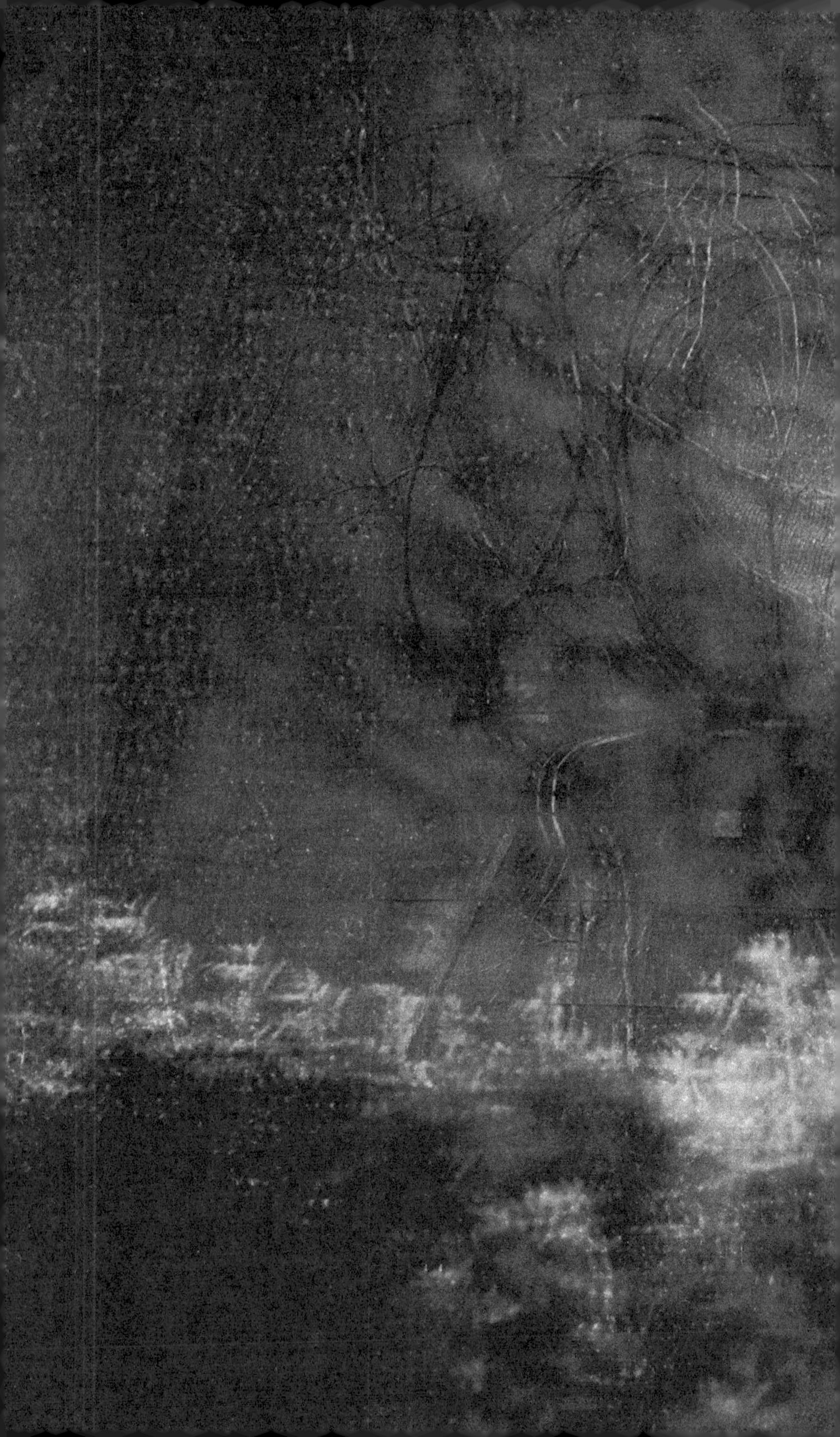

Mayhem Motel

Static

MARIE ANN

Copyright © 2026 by Marie Ann

ISBN: 979-8-950195-00-6
Cover design: waesmilesreads
Editing: Tiff Writes Romance
Formatting: Marie Ann

Blurb

The first time I laid eyes on Madison Payne, I knew he was mine.

He was such a surprising little treat to find within the walls of Mayhem Motel. Devoured by his fear, he became so malleable and submissive... *for me.*

I couldn't possibly let him go.

But then he left, and I had no other choice but to find him again—by any means necessary.

And I did.

His fear consumed him once more, but he fell into me with a beauty and grace I could've only dreamed of.

I finally found the parallel to my shadow.

And now, we return to Mayhem. Back to where we began.

Because he's the rapture I need, and I'm the nightmare he wants.

PLAYLIST

Knife Prty—Deftones
Foxglove—Boston Manor
Closer—Nine Inch Nails
Nazareth—Sleep Token
Consensual—Landon Tewers
What Do I Say (fear. Seanzy)—Landon Tewers, Seanzy
Slaughterhouse (feat. Bryan Garris)—Motionless In White, Bryan Garris
Cold—Static X
Discourse Is Dead—Architects
virgins go to hell—eli.
Custer—Slipknot
Your Dress—Unprocessed
Nihilist—Architects
Korea—Deftones
Unwelcome—The Plot In You
Stalker—J Swey, Azide, Blak Trash, Lox Chatterbox
Children Of Cybertron—Emmure
Infamous—Motionless In White
Disappoint Me—Left to Suffer
My Way—Limp Bizkit
Nocturnal Flame—The Word Alive
Left For Good—Bad Omens

You've Seen the Butcher—Deftones

Lost In The Static—After The Burial

Coming Undone—Korn

Sin—Serinx

Suck My Blood—Kuoga., Wite Katt

Loverboy—You Me At Six

BFBTG: Corpse Nation—Motionless In White

Glitch—Parkway Drive

City Lights—Motionless In White

Cracks—Killstation, Joei Razook

Freak On a Leash—Korn

Freakstreet—Highly Suspect

Scattered Shit—Landon Tewers

Infiltrate—OmenXIII

EYE SPY—Night Lovell

Bleach—Kingdom Of Giants

Boogie Woogie Wu—Insane Clown Posse

Middle Fingers Up—Attila

Ted Bundy—socliché

The Cycle Of Violence: Chapter 1—Varials

Outsider—Veil Of Maya

Rocket Skates—Deftones

Bodies—Drowning Pool

Angel Eyes (feat. Chris Motionless)—New Years Day, Chris Motionless

Voices And Vessels—A Bullet for Pretty Boy

Cry Little Sister—Marilyn Manson

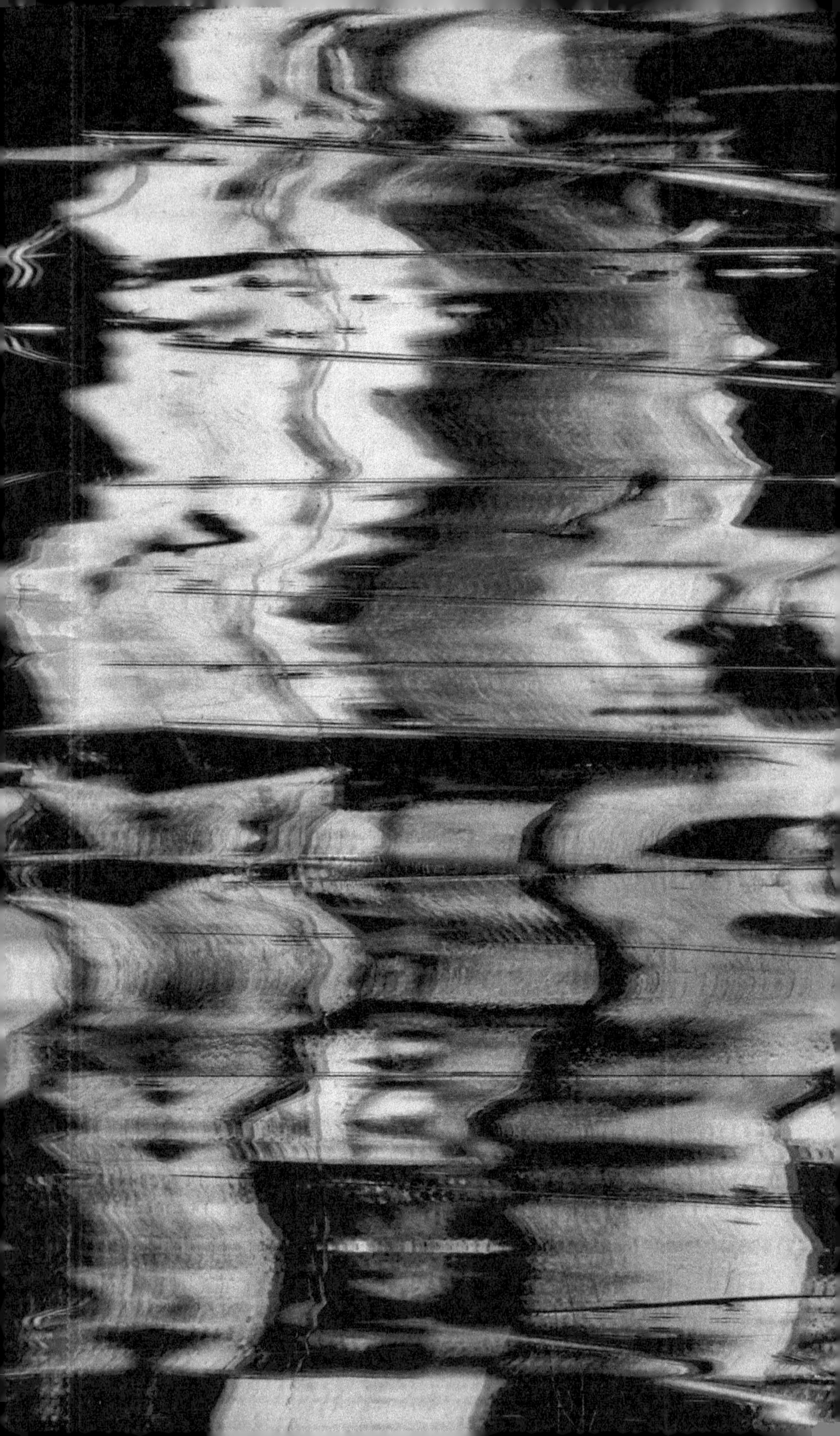

# Dedication

To Rae. Static is forever yours.
And to Cait.
Thank you both, so much.

"Hey, wanna play? And yes I do wanna play. I really really do."
—Dexter Morgan, *Dexter*

Author's Note

Are y'all ready for my crazy boy Static?

If you read the Phobia Anthology I was a part of, then you know this has been a long time coming. It took me a while to get here, but I finally did—with the support of all of you, so thank you for that.

In this story, you'll meet Cedrick Vinton. *gasp* Yes, that's Static's name. And you will see how absolutely *obsessed* and lovesick he is for Madison Payne.

And Madi... Well. The poor boy is just really going through it. But the way Cedrick is there for him... Fuck. I am not kidding you when I say they are so sickly sweet, it'll make you sick.

Are you ready to be equal parts scared and turned on??? 🌝

Now, on the next page, you will find a list of possible triggers and other content warnings. It does contain spoilers so keep that in mind before viewing. If you have any questions, don't hesitate to reach out to me at authormarieann@gmail.com!

Content Warning

The content within Static is dark and may be triggering for some readers.

Below, there will be a list of possible triggers and specific content within the story, but please be aware they contain spoilers.

Coulrophobia (fear of clowns), haphephobia (fear of being touched), physical violence, dubious consent, non-consent, psychological/mental manipulation, stalking, bodily fluids, orgasm denial, jealously, sex with other people while MC's are not in a relationship, religious trauma, forced proximity, over the top possessive/obsessive behavior, mentions of past mental health issues, mention of alcoholism, anxiety/panic attacks, verbal/mental child abuse, reference to homophobic slurs, references to internalized homophobia, sadism/masochism, blood play, water sports, rope play, collaring/ownership, hide & seek, pain kink.

PROLOGUE
SWEET LITTLE SURPRISE

My sweet, little treat.
I've fuckin' missed you.

My lips twitch, curling upward as I watch him through the pane. Sweat beads across his forehead, glistening in the pale, yellow light above. His small, delicate hands press together, fingers wringing with uncertainty as he drops his head to stare down at his phone on the floor.

I know what he's staring at. What's making him act this way.

Me.

Always me.

I huff in amusement, dragging the back of my hand over my forehead to catch my own perspiration, uncaring that I'm smearing my makeup. My work clothes cling to my damp skin, made worse by my exertion and excitement as I shift on my haunches, gloved fingers wrapped around a thick branch.

It's fuckin' hot, even with the sun long gone and a cool breeze flitting through the branches I've made a home in. But it's worth it—just to see that look on his face.

"Fuck," I groan as Madison dips down to pick his phone back up, those blue eyes so fuckin' wide. My smile grows larger the longer he stares, that fat fuckin' lip clamped between those pretty, white teeth.

And then, his thumbs are moving.

"Gotcha, darlin'," I whisper, mouth filling with saliva.

My phone vibrates in my pocket. I drop my knee to reach inside.

> DARLIN:
>
> Please leave me alone.
>
> Look, I don't know how

Madison's text is cut off mid-sentence, but there are three bubbles underneath. I glance up, finding him pacing his room, hunched over with his chin digging into his chest as he types. I press my tongue to the roof of my mouth as I rake my gaze down his lithe body, vividly remembering his taste.

It's so easy to imagine him strapped to a leather table, completely exposed and vulnerable, his body trembling... *Or better yet... back on that dolly.*

Static sparks on my tongue, filling my brain and my blood.

> DARLIN:
>
> I think I do know how you got my number.

Laughter fills my chest. I wedge my foot between two thick branches so I can use both hands to type. But before I do, I look up at him to watch every emotion he possesses pass over his face in such a short span of time.

He has no idea how magnificent... how perfect *he is for me.* How he gave me something I've always needed *instantly.*

He's crazy if he thinks I'm going to give him up.

ME:

Hows that, darlin

His hands stop shaking for a moment, seemingly stilled by what he's reading. My heart chugs heavily beneath my sternum, the *glug* of my blood thicker than ever as it travels south.

And then, his eyelids flutter closed, dark lashes a shadow across his cheekbones. I skim my tongue along my teeth, burning to sink them into his flesh again.

The glass pane separating us is mere feet away... All I'd have to do is reach out, and I'd be able to get to him. To touch and taste and *take.*

My eyes roll back as I drop my head between my shoulders and sink my teeth into the flesh of my cheek. Copper explodes on my tongue, making me groan.

Every second that passes, it gets harder and harder to stay away.

But I love to play... *and he's finally playing back.*

My phone vibrating draws my eyes back open.

DARLIN:

You broke the rules.

I chuckle loudly, feeling mad. At this point, I don't care if he hears me right outside his window.

ME:

Did I

He has no idea how many "rules" I've obliterated to have him—the ultimate faux pas in my world... well, in both worlds. And I should probably care more than I do, which ain't at all.

DARLIN:

My information wasn't yours to take. It was
only for the experience thing.

His rounded jaw is set tight, and his knees are locked. But
his eyes... The eyes never lie. And his are still glassy with the fear
I remember tasting so good.

But fuck, it does feel good to fake it, so I can't really
blame him.

ME:

Everything of yours is mine to take

And I want another taste

Madison's phone drops from his trembling hand, landing
with a jarring thud on the carpeted floor beside his feet once
more. He turns his back on me to sit sideways on the edge of
his bed as voices shout from downstairs. They're barely audible
with the walls between us, but Madison yells in response before
falling back, his hand pressed to his sternum.

My fingers curl into my covered palms, the pointed tips of
my gloves pressing in. The pain is dull with the fabric between
the areas of contact, but I relish in it all the same.

I have the perfect view—from the crown of his head down
his entire body. Of his thick, mousy brown hair, which is plastered to his sweaty forehead, and his small hands, which
tremble as they lift the hem of his red t-shirt to undo the
button on his jeans. He plants his bare feet on his bedframe as
he snakes his arm over and down his stomach, fingers grazing
bare flesh before they disappear beneath his waistband.

My eyes light up, dancing with pleasant revelation as I
watch my little treat... *play with himself.*

Oh, he is such a sweet little *surprise.*

Teeth puncture the thin flesh of my bottom lip as I lean toward the glass, needing to touch him. My gloved fingertips nearly drag across the pane, leaving invisible streaks in my wake.

My mark. *One of many to come.*

Madison's neck arches, exposing tendons and veins and muscles that *need* to be sunk into. Bruised and bloodied and delicate. My cock is throbbing where it's trapped within my pants, and my fingers twitch to pull it out, but I suck in a breath, reining in what little bit of control I have left to *watch.*

Just watch...

Because he's the rapture I need, and I'm the nightmare he wants.

CHAPTER ONE
THE PROSPECT OF THE UNKNOWN

MADISON

THREE WEEKS BEFORE

"Madison, get down here!" Mom's shrill voice punctures my ear drums, yanking me out of sleep. In an instant, I'm on my feet, blinking blearily through dawn's early light as I stumble to the door. I'm running on years of pure instinct alone as I pull the door open and rush down the stairs, knowing my time is limited before she screeches again.

"Mad—"

"Sorry, Mother," I pant. "I'm here."

"Were you *sleeping?*" she asks, like it's such an improbable notion. I swallow down the urge to bite back, so I slip my bottom lip between my teeth and rub the sleep from my eyes. Once they're somewhat cleared, I look out the large bay window behind her and frown.

"What time is it?"

"Six thirty."

I blink slowly. "Okay... Y-yeah," I clear my throat. Might as well be honest. Either way, I don't get anywhere. "Yes, I was sleeping."

"Why on earth were you sleeping?!"

I wince. "I—uh, I'm sorry."

"You have that meeting with Pastor Laurence at seven to get your materials together for college!" Her face twists into an indignant frown of disappointment before she looks away to sip her tea, feigning cordial behavior once more.

My heart throbs in my chest, and I press my palm against it, but it doesn't ease the ache. It never does.

"I-I'm sorry. I forgot." *I can't tell her now. She's already so mad...* My eyes sting with the reality of what's to come. Of what I'm about to do to her and Father... to our family.

Their inevitable disappointment.

"Where's Father?"

"At the church," she sneers like I'm stupid. "They're setting up for vacation bible school, remember?"

"Am I to help with that, too?" I ask as I drop down in a seat opposite her. As I reach for the coffee that's set out beside the tea, Mom slaps my hand away with a loud huff. I retract with a wince, rubbing my hand. She grabs the juice instead and fills my glass without a word. I frown at the orange liquid, staring as it settles in the crystal.

"Watch your tone, Madison."

"I'm sorry. I'm tired."

"An excuse."

"Yes," I concede, because it is. *I am.*

"Well, eat! You're going to be late enough as it is."

"Yes, ma'am." I bring a piece of toast to my plate and take a bite of the dry bread, chewing through the paste with a lead weight in my stomach. As I'm shoving the last bite in, all too aware of Mother's eyes pinned to the top of my head, a knock sounds at the door.

"Get that, would you!" Mom shouts at Roman. My eyebrows furrow as I trace the wood grain.

"Pastor Laurence, ma'am." Roman nods before exiting, closing the sliding doors behind him. The large room, encased mostly with glass windows, suddenly feels so small, too hot. Goose-flesh prickles along my exposed forearms, and I'm more than aware of my messy bedhead. I reach up to smooth it the best I can.

"Hello, Pastor. Good to see you." My mother pushes from her chair. "Madison," she hisses, and I'm instantly reminded of my manners. I shove away from the table, and the scratch of the chair legs against the wooden floor brings a flush of heat to my cheeks as I reach out to shake the pastor's hand, hating the way my stomach aches and my body feels too hot, heart hammering erratically in my chest.

"Good morning, Pastor."

"Madison." He nods.

"What brings you by?" I feel my mom's glare like hot coals on bare skin.

Pastor Laurence can't hide his confused frown. "Our meeting, of course. With you starting college this fall, we've got to get your materials ready to go. Starting with your required internship with me throughout your first year, which is namely what I wanted to discuss today."

I incline my head toward the sitting room, adjacent to the dining room. "Let's head in here."

I feel Mother practically hovering on the other side of the

door as Pastor Laurence drones on about his expectations and requirements. I stare intently down at the paper clamped tightly between my fingertips to keep me from wringing them, but I only succeed in crumpling it.

Nausea swirls the more he talks, the guilt of what I've done. I can take it back—I don't even have to go. But the truth is, I *want to.* I don't want to be here anymore. I don't want to pretend I believe in a god that probably hates me.

I can't stand more of Dad's indifference and Mom's shrill disappointment. Of Pastor Laurence and the church, thinking they know best.

I just... *want to be free.*

The longer I stare at the black words on the crisp, white paper, the less I see. The less it all seems to matter.

I thought applying to university would be the scariest thing I'd ever do. Just taking that step of defiance, to prove I'm not so helpless, but then, I *got in.* I actually got accepted. And the rest... spiraled from there. It's all sort of a blur now. I'm not really sure *what* I was thinking, but it's too late to go back now —and I don't really want to, either.

I'm set to move in with my roommates at the end of the week because school starts in a month, and they all said it was okay if I moved in a bit earlier than normal. I wanted time to... *acclimate.*

The only problem is, Mother and Father don't know. And when they find out...

"Madison..." Pastor Laurence drawls, "are you feeling all right?"

I didn't realize before, but my breaths are labored, puffing out between my lips in loud exhales. Sweat clings to my skin, dampening my palms and making me feel clammy. I swallow tightly and lift my head with a weak smile I'm sure is more of a grimace.

"Actually, no. I feel quite ill. Would you mind if we continue this later?" His frown makes me wince. "Or, actually, this is fine."

"Of course not. Go on up and rest." He clasps my shoulder tightly, knocking me off balance as I try to stand on my shaky legs. His salt and pepper beard blurs before his lips move, but I don't hear a single word. And then, he's gone, and I'm alone in the large room, which feels more vacant, yet much smaller than normal.

"*What* was that about? What is going on, Madison? Why did Pastor Laurence just leave?" Mother storms into the room, hands on her hips, tendrils of her long hair billowing out behind her. I stare forward, not really seeing anything in front of me—but I can feel *everything*.

My heart *hurts*, hammering painfully against my ribs, the beat throbbing its way into my neck and up to my temples. My stomach lurches, cramping and twisting into a Palomar knot. I clutch my midsection, hoping to ease the pain with pressure.

"Madison Thomas!"

"I-I'm sorry," I stutter, my fingers joining to wring together. Blood rushes in my ears. "I have to go." I swallow against the lump lodged in the back of my throat.

"What on Earth are you talking about?"

"I'm leaving," I rasp, nearly passing out once the words leave my lips... but their exit is a crushing weight lifted off my chest. I suck in a startled breath, nearly laughing at how light I feel already.

For the first time in my life, my mother is quiet. I feel her eyes glued to my face, but my own are locked on the open door in front of me. I've had most of my things packed for weeks, not really ready to finish because I didn't even know if I'd be able to do this. Too scared of myself, but this fear is better than the fear they bring me, than being stuck in this life.

"*What?*" Mother's voice obliterates my train of thought. Every muscle locks tight, tensed in preparation.

I'm not sure how I manage to choke out the words, but somehow, I find the will. "I got accepted into university. I found a place to live, so that's where I'm going. I..." Tears spring to my eyes as I look around the room. The only home I've ever known, filled with more memories of fear and shame than anything remotely good. A home filled with a god I no longer believe in—and that almost hurts worst of all.

"I-I don't want to be h-here anymore, so I'm leaving. Today." That wasn't the plan, not even close. I only hope my new roommates let me move in a bit earlier... maybe if I give them a bit more for rent.

A newfound burning anxiety settles just beneath my flesh at the prospect of the unknown I'm about to traipse into. But I welcome the sensation with open arms—because it's better than this, than the look Mother is pinning me with. So like all the rest, cold and unloving.

I spin on my feet and race through the rooms and up the stairs, nearly slipping on the stone as I whip around the corner, choking on my heartbeat as it throbs in my throat. Mom is screeching my name, heels clicking loudly across the granite. My door clicks closed, and I turn the lock before reaching for my phone and dialing the number for one of my soon-to-be-roommates.

"Sup, man."

"Kane?" I croak. "It's, uh, it's M-Madison." My fingers clamp around my nape. Sweat clings to my clammy palm as I rub back and forth. "Madison Payne. We, erm. I'm—"

"Our new roommate, yeah, I know who it is. I have your number saved." He chuckles lightly, making me flush with embarrassment.

"R-right. Sorry, I—"

There's a short, tense pause. "Is everything good?"

"No, yeah. No, everything—everything's good. I was just, I just... I was hoping to ask a-a favor, if that's not too much—"

"'Course," he responds easily, making my breathing a bit easier.

"Right, okay. So, uh, something's come up, and well, I was hoping it..." The sound of Mom's heels sound in the hall outside my door, and my stomach lurches. I slam my lips together. Fearful vomit is going to spew up my throat any moment. I breathe heavily through my nose, forcing as much air in as I can, hoping it curbs the waves that nearly blind me.

"Madison?"

"Jus'a sec," I rasp as I sink my teeth into my bottom lip. Spots dance behind my eyelids as she hammers on my locked door.

"Madison, get out here right now! I'm on the phone with your father, and he'd like to *speak to you.*"

Oh, God.

"Is everything okay?" I can barely hear Kane over my mother. I drop onto my bed and yank a pillow over my head to muffle the sounds.

"Yeah. I'm sorry. Can I move in?" I blurt.

"Uh, yeah? I thought that's what was going on." He laughs, and it sounds warm.

"I mean like... now." I scrunch my eyes shut, preparing for the refusal.

"Yeah?" he says it like a question. "I mean, I don't suppose why not. It's not like anyone else is living here. Hold on. Let me ask."

I tap my fingers against the pad of my thumb, back and forth, over and over, counting to five and back down.

"Hey, guys!" Kane shouts. He must be holding the phone against his chest because it's muffled, but I can still hear everything. "Do you care if Madison moves in early?"

"Don't give a shit."

"Sure."

"Come on over, buddy!"

"Yep, all good with us. When were you thinking?" Kane starts talking again like there wasn't a lapse in the conversation. I heave out a large breath as tears spring to my eyes. My throat is closed off, but I try not to let it sound as I answer him.

"T-today?" I stutter. "I live a few hours away, and I have to finish packing, but I can be there later." It doesn't come out as more than a whisper, but that doesn't seem to bother Kane, which is... *nice.*

"Sounds good. Why don't you just text me when you're leaving so I can make sure we're all home to help you get your shit inside."

"W-wow, really?"

He chuckles. "Yeah, man."

"Oh, uh, okay."

"Cool. See you in a bit, Madison." A click sounds, and then, the call disconnects. I leave my phone pressed to my ear because the quiet lingering is a much better sound to focus on than Mother screaming outside my door. But after a few minutes of her continuous comments, I push the pillow away and walk to the door.

Placing my palm against the wood, I drop my forehead to it. "Mom."

"Madison!"

I wince, eyes scrunched shut. "Please stop." I hate the tears I feel brewing.

"I certainly will *not!* This is absurd! Your father's on his way home—in the middle of work, mind you—to deal with this!"

That means I have a half hour at most, with traffic this time of day. I let my head drag against the wood a moment before I push back to grab my bags shoved in my closet. They're heavy as I set them on my bed, then look around my room, feeling oddly detached.

Most of the things I own aren't even *mine.* They're just things Mother used to "decorate," and I don't feel much of anything knowing I'm leaving it all behind.

It takes less than ten minutes to gather the rest of my things, packed in one last smaller bag. My eyes catch on my Bible on my nightstand. The weathered, maroon cover, the thin pages filled with highlights and pen marks, tabs in place for reference.

A book of *lies.*

And yet, I still grab it anyway, shoving it in the front pocket of my backpack beside my phone charger.

With my keys fisted, I grab all four bags and hobble toward the door, already feeling the strain in my arms. Mom's eyes shoot wide when she sees me, stepping back. Probably more out of shock than anything else, but I try to ignore it, regardless.

I don't make it more than three steps down the stairs before she's trailing me, screeching and screaming. I can't even make out what she's saying through the blood rushing in my ears and the curdling in my gut.

My car is a beacon as I hobble down the stairs, focusing on

not slipping and breaking my neck—which seems entirely plausible. God has an ironic way of punishing those he deems have wronged him, and I'm sure me turning my back would constitute as such.

When I reach the foyer, my gaze catches Roman's, the butler, where he stands near the front door. His old eyes are crinkled at the corners. They seem a bit sad but a bit proud—or at least, that's what I hope. I offer a weak smile in apology, which he returns with a silent nod of his head, and then, he holds the door open for me... *At least one person wants me to go.*

The acceptance of that is enough to fuel me the rest of the way as I step onto the concrete steps. The air is humid and stifling as I breathe it in, feeling too queasy for much else. Gravel dust plumes upward as I drop my bags at my feet to open the trunk. I keep my eyes downcast as I arrange them, keeping my backpack on my shoulders.

I round the car and open the driver's side door, hesitating for a moment. I know I shouldn't look, but I do anyway.

Mom's standing at the top of the stairs, arms crossed tightly over her chest. Her face is twisted in a fit of rage—silent for once. Roman's at her back, hands clasped in front of himself, but with my mother's back turned, he allows his smile to be shown—just for me.

I try not to cry as I look at the house, the *estate,* I grew up in—an expensive house far too big for just the three of us, the large garden I loved to spend most of my time in on the left, the garage housing multiple cars to the right.

So much green but so little *color.*

"I'm sorry," I say just loud enough to be heard.

"You will lose *everything,* Madison."

I swallow through the closure in my throat and force a slow breath through the weight pressed against my chest. "I know."

"What will you do without our help?" she sneers.

"Survive, I suppose."

And then, I drop into my seat, take another breath, albeit just as hard, and pull around the circular drive just as Father pulls in. He slams on his breaks, sending dust billowing upward. I lift my hand in a small wave, face pinched tight as I say goodbye to him and leave the only world I've ever known behind.

CHAPTER TWO

JUST AS SICK

CEDRICK

"You're a sick fuck."

"*Mhm*," I murmur as I smear white paint across my forehead, holding my hair out of the way of the brush. "So are you."

"Well, yeah." Kian waggles his brows. "But you'd piss on someone?"

I lift a brow as I glance at him through the mirror we share. "On them, in them." No point in arguing that. Everyone in this room *does* know what a sick fuck I am, but probably not *how* much of one...

He shakes his head. "Crazy, dude. Crazy."

"It's not your kink, so 'course you wouldn't." I click my tongue. "But you're missin' out," I drawl.

"I would," Wesley pipes in, making everyone roll their eyes.

"Yes. *We know,*" we all say in unison.

"Fuck off," he mutters, feigning indignance as he pops his contacts in his eyes, but we all see his smirk.

"So apparently, you fuckers are just pissin' on people." Booker chuckles, as blatantly curious as ever.

I just shrug. Ain't nothin' wrong with having kinks—the nastier the better if ya ask me. But that doesn't mean I'm giving these assholes more ammo to fuck with me. They know too much as it is.

But we're all some degree of immoral and debauched to do what we do—and enjoy it. It's why we work at Mayhem Motel, surrounded by other people who just fuckin' get it. Who all get off on—in one way or another—bringing people fear unlike anything they've ever experienced and the release that comes with that. And I have Kaser to thank for it.

We grew up living next to one another in the trailer park back home. I don't really remember a time before them and their ma, Lillian, moved in, but I remember everything after. It's pretty much always just been me and them. Kaser knows me better than anyone—who I am and what I need—and they've never judged me for it.

I know that if I didn't have them, I'd definitely be in fuckin' jail—and it's because of a close call I had a few years back that we both ended up workin' at Mayhem.

I may be the one who's fucked in the head and who needed a "healthier outlet" as Kaser put it, but they've got their own shit, too. And when we heard while working the carnival back home that a place like Mayhem was openin', it felt like somethin' we couldn't pass up. Especially after Kaser explained all the good it could give us.

I nearly gave up when we found out how intense the hiring process was, but the fucker never let me. It took fucking forever because we had to do background checks and pull references— and I'm not a patient person. If somethin' doesn't give me instant gratification, I lose interest faster than I can blink.

When that shit came back, we then had to get a physical and a fuckin' psych evaluation, but when I passed—to my own surprise, honestly—there was nothin' holding us back, and the buzz of something new festered beneath my skin.

It was kinda hard to move away from home, from Ma, but there wasn't much left for me there, anyway. And Kaser was more than willing to jump ship since their Ma died a handful of years back.

The thought of Lillian dying—how bad it had been—has me dropping my head back between my shoulders and rolling it back and forth to release the tension, pushing the thoughts down deep.

When I sit back up, I open my eyes and look behind me into the mirror, watching as everyone gets ready for the long day ahead.

Graves is the SFX makeup guru for himself, Kian, Wesley, and Booker. Then me and Wesley help Kaser into their suit—and let me tell you, latex is a fuckin' bitch. We've pretty much got it down pat at this point, but it made me realize that's definitely *not* a kink of mine... though I'm sure it *is* Kaser's. It wouldn't surprise me if *that's* the shit they're into, the fucker.

I'm the only one that doesn't need special effects makeup or help gettin' into my clothes. My style is one I've made into my own. With my gothic clown makeup and tattered, striped clothes, it doesn't take me long to get ready. It also helps that I'm a naturally eerie lookin' guy.

I smile wickedly at my reflection, running my tongue along my fake, sharpened teeth. My gaze catches on Wesley, now covered in green from head to toe. He catches my gaze and smirks, eyebrows wagging. Something restless but heavy settles in my chest.

I've found what I need within these walls, with these people.

Each one of us is just as sick as the other.

But I'm still missing something, a gnawing itch beneath my skin I can't fuckin' scratch, no matter how deep I dig, *how bloody I get.*

A sharp rap of knuckles on the door makes me blink. Kierra pushes the door open. "Y'all about done? There's a line across the parking lot."

"'Course there is," I mutter, but my heart jackknifes, adrenaline surging through my bloodstream. My skin starts to tingle as I push out of my chair, dipping down to double check my face in the mirror before grabbing my axe and filing out behind everyone else. Graves chugs the rest of his Redbull before tossing it in the trash on the way out, nearly elbowing me in the gut as he trips over the threshold.

I lift a brow, and he smirks, but with his heavy, grotesque makeup, it makes him look every bit the cannibal he's portraying.

"Woo!" Wesley singsongs down the narrow hall, voice echoing as it bounces off the concrete walls. It's the same thing every day—like a mantra of sorts. Or somethin' like that. But I've never asked.

Even beneath Kaser's mask, I can tell they're rolling their eyes. I huff, which makes them shake their head, dropping it slightly so their chin drags over their chest, creating an eerie creak of latex. I shudder at the noise as we file through the single door, all veering off into different directions without a word spoken, our bodies tense and ready as we delve into the mindset to do this.

For me, it's this dark, consuming, *obscure* place I feel I can rarely venture into even though I do this nearly every day.

But when I can delve into it, it's a high unlike anything else—or it would be if I could just *scratch that fucking itch.*

I watch as everyone else disperses. They all tend to go to different areas every day—preferring to switch it up—but I always stay at the basement level, loving to see our newest victims come in and experience the black-out rush, the initial blanket of horror. To relish in their *"Oh, shit, I really fucked up"* moment.

Once that's over, I always find my way to the rooms where most of the suicides occurred. There are still ropes hanging from their endeavors, and while it sickens most, I quite enjoy the theatrics since everyone that walks through the doors of Mayhem Motel know what happened here before we came along.

Screams echo down the corridor, and I allow my laugh to spill from between my lips, loud and demented as it bleeds with the newfound silence. A promise of the horrors to come.

The strobe lights flash as I walk down the hall, closer to the first group of the day. My heavy boots *thunk* on the damp concrete below, resounding and undeniable. As their harsh whispers meet my presence, I slow my descent and drop my axe to the floor. The scrape of the blade against the ground sends shivers up my spine and blood rushing down.

I jump inward, crouching low with wide eyes to meet their frightened gazes. My lips stretch wide, sharp teeth fully exposed as I shout, "Don't ya know you're supposed to *smile* when ya see a clown?"

Their screams pierce my ear drums, making me cackle as they all scramble to disperse, slipping and stumbling around as water leeches across the floor.

"Oh, God. *Oh, my God!*"

I lunge forward. My gloved fingers graze an ankle.

"Please, no! No!" They kick their legs frantically as I drag them closer, easily dodging each intended jab.

"Holy fucking shit," someone heaves.

"Gotta do better than that," I cackle.

The screams get louder as we're left alone, the others having disappeared, just as I intended. "Your friends left ya behind," I drawl, letting my accent bleed a little thicker than normal, taking on a bit of a rasp. I *tsk*. "Not very good friends, if ya ask me."

"P-p-please," they wail, nails scraping along the concrete as I drag them to a room.

My eyes light up at their plea, dancing with pleasure at what that simple word gives me.

I spin around and drop to my knees on top of them, making them scream right in my face. Their hands come up to cover their eyes, but I grab both wrists in my left and slam them above their head before they can even blink.

I dip low. Low enough for my black-painted nose to graze theirs. Their dark eyes are bulging, glassy with the tears that won't stop spilling down their temples. I drag my tongue along the fronts of my teeth, nearly hissing as one pointed edge pierces the muscle before I slip it out between my lips to drag it along their cheek.

I groan at the salt of their tears.

"Careful what ya wish for."

A scream pierces the air, and then, their eyes roll back.

"How was today?" Kaser asks as we walk toward the room to undress, the moon high in the sky as darkness descends through the shattered, boarded up windows.

"Good." My eyes close briefly as I picture their screams again, how fucking *sharp* they always are. And how empty it always leaves me feeling.

It's good while it's good. And when it's over, it's... not.

They lift one dark brow but don't say anything else. They know I'm lying—probably. I think I should feel worse about that, but I don't. Everyone lies when they need to. Just like *I* know they're lying to me.

"How're you today, then?" I ask, waiting for the blow-off they always give.

Their steps falter, but they right themself quickly. "Fine."

"Jus' fine?"

Kaser's back is ramrod straight as we round the corner, black door in sight. "Yeah, Ricky. I'm okay."

"You're never okay," I respond, just as dull as they did. But we're both aware of how serious the other is. It's just one of those things we live with. That we know but don't talk about because what the fuck is there to do about it? Kaser's depressed, and I'm pretty sure I'm some kind of fuckin' crazy. It's just the way it is. We do what we can to survive each day.

"Fuckin' tell me about it," Wesley babbles, interrupting us as he runs up between us and throws his arms around our shoulders—or tries to. I'm the tallest guy here—a few inches taller than them both—so Wesley ends up leaning cock-eyed.

Kaser looks over at him, deadpan as usual. I grunt, shaking out from under his touch before pushing the door open to our room where everyone else already is.

After I've gotten the paint off my face and taken off my work clothes, I help Kaser out of their latex contraption, trying to ignore the restless buzz in my blood. It's quiet between us as I peel the material from their naked body. Once it's down to their ankles, I push myself up from my knees to high-tail it for the exit.

"Goin' somewhere?" Kaser asks as they drop down onto the chair, their accent coming out strong again for the first time in quite a while. It usually only ever happens when they let their guard down, which is what has me pulling to a stop.

Ever since we moved, Kaser's worked hard to force it down so it's a barely recognizable drawl. I've never asked why, but I can guess.

I swallow the smallest flare of guilt as I answer them. "Yeah." I glance over my shoulder, teeth tugging on one of my lip rings.

They look like they want to say something as they run their hand over their shaved head, but they must decide better of it because they drop their arm with a nod, looking more tired than usual. "Be careful, Ricky."

That kinda hurts, and I kinda want to rub the ache now in my chest, but it's easier to ignore it, so I flex the muscles in my back as the pain works its way down, where all the rest of it is.

I flash my eyes, giving Kaser my signature Mayhem grin. "Always, baby."

Their huff follows me out, a soft caress as my heavy boots *thunk* on the concrete. The summer night is comfortable as I walk through the gravel, watching plumes of dust kick up with every step. The air in my car is thick with the day's humidity as I drop down into the seat. Once the windows are down, I pull out of the lot to start the hour drive back home to Arcane— only I'm not going home tonight. Just like I don't go home most nights anymore.

The club is quieter than usual as I step inside, and I already know tonight's gonna be a bust.

I huff out a breath, barely able to contain my groan. My skin itches and tingles, making my stomach turn uneasily as I lean against the sleek, white counter.

"Pretty sure everyone knows you by now, Cedrick," Ethan says as he slides a beer over to me.

"Doesn't stop 'em from coming over here, does it?" I mutter.

Ethan's eyes narrow slightly as he leans across the bar top. "Not usually, no," he says.

The neon lights are bright as they slash through the shadows, obscuring my view of the upper VIP floor, so I give up and scan the dance floor. It's busy with most of the people here in that area, but it's not crowded, so it's easy to see most of their faces. No one immediately catches me eye, which is disappointing.

"No one good enough for you tonight?"

The sound of Ethan's voice has me spinning around. I stare at the round, tanned face in front of me, but he surprisingly stands his own as he stares back with pursed lips.

"Seems there's only one—and he's standin' right in front of me," I tell him with a smirk. We've talked before, but he's never acted interested. My eyes dance at the newfound prospect.

"A bit presumptuous, no?" He quirks a brow. "I heard you're a bit of a slut," he says, but he's smirking still.

He's done more than heard, I'm sure, but I'm not offended. Can't really be when I come here almost every night to fuck. In the bathroom, in the alleyway, in a fuckin' car in the parking lot. I'm not picky. I just need to come—and I like a nice body to do it with.

And it's good—enough to get me where I need to be until the feelings start itching again. When they do, I'll be back at Mayhem, where Static gets to come out and play.

I just wish I could have both, *be* both.

"Sluts know what they're doing," I tell Ethan bluntly. He laughs.

"That they do."

"What're you into?" I ask, getting to the point. My dick's already getting hard, and I don't feel like playing much tonight —at least, not this kind of game.

Ethan pulls his bottom lip between his teeth. "Whatever gets you in me."

My eyes widen with delight. *Oh, how fun.* "Well..." I lean over the counter and run my tongue along the fronts of my teeth. "How about you come with me?"

His throat bobs, and he nods before going over to his coworker. They exchange words, both pairs of eyes flicking to me and back. I stare back, unperturbed. After a couple of minutes, Ethan's rounding the countertop, face illuminated in the neon glow as he looks up at me.

Damn. Eye contact really fuckin' gets me. I reach down and readjust my dick, groaning when the zipper of my jeans bites into my flesh.

I grab Ethan's hand and drag him toward the back, meandering around the few bodies in our way.

"Where're you taking me?" he asks as he trails behind.

I stop in my tracks, causing him to collide into me. *Time to test just how much of me he can take...* I reach around and wrap my fingers around his throat—ensuring I keep my grip light, even as I actively fight against the urge to just fucking *squeeze.* To steal his breath until his face turns red and he writhes, body screaming with the overwhelming need for oxygen.

"S-shit," he gasps, drawing my attention back to the moment. His eyes are wide, but it's not in fear... *mostly.*

"You look like a good bathroom fuck to me, don't you think?" I drawl softly. His throat bobs beneath my palm, drawing my attention to where I know his pulse is hammering away in his neck. I wish I could see it, but it's too fuckin' dark in here.

That's probably best.

I tend to... lose my shit a bit when I see things like that.

"Don't worry..." I whisper. "I won't hurt you." *Much.*

CHAPTER THREE

A GREAT WAY TO MAKE FRIENDS

MADISON

The door is yanked open before my foot even touches the first concrete step, startling me.

"Heyyy, roomie," a voice drawls as someone leans over the threshold.

I open my mouth to respond, but the words catch in my throat as my eyes land on the person standing in front of me, *completely naked* apart from a towel slung low on his hips. His dark, wet skin catches in the afternoon light, and my mind blanks out.

"Hellooo." He waves his hand in front of my face.

I struggle to meet his gaze, caught in the planes of muscles, but somehow manage to unfocus my eyes so I can look away. When I meet the other's eyes, my own widen, and my face flames with heat. I somehow manage to stutter out a pathetic, "H-hi."

He smirks, and it's lopsided and kind of wild. "Awe, you stutter. That's cu —"

Someone smacks him, the skin-on-skin contact a sharp crack in the air. "Don't be an ass, Lenny." A voice I recognize.

"Ow!" *Lenny* shouts, whipping around to glare at the other guy while rubbing his bicep. "I wasn't!"

My attention is drawn from Lenny to the man beside him as he makes his way toward the steps. His dark hair is hanging in disarray across his forehead. He reaches up to push it back before offering his hand. "I'm Kane, and that's obviously Lenny. Ignore him. He's a dick. Glad you had a safe trip."

There's so much going on, it takes me a minute to catch up. "Oh!" I start. *This* is Kane? My eyes dart back to Lenny, who's now sitting on the porch's handrail, just watching me. I quickly look away, focusing my attention back at the hand stretched before me. My manners kick in, and I take it with a sweaty palm, wincing when I realize how rude that is. I should've wiped my hand first.

Jesus, I'm really messing this up already.

"Y-yeah, yes. Kane, h-hello." His hand is warm and dry. Nothing like my small, clammy one. I suck my bottom lip between my teeth, hating how hot my face is feeling. I'm sure my pale skin is just *bright* red. Awesome.

Even as I berate myself, my eyes wander again.

Is... everyone that lives here so... nice looking?

"Depends on personal preference, I guess," Lenny says with a shrug as he hops down, brown eyes dancing.

"O-oh," I squeak. What in the world is *wrong* with me? I'm going to get kicked out before I even get the chance to move in. I'll have to crawl back to Mother and Father with my tail between my legs. I'll have to... to *grovel.* Tell them I was wrong...

I let my head hang between my shoulders. My fingers fist

my backpack tighter, needing the feel of *something* against my fingertips to help ground me.

A hand clasps my shoulders, making me jolt forward. "Hey, don't sweat it," Kane says with ease. His smile is small but kind. It helps.

"Sorry," I apologize. *Might as well get this over with. I knew it would be a problem.* "I, erm, as you can probably tell... I have, uh..." I grab the back of my neck and drag the tip of my shoe over a plank of wood to avoid both pairs of eyes on me. My stomach cramps.

"I've lived a pretty sheltered life. I don't... r-really know what I'm doing," I quickly blurt the second part out. The pressure of my fingertips against the ridges of my cervical spine makes me grit my teeth, but it's a pressure I *need.*

"You have come to the right place, my friend," Lenny says loudly. "We shall teach you!" I look over at him, smiling, but it probably comes off as more of a grimace. Lenny winks and then disappears back inside. I'm grateful for that because his naked body is quite distracting.

"Ignore him. He's the dumb one," Kane says with a huff of a laugh. He makes me feel at ease. Maybe it's because he's the one I've been talking to, but I try not to question it when it's such a relief.

"C'mon, let's go get your stuff." He starts down the steps, leaving me to follow. When I open the trunk, I notice his slight frown. "This is all?"

I wince and pinch my nape. "Erm... yeah. Sorry I came early. T-things got... *bad.*" When he looks over at me, I stumble to explain—and end up oversharing. "Mom and Dad wanted me to stay and go to this Christian university, and I just—I couldn't. I couldn't be there anymore and keep *hating* myself so much, so I needed to leave before I couldn't and—"

Kane's wide-eyed stare cuts me off mid-sentence. I blanch when I realize everything I've said. I open my mouth. To say *what*, I don't know, but Kane beats me to it.

His smile is small but sincere. He pats my shoulder gently. "I get it. I'm glad you're here." It's nothing profound or even that deep, but it means so much, my eyes instantly burn and fill with tears. To be accepted so easily is a gift I don't think he truly understands.

I blink rapidly and clear my throat. "Th-tha-thanks," I stutter, not feeling embarrassed about it for the first time.

"Sure thing." His smile is too much. "Let's get this stuff inside, and I'll show you to your room."

"Cool."

As I follow Kane into the house, bags in hand, I can't help but think maybe this won't be so bad.

Maybe I can finally relax.

"Sup, Mads," Kane says as I walk into the living room where everyone seems to be congregated. I blush at the nickname but nod my head with a tight-lipped smile. Everyone's eyes track over me, and the heat blazes hotter from their attention.

After a quick exchange of "hi's" and "hello's," I plop down onto the worn couch beside Kane, grunting slightly as the broken wires poke me beneath the thin, fraying fabric. I readjust with a wince.

"You get unpacked okay?" he asks with a quick glance as he scrolls through his phone.

"Yeah, thanks again for your help." I try not to twist my

fingers together in my lap—another habit I'm trying to break —but my nerves are shot after what happened with Mom and Dad and then moving into a house full of strangers on top of it.

But this *is* better than being at home, and I keep trying to remember that. They won't be strangers forever.

And I need this. I need to be three hours away from them, starting a college I chose and doing it all on my own. I know it'll be hard to work while in school, but I have enough money saved to last me for a while. But no matter what happens, I know I can't go back. This... decision was final in every sense of the word.

They would accept me back if I admitted they were right, but I can't because they never have been. And I never realized how detrimental their "love" was until I actually had the freedom of being a legal adult. Or any freedom at all. I never thought making my own decisions was something I could do... but then, I did it, and it changed *everything*.

I just hope I'm strong enough for this... I've never been very courageous. Or confident.

"Sure thing. Happy to help." Kane nods his head in response to my thanks. The movement sends some of his dark hair flopping across his forehead. My throat bobs as I watch the tendrils brush his smooth skin before I force my eyes away, heat settling just beneath my skin. Not because it's wrong but because it's *so* inappropriate. *My roommate!*

Jesus Christ, Madison.

Thankfully, no one seems to notice my recurrent blushing —or if they do, they don't comment on it, which I appreciate.

Being around other people who are just... *normal* is still so new. I don't know if I'll ever get used to it.

After a few moments of subtle breathing, I finally take a

real look around the room. It's big and open. The white paint on the walls isn't bright anymore, and there are stains in the carpet. Every piece of furniture is old and falling apart and smells kind of musty, but it's nice. Feels real and honest.

Not like the pristine, stiff contents of the home I always knew...

I shake those thoughts away—which is harder than I thought it'd be. It takes me a few moments to realize everyone is either on their phones or they have their laptops out—and they're all staring at the screens with rapt attention. "Is something going on?" I ask hesitantly.

"Yeah." Lenny nods excitedly. I eye him curiously, trying not to remember him naked—or almost naked. Instead, I focus on his eyes, which are wide and glassy, the screen of his computer reflecting off of them. His dark fingers hammer over the keys with giddy glee, magnifying my curiosity. "Here." He shoves his laptop toward me. "Look at this, dude."

I wince as it scrapes across the wood, sending the worst nail-scraping noise reverberating throughout the room. Shaking off the chill, I lean forward, pressing my fingers against the coffee table to ground me as I look at the web page in front of me. It's dark, muddled with an ambiance of colors that are nearly indistinguishable, but all that does is highlight the photo in the background.

I blink as my eyes zero in on it, throat bobbing as my skin prickles with unease.

It's a motel, which looks to be abandoned—run down and decrepit with peeling paint and doors hanging off the hinges. There's a large, broken neon sign with only the letter M glowing through the black and white, standing out like a haunting beacon in the darkness.

It's not until I shudder, and a single tear falls from the

corner of my eye that I realize they're burning. I lean back with a sniffle, dragging the back of my hand over my eyes in a rush as my face floods with embarrassment.

"Uh..." I clear my throat, resisting the urge to tug on my collar. Unwittingly, my eyes drop back to the words beneath the photo. They're bold and dingy and... creepy. If words can even be those things.

Welcome to Mayhem Motel.

A bead of sweat drips onto my quivering bottom lip. My tongue swipes across it absentmindedly before I suck it into my mouth and sink my teeth into the flesh.

"Wanna come with us?" Collin asks, startling me.

"M-me?" I balk, eyebrows sky high. My three new room-mates jerk their heads up to stare at me.

"Yes..." Kane replies hesitantly with a brow wrinkled in question.

"Who the hell else would we be talking to, bud?" Collin chuckles, and my face flames. I lean back into the couch, trying to bury myself in the deformed foam.

"But why would you want me to go?" *This is a great way to make friends, Madison. Great job.* "Erm... sorry," I blurt shakily. A few of their gazes narrow slightly in confusion, making me squirm harder.

"You're a bit of a loner, huh." Kane bumps his shoulder into mine, making me nearly gasp in surprise. I find his eyes on me, but his gaze isn't cruel. It's curious.

"Uh, yeah. I've..." I rub the back of my neck—yet another nervous habit. I drag my fingers through the short, nearly dried strands there, letting the soft, fuzzy texture calm me some. "I've kinda lived a sheltered life and whatnot, so this is all sorta new and strange to me."

"Eh, that's okay, buddy," Lenny pops in. "College is great.

You'll have loads of fun. Especially since you're living with us." He waggles his brows suggestively—or, at least, that's what it seems like—making me blush. He chuckles, shaking his head.

Kane leans forward and smacks Lenny across the arm. "Leave the poor kid alone, Len, for fucks sake."

Lenny holds his hands up in a mocking gesture. "Sorry, sorry. So, anyway, do you want to go with us, Madison?"

I blink. "Go with you where?" Lenny leans back and shoots Collin a look where he's seated in the reclining chair.

"To Mayhem Motel, loner boy. You know..." He rotates his hands in the air like that's supposed to tell me something, but then, his eyes dart to his laptop.

"Ohhh." My face flames hotter. *Jesus Christ, you're daft, Madi.*

"We've always wanted to go, and they finally fucking have tickets available," Lenny exclaims. "So, we have to snatch them up before they're sold out for the next six fucking months again."

"Uh..." *Shoot.* How do I tell them I'm completely and utterly broke without sounding pathetic? All the money I have is saved for college and rent. "I don't really have the extra—"

"I can buy yours for you—no big deal," Kane offers without hesitation. He gives me a smile, which only increases my blush—and embarrassment.

"It's gonna be so fucking creepy." Collin cackles. "I'm gonna make Brianne come, too." Everyone dips back to their phones, and the ball starts rolling at break-neck speed.

"How many are we getting? Mads, do you want me to get yours?" Kane asks.

"I've got two," Collin blurts. Kane nods his head, thumb scrolling across his screen.

"Just..." Lenny sinks his teeth into his bottom lip as he

clicks away on his laptop. "Got mine." He looks up from his screen, eyes on me. Collin's looking, too. So is Kane.

I glance around at all of them, hating the way my heart is hammering against my sternum, making my breath come out in short, obvious pants. *Ugh,* just the thought of that place makes me break out in hives, and now, they want me to go.

"I don't know, guys... It's not really—"

"Oh, come *on!* It's a once-in-a-lifetime opportunity!"

"No, I know. I just—"

"Please..." Lenny resorts to puffing out his bottom lip. I wring my hands together in my lap, tugging on my fingers until my muscles ache with the strain.

How do I explain that the mere thought of this motel makes me want to cower under my blankets and never steal a peek at sunlight again?

I peer through my lashes, finding three sets of eyes on me all over again. Each one is heavy, making my skin crawl and roll under the pressurized sensation, like worms digging through dirt.

I moved here to make friends, I remind myself. A pathetic attempt to mentally steel my spine. This is supposed to be my fresh start. I may be in the same state, but I'm hours away from my hometown, from my not-*exactly*-abusive parents but close enough.

College is supposed to be the beginning of my new life. A way for me to get out from underneath the shell I've lived under for as long as I can remember. And what better way to do that than to go with my new roommates-slash-possible-friends to a horror attraction that might—okay, probably will —kill me?

"Fine," I whisper in hopes no one will hear me, but they heard each hesitant decibel like their ears were straining for it.

"*Yes!*" Lenny screams and jumps to his feet. He knocks a knee against the coffee table on his way up, howling and clutching the bone with a pained grunt. We all chuckle and snicker as he bounces around with a flushed face and puffed-out cheeks.

"All right—got ours," Kane says a minute later, pocketing his phone. The couch dips under the shift of movement, causing our shoulders to bump. "You look ecstatic," he drawls. I can't help my snort.

I pick at the frayed end on my drawstring, pulling a thread loose and winding it around my finger until the skin turns white beneath. "Oh, totally." My voice quivers a bit, and I'm forced to suck in a breath to keep the panic from my voice.

"It'll be fun."

"And scare the piss out of us—literally," Lenny cackles after he finally catches his breath.

"Wait, are you serious?" I balk at him. He nods enthusiastically.

"Oh, yeah, dude. One hundred percent. Mayhem is famous for a reason."

"It's famous?"

"Have you never heard of it before?" Collin asks. I shake my head. I'm regretting my decision more and more with every passing second.

"Welllll, shit, dude. You're in for a treat tomorrow."

"Um... Usually, a treat implies something good." I laugh lightly just as the doorbell rings.

"Pizza!" Lenny shouts and scrambles over Collin's spread legs as he races for the front door. He comes back carrying two large boxes and bringing the smell of tomato sauce, meat, and melted cheese.

He plops them down on the table, flips the lid on the top

box, and dives right in. Everyone else follows suit. I stay in my spot, my mind reeling with questions. It's not until a slice of pizza is being waved right in front of my face that I blink through my stupor with a sheepish smile.

"Thanks," I mumble and take the floppy piece from Kane before taking a hesitant bite. The second the tangy sauce explodes on my tongue, I nearly groan.

I can't remember the last time I had pizza—it's been so many years.

The evening passes quickly. The chatter amongst my new roommates is fun and teasing. It's actually very weird to observe the banter between them, but I find myself smiling more often than not.

I think I'll really like it here.

"All right, well, I'm gonna head to bed. Goodnight." The soft cacophony of mumbled replies follows me as I make my way up the stairs to my new bedroom. Once the door is latched behind me, my eyes flutter closed, and I take a deep breath.

My hands tremble slightly against the door at my back. My lungs deflate as I push out every ounce of breath inside my chest. I wait until my head swims with pressure before I gasp in more oxygen.

The relief in my chest is instant, and it nearly makes my legs buckle.

With a near-silent grunt, I take the few steps to my new-to-me twin-sized bed and flop down face first. My blanket smells like the flowery laundry detergent my mother uses, and my stomach flips with the vacant feeling of missing home—which is ridiculous because I don't miss anything about it, especially my parents, but my brain doesn't seem to care.

Still, I allow myself a few extra inhales before I'm pushing myself up and shucking my clothes, letting them fall to the floor in a pile I promise myself I'll pick up first thing in the morning.

Lying beneath the now warm sheets, I stare up at the foreign popcorn ceiling, my mind churning with the events of the day. How rejuvenating it felt to drive my very own car here that I spent nearly five years saving up to buy, packed with everything I own—which, pathetically, isn't much.

How I'm now living in a strange house with people I barely know. How *good* it feels to be on my own with no one to tell me what to do—except, apparently, my own subconscious and my deep-seated desire to be accepted.

Which has, *so* fortunately, landed me in a very precarious predicament.

I agreed to go to the state's most haunted house—or whatever—when just the sound of the wind blowing against the windows wrong nearly sends me into a panic.

Not my brightest moment, but I'm hoping once we get there, my resolve will steel and I'll at least be able to walk inside without peeing my pants.

I know for a fact I won't make it longer than two minutes, but I think if I make the effort, that will be okay. I'll just go in last so no one else knows how much of a pansy I am.

But first, I need to know all that I'm getting myself into.

Rolling onto my side, I reach toward the small stand near my bed and grab my phone. I pinch my eyes closed as the brightness of my screen temporarily blinds me. I type in my password and open the browser. The search bar stares back at me, taunting me. My thumb hovers over the blank space, trembling a hair's breadth away from the screen.

The haunting picture of the motel flashes through my mind's eye, and I shiver, nearly choking on the lump lodged in the back of my throat.

The click of each letter resounds through the room, charged and permanent. With a bated breath and a vacant little *thump,* I hit search. The first thing that pops up is some random ad, so I scroll past to the link for the website just beneath.

The photo of that godforsaken motel loads in the background, surrounded by all different shades of black. Clicking on the menu, I scroll through each option with hesitant interest, wincing as that freaking photo *follows me.*

I click on the tab that says *FEEL US,* unsure as to what that means. "Welcome to Mayhem Motel. *Beware...*" I read aloud, choking on the word as my eyes rove faster than my brain can keep up with.

"You will feel like a victim—because you are."

Oh... my God.

My intestines wrap around my heart.

"You're our victim now... Prepare to die... Oh, shit. *Jesus,* what does that even mean?" I sound hysterical to my own ears. My eyes sting with the unexpected pressure of tears, but I barely manage to bite them back with a grit I didn't even know I had.

I am *not* going to cry over reading a little freaking introduction paragraph—even if it does make me feel like I'm volunteering to be *murdered.*

"It's just part of the gig," I whisper to myself, not feeling the slightest bit of reprieve at my faint, pathetic words of consolation. "Yeah, I freaking *feel you* all right," I grumble as I click on the next tab, *YOU MUST*—whatever the heck that means.

The Mayhem Motel experience is only suitable for persons aged 18+.

You must read and sign our WAIVER AND RELEASE,

EXPRESS ASSUMPTION OF RISK, INDEMNITY, AND VOLUNTARY CONSENT AGREEMENT. If you choose not to, you will not be allowed to enter.

I blink slowly, lips parted as I reread the paragraph two times over. A *waiver?* We all have to sign a waiver before we can enter. The thought makes me want to throw up. It certainly can't mean anything good.

With hesitant, shaky fingers, I click on *HISTORY,* immediately curious as to what that could mean.

What I didn't expect to find was an endless scroll of paragraphs explaining the history of the *original* motel—before it became *Mayhem.*

Gooseflesh devours my bare skin as I absorb every word. Each one settles deep in my gut, adding more weight with every passing minute.

By the time I reach the bottom, I try to keep scrolling but come up empty.

What... the heck. I blink helplessly at the dimmed screen as the glowing, white words blur, my eyes unfocusing.

Apparently, not even five years ago, all it was, was a sad, news-riddled motel due to the endless cycle of apparent suicides.

There was at least one suicide a week, which gradually turned to two. And then, when lucky number three became the pattern, the owner, Mr. Haynes, decided to close up, not even bothering to sell.

It stated in a direct quote that he didn't want to sell because he didn't want the *"bad juju"* to continue.

But what Mr. Haynes didn't predict was that he'd die, sooner rather than later. Which then left the motel up for sale by the bank.

And that is apparently how Mayhem Motel came to be.

Two years later and it's now one of the country's most known horror spots. People come from all around to experience the terrors within the walls of Mayhem.

Now that I know, I feel like I *should've* known this whole time since I have lived here my entire life, but I guess I can blame my suffocating parents for my lack of knowledge of obvious state attractions.

And now, I am one of those stupid, *stupid* people.

I mean, *Jesus*, a building with a history of dozens of suicides is now a haunted attraction, where you have to sign a *contract* waiving your right to legal action.

Apparently, Mr. Haynes was right about the *"bad juju."*

Backing out as soon as everyone goes in is seeming like a better idea by the second.

Clearing out of my browser with a shudder, I stare back up at the ceiling. Only this time, my mind is reeling for an entirely different reason.

And I can't get the image of that motel out of my mind, long into the darkest hours of the night.

CHAPTER FOUR
WELCOME TO MAYHEM MOTEL

MADISON

I shudder visibly as we pass the welcome sign for Vitriol, the small town just off the interstate that has famously become known as Mayhem Motel's home. But even that fame isn't enough to upgrade a single thing.

It looks like a freaking ghost town, which I suppose is apt.

"You look like you're going to throw up already," Kane remarks. The car dips as we hit a pothole. I jerk, nearly smacking my head against the glass window.

We pass a green, moss-covered pond a few dozen feet off the road. Weeds nearly as tall as me line the body of water, only broken in segments where geese waddle through, honking and flapping around.

"I feel like it," I mumble pathetically as I crank my head back, watching the aggressive little things disappear in the distance.

My stomach's been in knots since the moment my eyelids

cracked open to the mid-morning sunlight streaming through my curtainless windows.

I didn't fall asleep till near sunrise, so exhaustion is already weighing heavily on me. Add that to my undiluted apprehension about where we're headed, and I'm a pathetic, jumbled mess.

"You should've eaten something before we left, but here." Kane hands over his half-eaten bag of Funyuns. "Eat something now. It might help with the nausea."

Flicking him a grateful smile, I take it and munch on one, thankful for the obnoxious crunching now reverberating in my skull, drowning out the echoing noise of fear.

"Thanks," I say once my mouth is clear. "But I don't think this'll help much. I was looking into this... motel—" the word sounds far too heavy on my tongue—"last night, and did you guys know we have to sign a waiver before we can enter? Because they, like, touch us and stuff?"

Lenny whirls around in the passenger seat. "Uh, yeah, dude. That's the whole point." Collin snickers, shaking his head as he flicks on his turn signal. Even his girlfriend, Brianne, laughs quietly from the other side of Kane.

My face burns with heat, so I turn into my bicep and rest against the door panel. "Guys, for fuck's sake, quit giving the new kid a hard time." Kane bumps against my side, making me glance up.

"You don't have to do this if you don't want to." He seems genuine, which makes me smile out of sheer gratefulness. Before I can even open my mouth to respond, Lenny's shouting in a voice much too loud for the small space we're all trapped in.

"Absolutely *no* backing out! For anyone! This is a once-in-a-lifetime opportunity, and we're all gonna do it together." He shoots his index finger out, pointing straight at me through the gap in his headrest. "Even you, new kid."

I lift my head with the world's most pathetic fake smile plastered on my ghastly face. "Nope—not backing out." The words make me want to spew the single Funyun ring I managed to choke down.

Kane just snickers beside me.

Oh, God, it's even worse in person.

My eyes catch on the broken, neon motel sign and the way that singular M is illuminated. The car dips as Collin pulls into the packed parking lot. Not that it's very big to begin with, but nearly every space is filled with every kind of car imaginable. My eyes rove over the cracked, stained concrete leading to the front entrance, where I'm assuming we all go to sign our souls to the devil if the long line leading to said door is any indication.

Gravel kicks up around us as Collin maneuvers into a tight space near the opposite end and slams the old, maroon Pontiac into park. He fiddles with the keys, wiggling them out of the ignition before he drops them into the center console.

He turns around, eyes immediately finding Brianne's. "Ready to piss yourself?" She laughs and shakes her head. Her perfectly shaped brow arches in a challenge.

"That'll be you, babe." He scoffs but doesn't bother denying it, which would make me laugh if I didn't feel like I was about to have a panic attack.

Everyone's digging through their bags, pulling out their

IDs, and I'm just stuck staring at the gray, cloth fabric of the seat in front of me.

My breath feels faint as it rushes in and out of my lungs. Even my blood seems to have stopped flowing in my veins.

"Hey, you good?" Kane asks.

I shake my head. I can't speak.

This is such a bad idea.

"Jesus, it feels like I'm about to walk toward my death." I laugh shakily, eyes wide and staring straight ahead. Silence rings out around me, lulling me from my reverie. I glance around the car, finding everyone's eyes on me once again. The weight of their stares makes my skin crawl worse than the prospect of getting out of the car, so I yank on the handle and shove the door open.

"Well, let's go." I don't know how I manage to talk, let alone move, but everyone easily follows suit. The sun is nearly gone from the sky by the time we make it to the end of the long line that winds around the front of the motel.

Aside from the hushed murmurs of conversation, it's surprisingly quiet. I thought we'd be able to hear screams from people inside, but there's *nothing*. Just eerie silence.

That bodes well.

Not.

My roommates all start in on some conversation I *try* to follow, but it's way past my capabilities. My eyes wander around the expanse of Mayhem. The motel is two stories with a level right off the ground and the other just above with a sawed-off guard rail. The building is long and narrow, covering a large expanse before it cuts left, wrapping around to where it ends a short distance later. The faded, baby blue paint is chipped off and missing across most of the building, leaving splintered wood panels exposed. The windows are coated with what appears to be years of dirt and grime; it's impossible to see inside, which I'm sure is entirely on purpose.

"Yo, Madison." The sound of my name has my whole body jerking. My feet twist in the gravel, sending a plume of dust into the air.

"Yeah?" I croak, tugging on the collar of my shirt. I shove my hands into my jeans pockets. The fingers on my right hand clamp tight around my ID—the only thing I have on me. It doesn't do much to ground me, but it's something tangible at least.

"Did you happen to look at Mayhem's gallery last night when you were doing your research?" Collin asks. I shake my head before he's even finished talking.

"No, I, uh, didn't think I should."

"Better to be surprised." Lenny waggles his brows.

"No." I shake my head. "But after what I read, I was too scared to," I blurt, then immediately clamp my mouth shut.

"That's smart 'cause the pictures alone would've talked you out of it," the person in the line in front of us chimes in on the conversation. Everyone turns to face them as they talk. I'm just grateful we skipped right over my stupid admission. "There's Static, the clown, though he's like, *way* creepier than a regular ol' clown. And then there's Phantom, the ghoul, which is pretty self-explanatory. Maggot is the Boogeyman. He's absolutely terrifying. All green with exposed teeth and shit." They visibly shudder.

"But my favorite is Vulture. He's the vampire." Their eyes flash, making a few in the group laugh.

"I like Ravage," Lenny adds.

"Ohhh, the cannibal. Nice."

"Cannibal?" I squawk, eyes shooting wide. Everyone turns to peer at me with amused expressions that make my face heat.

"Yeah, and there's a puppeteer, too. Ligature."

Cannibal, the Boogeyman, and a freaking clown.

I heave out a breath, hunching over as my stomach revolts, my uvula twitching away.

They shake their head with a laugh. "Sorry—should've left ya in the dark."

I hold out a thumbs up with a mocking smile. "Wish you would've," I mumble and effectively tune out of that conversation.

The line takes forever to shuffle along. Apparently, they only allow a certain amount of people in at a time, so it takes a while to get through. Which makes sense, but with this supposedly being a two-hour ordeal, you'd think it would actually move slower.

I mean, we're not even seeing people exit, which they'd have to be to allow more people in.

Ugh. I groan and clutch my midsection. My stomach flips and churns as we near the black-painted front doors. Kane rubs his hand between my shoulder blades.

"Take a deep breath, dude. You're overthinking it."

"No, I'm pretty sure I'm underthinking this whole thing," I mumble but take his advice, regardless. The people in front of us disappear inside, spiking my adrenaline tenfold.

"Ohhh, shit, we're nearly there!" Lenny rubs his hands together in a pose that closely resembles a praying mantis. It makes me laugh in spite of everything.

I time each breath to the mental tick of a clock, wishing I had my phone to distract me, but Collin advised us they're not allowed, so we left them in the car. *No way to call for help...*

Another piece to the bone-chilling and absolutely terrifying scenario.

"Next five people," a voice booms out, and I nearly jump

right out of my skin. My hand slams across my sternum with a resounding crack, even through the fabric.

"Damn, Mads. Chill, dude. We're just signing paperwork," Collin so helpfully adds as he walks through the entrance to hell.

Yeah, I'm working on chilling.

Kane swings his arm out. "After you."

"Oh, how freaking courteous," I grumble as I shuffle over the split concrete, nearly tripping over an elevated slab. Kane laughs loudly as he follows behind me.

The lights inside are much brighter than I expected them to be. The walls are painted black, making the surprisingly large room appear smaller.

Another purposeful illusion of the mind, I'm sure.

Collin saunters right up to the counter. He tells the person his name, and they pull up his tickets on their system. Once he's checked in, both he and Brianne are handed clipboards, along with a short, scripted explanation similar to the one I read online.

They both nod and take a chair along the far corner to start reading. The process is repeated for the rest of us, and the next thing I know, my shaky legs have some reprieve as I plop into a chair with a hesitant inhale.

Everyone's already bent over their paperwork, eyes scanning the small print of legal mumbo-jumbo.

Since no one's looking at me, I close my eyes for a moment, hold my breath for *one... two... three...* I open them and release it, eyes dropping down to the white papers.

<u>WAIVER AND RELEASE, EXPRESS ASSUMP-
TION OF RISK, INDEMNITY, AND VOLUNTARY
CONSENT AGREEMENT</u>

Oh, fuck. Here we go.

This event is only suitable for persons aged 18+.

You will be asked to verify your age, and if you are unable to produce a valid photo ID card, you will be refused admittance.

<u>WAIVER AND RELEASE AND EMERGENCY MEDICAL SERVICES</u>

Releasing Party hereby RELEASES, WAIVES, DISCHARGES, AND COVENANTS NOT TO SUE MAYHEM MOTEL...

<u>EXPRESS ASSUMPTION OF THE RISK</u>

Releasing Party hereby acknowledges and understands participating in the Mayhem Motel Immersive Experience can be EXTREMELY DANGEROUS and could result in PERSONAL INJURY, DEATH, AND/OR PROP-ERTY DAMAGE.

The Experience may involve and is not limited to: fog, insects, strobe lights, lasers, foul scents, loud noises, electrical shock, foul language, touching, clothing removal and nudity, sexual contact, dizziness, claustrophobia, suffocation, water and/or water inhalation, brutal aggression, projectiles, psychological distress, use of equipment and facilities which can result in DISABILITY, DISFIG-UREMENT, SERIOUS PHYSICAL, MENTAL, OR EMOTIONAL INJURY, DEATH, OR PROPERTY DAMAGE.

<u>VOLUNTARY PARTICIPATION AND CONSENTS</u>

Releasing Party further acknowledges that by participating in the Mayhem Motel Immersive Experience, Releasing Party may be asked to but is not limited to:

crawl, jump, fall, and hold their breath. They may be touched, moved, and yelled at.

You can revoke your consent to the above at any time by using a safe word ("RED").

Once your safe word has been deployed, the experience will stop as soon as it is reasonably possible, and you will be escorted out of Mayhem Motel.

AGREED TO AND ACCEPTED BY:

____
RELEASING PARTY (PRINT)

________________________________ SIGNA-
TURE OF RELEASING PARTY

________________________________ DATE

________________________________ DATE
OF BIRTH

________________________________ TELE-
PHONE NUMBER / EMAIL ADDRESS

____
EMPLOYEE SIGNATURE OF APPROVAL

____
EMPLOYEE DATE AND STAMP OF APPROVAL

WHAT. In the *actual hell*. Did I just read?

My mouth is hanging open as my eyes scan the words I just carefully devoured. *Electrical shock, suffocation, water inhalation… Sexual freaking contact.*

There is no way in hell I am signing this. *Especially* because it mentions *death*—actual, literal death. As in dying. As in no longer *breathing*.

The scratch of a pen makes me jerk my head toward the

noise. Lenny's writing on his paper…. "You're not actually signing that, are you?" I ask, balking.

"Duh, dude. It's why we're here." He shakes his head without even looking at me like *I'm* the one that's out of my mind.

"Did you even read it?"

"Of course, I did. I'm not that stupid."

"It literally says *death*," I remind him.

"Yeah, but that's not going to happen." He finishes writing and snaps the pen against the clipboard. "This is all just legality shit, so they don't get sued."

His words do absolutely *nothing* to appease me.

"Okay, maybe, but has anyone actually died before?"

"Not that we know of," Collin so helpfully adds.

"Oh, that's just great," I grumble. "Really reassuring."

"Lighten up. This is supposed to be fun."

"I thought it was supposed to be terrifying."

"Yeah." He smirks as he strides toward the front counter. He hands over the papers and pulls out his ID. After a minute of them checking and verifying, it goes through, and he's escorted toward what I assume is the entrance.

Everyone else is close to follow, leaving me still sitting in my metal chair, chilled to the bone while the humidity clings to me like plastic wrap. "Mads, you comin'?" Kane asks from across the room.

I wave around my clipboard, watching the tail-ends of the paper flutter from the movement. *Ugh.* My eyes pinch shut. My lungs contract. Deflate. My legs hammer against the floor.

"Mads." I hear my name again.

Please don't die. Please don't die. I repeat the mantra over in my head as I scribble my signature at the bottom. *My death warrant.*

I can't help the grave thought. I even try to shove it down deep as I show them my ID, watching as they verify my name on both, make a copy, and place my actual card in a file. But still, that feeling lingers.

"Follow me," a voice sounds out, drawing everyone's attention. Feet are tapping anxiously along the floor. I can feel the adrenaline surging in the air, akin to electrical sparks.

Like static.

Hushed conversations cease to exist as we follow through the narrow, unmarked black door and down a dimly lit hallway that smells like a wet basement.

My eyes scour the cement walls, tracing over every crack and stain, every cobweb, and suspicious low-hanging beams.

The floor seems to slope downward as we walk, making my feet stutter. I stop and glance around. *Uh... is the hallway getting smaller, too?*

Air whistles out of my nostrils as my head whips around. Everyone else keeps walking, their steps echoing. A light flickers in the distance as the group pulls further away. I kick my ass into gear and rush to catch up, keeping my gaze pinned to the ground.

But it's still sloping. *Has no one else noticed?*

I should've stayed behind. This was so stupid. I don't need to make friends *this* badly. "Did you guys—" Darkness descends on us in an instant, dousing the entire hallway in inky black. A thud resounds, bouncing off the cool, damp concrete, sounding louder, even as it fades. Someone gasps, making my hair stand on end. A sharp prickle.

It burns.

I reach out in front of me. When my pinky grazes something, I shriek and jerk away. My body slams into the wall, which I clutch desperately, needing the stability as the unknown unfolds right in front of me.

I *knew* it.

"Collin!" Brianne screams. I slam my hands over my ears to block out the magnifying screech.

"Bri?" Collin shouts back, sounding further away. My stomach plummets.

"Uh, can anyone see?" Lenny so helpfully asks.

"No, Len. None of us can see a fucking thing." That was Kane. I'd laugh if I wasn't about to piss my pants.

I squeeze my thighs together and shove a hand between them, needing as much pressure as I can to keep my urine *in* my bladder. Jesus, I should've gone to the bathroom first.

Actually, I should've just locked myself in there until this was all over.

"Where'd that guy go?" That was definitely Lenny. Shoes scrape across the floor. Scuffles and the drag of nails scoring over the porous cement.

"Did you forget none of us can see?!" Collin shouts, sounding so far away.

"We should try to stay together," I try to say, but my voice comes out in a meek whisper.

"What! Oh, fuck, what is—" Screaming silence descends. My breath halts in my lungs, mid-inhale. I choke on the pressure and the sound of my raging heartbeat hammering in my ear canals.

A slow yet impossibly rapid *chug, chug, chug.*

I plaster every inch of myself against the damp wall, still pressing harder even as my feet slip.

"Kane?" I rasp on a cough.

Nothing.

"Kane! Lenny?"

Silence.

I can hear the sound of my own panting, loud and rushed as it fills the staticky air. I slowly slide my foot out, away from the wall, hovering it around. When I meet no resistance, I slam my molars together and force myself to push off the wall.

Leaving the stability makes my skin crawl. Something rushes in the distance—a long, echoing sound that grows closer with every step. I swing my arms out around me, blinking rapidly with wide eyes in hopes I can catch a single glimpse of *anything.*

I've never experienced a darkness so absorbent, like *nothing* exists but me inside a black hole.

It's the most terrified I've ever felt. To be so hopeless and helpless.

As stupid as it is, I close my eyes. Psychological torture is one of their things. This is all this is. A sensory deprivation. A way to knock me off balance.

You can do this, Madi.

Even the voice in my head sounds unconvincing.

"Guys? Are any of you here?" The heel of my palm slams against something, sending me reeling back with a scream. My arms flail as my feet slip, and I tumble to the floor. There's a creak and a snap, followed by a deep, shuddering groan, like a heavy door being shut.

Something long and thin wraps around my bicep. The foreign touch rips a scream from my throat—a sound so brutal, it splits my vocal cords—and I think I taste blood. I try to yank out of the hold, using every ounce of strength I have, but it's fruitless.

Wetness trickles between my fingers, making me gasp. It oozes over my palms. I push down to get away from it, but it starts flowing faster, soaking my jeans in an instant. The sound of it dripping somewhere in the distance is a focal point as I trudge through it on my hands and knees, swallowing down gags as the thick sludge coats my fingers.

The smell of sulfur wafts in my nose, making me gag. My whole stomach convulses as it only grows more potent. It clogs the air, and I swear if I could see, there'd be a haze in the air.

My chest contracts with the effort it takes to inhale, the stench so repulsive, my body begins to fail its most basic instincts.

My limbs slow of their own volition, even as my mind is screaming at me to keep moving toward what must be a drain. A door. Something—*anything*. But I can't think. Not when everything is burning.

My fingers flex through the wetness, pressing against the concrete beneath. It's low enough it doesn't go very far up my hands, but it covers my fingers completely.

With a pained whimper, I slowly lower my upper half to the floor. By the time my chin grazes the liquid, I'm bawling, full, body-wracking sobs. My head dips on a slow incline, but when the foreign wetness covers my face, from chin to forehead, I cry internally.

I still can't breathe, but *fuck,* the relief of keeping the potent stench from seeping into my pores is nearly life-changing. My lips graze the rough textured cement as I bury deeper in the liquid still rushing across the floor, but I don't even care.

My heart is still hammering but seems to slow infinitesimally. A slow chug. A despondent lurch.

"Have you ever thought about drownin' in your own blood?" a dark, hollow voice grazes the shell of my ear, splintering my brain. Just as my head jerks back, a scream already exploding, my forehead drills back against the floor. I inhale whatever liquid is suffocating me.

I splutter, gasping and choking on... *blood.*

My eyes roll back just as my back bows, my stomach concaving in a desperate attempt to gain the faintest traces of oxygen.

The fingers gripping the back of my head have an iron-tight hold. They slowly drag down, scraping over my scalp until my nape is gripped, and I'm jerked up with a weak gasp, uncaring that I'm probably swallowing blood because... *Air.*

It fills me rapidly, each inhale burning and aching like my body regrets it as much as it needs it.

"*Hmm...*" The talons scrape across my skin. I jolt and try to pull away, but I can't move. I'm held exactly where I'm wanted.

"W-what do-do you w-want?" I choke on my own sobs, hiccupping and wailing. A singular finger pricks at the divot just above the start of my hairline, right in the center of my neck. My legs lock, curled inwardly and twisted back in my awkward position.

A whimper bleeds out of me as the sharp point presses deeper, surely cutting me right open. I hold as still as possible in hopes they don't puncture to my freaking spine. Trembling and throbbing.

"To hear you scream." The blade scores my flesh, and I scream as I drown in my terror.

CHAPTER FIVE

THEY'RE SO... BLUE

STATIC

I slam the door and crank down the bar lock behind the fifth—sixth?—group of the night. They all safe worded no more than fifteen, twenty-something minutes in. I roll my eyes as I round the corner, back to the start. All over again.

I fuckin' love my job, but sometimes, I really hate it. Can no one stand being scared anymore? Hell, just a little trickle of piss running down their leg, and they're blurting "Red" in their next breath.

"You look pissed," Vulture snarks as he comes up beside me. I don't even spare him a glance as we both make our way toward the front so we can work the next group through, though I don't have high expectations.

"I swear the safe words are comin' faster and faster now," I grumble. "It sucks bein' pulled out right in the middle of it."

"Yeah, I feel you." Vulture slaps my back. I shrug him off with a glare. Our earpieces crackle as Kierra lets us know they're bringing in the next group.

"It's *showtime*." Vulture waggles his fingers, mocking Beetlejuice before he shoves through the hidden door just ahead, his black cloak fluttering outward. I watch it click shut before I veer left and take the steps toward the lower level that they bring them in at.

I like watching their initial reactions to the introduction.

The way their eyes light up with equal parts fear and excitement. Their pure, foolish innocence. Because they have no idea what's comin'. Even if they *think* they know, they *never* do.

HIS EYES...

They're so... blue.

I stare down at his limp body, crouched over his face. Two of my fingers hold open his eyelid so I can watch the way it rolls around inside his skull.

He passed out. Just from a few pricks of my pointed, gloved fingers and the scrape of my axe.

Amazing.

I'm beaming at his lax, twitching face, relishing in the fear that absolutely consumed him. Fuck, there aren't many that just bear with it like he did. It's like he forgot he even *has* a safe word—not that I'm going to remind him.

I'm having too much fun with this little surprise.

He groans weakly and rolls over onto his side. I release his eyelid with a frown and step back into the corner of the room where the shadows still linger.

A single dimly lit, yellow bulb hangs from a cord in the

center of the room, a few feet in front of him. I tap it as I pass, sending it swinging into the air.

"*Nngh,*" he groans as he rouses, sending a spike of adrenaline to my heart. He slides his palms across the floor, wincing. It takes him a few long, agonizingly slow moments to right himself, but the second he's vertical, it's like it all slams back into him at once.

My lips twitch and slowly curl upward.

"Oh, shit." His feet shove him backward, where he slams into the wall, his skull bouncing with a crack that echoes so wonderfully. A symbol of our isolation. He cries out and drops his head between his raised knees with a whimper.

Shuddering, he jerks his head back up just as fast, as if suddenly remembering he's not alone.

His eyes are wide and glassy, pinned with potent fear.

My heart rate accelerates.

I cock my head to the side. This boy is just a mess. I almost don't have to work to scare him—he's doing enough of that all on his own.

His brain must be a wildly mesmerizing place. But that just won't do...

No, that won't do at all.

I purposefully rap my knuckles against the wall before I shove back, sending me out of the room. I cackle at the sound of his scream. The way it echoes through the halls of Mayhem. The way it echoes right into *me.*

The door he was pressed against creeps open. Footsteps thunder down the warped hall, taking him deeper into my domain.

Time to chase my little prize.

Chapter Six
Please Be a Dream

Madison

Blinding white light flashes in a disorienting rhythm, making the floor and the walls skip as I try to blink through it.

It only makes it worse.

But then, the fog starts to seep out from the cracks in the walls. And a high-pitched wail screams from above me.

I'm attacked from all sides—but not physically.

It's all in my head, and I can't fight it.

The wet slaps of my shoes against the black and white tile floor resounds in my head. It's a distorted, warped, white noise as I push down with every ounce of strength I have, but just as I think I'm finally gaining distance, I collide with a wall.

"*Nngh,*" I groan as my face smacks into the splintered wood. A sliver pierces my nose. I wince.

My hands finally catch up with my brain and slam against the wall, two seconds too late. My nose throbs and burns.

Wetness trickles out of my nostril. My cheek stings from the fresh scrape.

The wetness slips into my mouth, and I shudder at the tang of copper as it slides over my teeth and seeps into my porous tongue.

A bellowed wail sounds somewhere to my left. Or maybe my right. *Jesus,* is that coming from above me?

Slaps of shoes hammer on the floor. More follow. A flash of movement has my every muscle tensing, locked in place. "Shit! Fuck!" Panting breaths so close. "Oh, God, no!" someone howls. I barely hear, let alone recognize their voice through the racketing clamor blaring.

A vibrating growl accompanies. I grip the wall, curling my fingers around an exposed beam as I try to scale it, to get the *hell away* from whatever's coming. My feet leave the ground just as a shadow moves through the drowning fog.

All I see is black. Flashes of white. No eyes. Just black, soulless holes. My chest heaves and contracts as air whistles out of me, faster than I can replenish it. Sweat slicks my palms. I can't look away from the horrifying creature coming right for me.

Oh, my God, I'm going to die.

My breath stutters. Tears spring to my eyes. I slip from the wall and cower, curling into a ball. Wind whips past me. The flash of cold amongst the heat singing my skin makes me jerk and whimper.

Then someone—some*thing*—much heavier, bigger, all-consuming presses closer. There's a shift of fabric against my soaked jeans. They stick to my legs, making my skin itch and crawl even worse. Hot breath blows in my face, inches away from my hands and forearms.

My eyes are squeezed shut so tight, I see white lines zigging and zagging behind my closed lids. The pressure in my skull magnifies, my optic nerve the radial point.

A voice hitches. Then, a cackle unlike anything I've ever heard before blares in my face, right on me. Into me.

A shriek of my own rips from my vocal cords as spittle flies across my cheeks, my lips. Inside my mouth. Coolness douses me in an instant. Liquid pools over my head and flows downward. I inhale and splutter, choking on water as I breathe it in.

It keeps coming.

It doesn't stop.

My arms flail, reaching and grasping for purchase anywhere. Somewhere.

I can't breathe. I can't see. My heart jumps into my throat, hammering away, reminding me how real this is.

The suffocating presence looming disappears in an instant. So does the water dousing me. My eyes fly open—and I've never regretted an action more.

I should've stayed in the dark.

I should've never walked through the doors of Mayhem.

My eyes lock on the figure at the end of the hall. It's... oh, *Jesus,* it's tall. He takes a step forward with a sharp, grating noise. The strobe lights make my head pulse, and my eyes burn as I try to focus.

The figure is leering, head cocked to the side as it comes closer.

Another step.

I press back into the wall. It doesn't make me feel any safer. My feet press and drag along the slick, chipped, tile floor as I scramble to push myself upright.

I force my eyes away from whatever is coming for me. To escape. With my life.

A life he wants for himself.

More screams and rips of terror echo out. More high-pitched, booming laughter. Taunting bellows.

It's all too much. I'm dizzy and disoriented with the intensity of it all.

The water beneath my hands makes it impossible to gain any traction. I can feel the figure gaining distance with every wheezing breath. The scraping gets louder. More pronounced. Like the sharpest nails on a chalkboard. Each long, drawn-out decibel another stitch in the fate I sealed for myself.

One second, I was safe. In distance, but maybe not in sanity.

The next, the most haunting, horrific, entrancing clown I have ever seen is in my face, large mouth spread into a manic, crazed smile, two full rows of pointed, white teeth on display and flashing in the light.

My eyes dart over every inch of his white-painted face. Over the coal black smudges around his eyes and mouth. The way they flicker up in distorted lines, adding to the horror.

The collar around his neck is black and frilly, shredded and sleek with something... *oh, God.* My stomach revolts, and the urge to hunch over is nearly too strong to resist.

But if I move, I'll touch...

"Scream for me." A wickedly long tongue sneaks out and swipes across my stinging cheek. My eyes slam shut on a pathetic whimper just as fingers delve into the hair on the top of my head and yank, making me do just as he demanded.

His mouth stretches even wider. *Shit, that's not normal. Is he real?*

I never believed in ghosts until now, but hell.

His tongue scrapes over my chin. My bottom lip wobbles.

I tremble and moan. Small whimpers that are barely audible.

Long, thin fingers clasp my throat and steal what little oxygen I had left. My eyelids fly open in a panic—a worse one than I'm already wracked with. The clown in front of me beams. His white eyes glow, nearly iridescent.

Tears spring to my eyes as he clamps down on the sides of my neck. My blood chugs. I can feel each heavy pulse as it slows, drawing to a stop.

My lungs deflate, contract. Scream.

His fingers tighten, grazing the hair at my nape.

"Sweet dreams, darlin'."

THE FIRST THING my brain registers is that it's quieter. The high-pitched wail is gone, and in its place is a deep, thundering bass. It's heavy, vibrating into me, into my lungs.

Breathing hurts. My throat burns and aches. I swallow the lump down, but it stays lodged against my uvula.

My eyes are much harder to force open. To see what I saw before.

Please be a dream.

I lean forward, only to be slammed back at my efforts. I wriggle my shoulders, feeling tight bands wrapped around my biceps. My stomach.

Hell, my feet, too?

Dropping my head until my chin bumps my... My eyes fly open at the feel of my bare skin. I blink through the lights still flashing and the fog still lingering.

My stomach is contracted, heaving and waving with my stuttered pants.

My jeans are long gone, leaving only my wet boxers plastered to my thighs.

"Welcome back," a heavy voice drawls in a... southern accent? My head jerks up at the sound, finding the clown pacing the space opposite me. The room we're in resembles a regular motel room, only... not.

What once was wallpaper is now bare, ripped open walls, gaps in wood separating rooms. There's a bed. It's stained. Black speckles, red puddles, and... yellow blobs.

A rope hangs from the banister. A gut-punch reminder of the suicides that happened here.

Evil churns all around me, forcing itself into me. Tainting my blood. Blackening my organs. Eradicating my soul.

I glance down. But it's still so impossible to see with that godforsaken, flashing light. My eyes burn so badly. The tears never stop flowing.

"Please," I whisper. My voice cracks. A loud cackle booms out.

I wince and hunch inward. The sound creeps up my spine, slithering slow and daunting. A slow descent into madness.

That scraping sounds again. A glint of silver. The clown... *shit,* what was his name? It was creepy. Made my skin crawl.

He lifts his arm into the air, casually swinging... *oh, Jesus, is that an axe? That's an axe...*

Flashes of red streak as he swings it around. My eyes draw toward the wooden handle, where there's even more red. It's stained into the grain.

It's fake blood. It's fake, it's fake, it's fake.

My yelp is muffled when he lunges, the handle of his axe aiming right for my mouth. It slams against my teeth, rocking my head back as they clank together. He pries my mouth apart and shoves the wooden handle inside.

Copper.

Oh, my God, it's real blood.

I start hyperventilating. My vision swarms as I choke, gagging as he shoves it deeper, the curved end splintering my flesh. My throat contracts, preventing entry, even as vomit threatens, creeping up.

My eyes are wide, blurry with wetness as I stare at... Static.

Static the clown.

His black-painted lips are stretched thin, those long, sharp, white teeth on full display as he holds the bloodied axe head in his hand, sharp edge pressed against his covered palm.

He rotates it, twisting the handle inside my mouth—a mouth far too small for such a large piece of wood. I whimper and blubber, trying to speak around the wood gagging me, my eyes never straying from his white ones.

"What was that?" He presses closer and yanks out the handle. I gasp, splutter, and retch as vomit spews from between my lips and splatters on the worn, shredded, exposed carpet below.

With the strobe flashing behind him, Static comes into view in fractured segments.

A black and white striped shirt with the collar donning his neck... I shiver, my body twitching from the force. His hair is black and thick and pushed up into thick spikes in haunting disarray.

Pants with one half a solid black, the other striped to match his shirt. Thick, black boots with what I think are buckles... I crane my neck, but from the way I'm pinned against *something*, I can't make out more than that.

He steps around me, drawing closer. Hot air wafts across my face, and the dampness of my tears only heightens the sensation.

I try to squeeze my legs together against the pressure in my bladder, but it surmounts my capabilities. And the sharp scrape of that blade's edge against the back of my neck followed by my hollowed screams has my bladder releasing.

At first, the warmth is almost comforting against the haunting chill of the room, but then, my lagging brain registers that I'm peeing all over myself, and I start sobbing.

They wrack my body. My lungs concave. My ribs protrude from my body. All as my urine streams down and soaks into the carpet. The smell... oh, *Jesus,* the smell wafts into the air, lingering with the fog.

A deep inhale sounds right next to my ear—a sharp whistling noise. The drag of a nose. A tongue. That axe...

All marrying to demolish my psyche.

Chapter Seven

The Perfect Victim

Static

"I can taste your fear on my tongue..." I lick my lips. My tongue grazes the side of his sweaty neck. "And the scent of your piss. Fuck, you're really scared, aren't ya?" I throw my head back with a cackle, relishing in the merriment.

"P-p-please," he begs helplessly, cowering away as my large frame rounds the dolly I have him strapped to.

Strobe lights flash around us, clogs of smoke thick in my lungs as I breathe him in. *All* of him.

Ammonia, sweat, and terror. *Fuck, that's good.*

"Please what, darlin'? Please don't cut you with my pretty axe? Please don't take your blood as my own? Please..."

His eyes are scrunched shut. A weak block of his reality.

It makes my blood thrum excitedly.

His ribs stick out from his midsection, forming a perfect hollow. I swipe the slick handle of my axe along a deep groove, relishing in the way he squeaks and shudders, trying to suck in even more to get away from the touch.

My eyes flicker back up to his mouth. The way his lips are stretched so thin, they turned white. His jaw was nearly unhinged as it opened wide for my axe.

My gaze drops to the floor, eyeing the small pool of watery vomit. I smirk. Took him longer than I thought.

But let's not forget the piss staining his legs. The perfect puddle leeching into the paper-thin carpet beneath his feet. Into the wooden slats. The slow trickle as it continues to drip from the steel bottom plate of the dolly.

He's the perfect victim. Or he would *be if…*

I step close, uncaring of the piss dripping onto the sleek leather of my boots. They're waterproof for a reason.

I drag my hand over his bare chest, swiping through the dribbles of vomit and sweat clinging to his smooth flesh. I drag my gloved hand across, ensuring he feels the light scrape of my pointed fingertips as I circle him, round and around.

At first, he tries to follow me, eyes straining in their sockets as I disappear from sight. Head cranked back, turning left and right, seeking every visible inch I give him.

His attention is magnificent.

I'm so happy I stole him away from the rest.

He's all mine.

Every pass, my hand drops lower. My index finger dips into his belly button, and he hisses, then whimpers. His head shakes back and forth, sending a few droplets flying from the ends of his hair.

My tongue flicks out over a drop that landed on my upper lip.

Mmm. Nothing tastes better than fear-induced sweat.

Sickly sweet and slightly sour.

I'm at his back now, my stomach pressed against the bars, keeping him exactly where I want him. Trembling, whimpering with snotty sobs, seeking me out even as he doesn't want to...

Yeah. With him, it's *all* already so different. I don't want to make him my victim.

I want him to *want* to be.

So, for the first time in the few years I've worked at Mayhem, scarin' the shit out of people—sometimes literally—I'm going off script. To do something *really* fun.

All for me.

"Tell me your name." I bend over to whisper into his ear, scoring my teeth over the edge of his earlobe. He shrieks and jerks to the side, banging his other ear against the metal bar. The groan that escapes from deep in his gut reverberates off the walls and into me.

"Tell me," I hiss. He gasps, the sound wet and filled with tears.

"M-mad—"

"M-m-m," I mock him with a snicker as I round his right side.

"Ma-Madison," he finally chokes out, eyes comically wide as I step into view again. And I know exactly what he's seeing, too. The face that fills most nightmares.

Coulrophobia in the horror industry makes for a great line of work. 'Cause as much as people are terrified of clowns, they fuckin' love being scared by 'em, too.

Especially one that looks like me.

Madison's eyes lift up, locking on the thick, spiked horseshoe ring hanging from the center of my nose. Then, they shift to the spikes in both sides of my bottom lip. I smile wide, flashing him my fake, sharpened teeth, spreading my mouth as wide open as I can. A small flick of my tongue. I even widen my eyes too, lunging forward for effectiveness.

He screams and slams his eyes closed. His whole body wracks with tremors. I ease forward, towering above his small frame as I run my fingers over his shoulder and down his bicep. His skin is smooth. Slick. I dig my index finger in, just to watch his flesh bloom with a stripe of crimson.

The lights flashing distort the terrified boy in front of me, but there's no turning it off. And it actually might work in my favor...

My groin furls with warmth as I work my hands over him, scraping lightly as I make my way down, following the center line leading toward his boxers. His body is supple. Not well defined with a layer of softness above the muscle.

Perfect for splitting open...

I step through a plume of smoke lingering a few feet off the floor. It dances around, curling and morphing into different designs that add a layer of density. I dip down to pick up my axe, gripping the end of it with loose fingers.

Swinging it back and forth, I let the blade scrape against the floor. The shredded carpet below exposes the wooden underlayment beneath, giving a nice, sharp hiss with every swipe. Poor little Madison is stuck between keeping his eyes scrunched tight and eyeing the motion of my axe warily.

Like the prospect of blindness is just as scary as the blatant reality.

I let my eyes drag over his body, nearly fully exposed to me. His chest is heaving, even though he hasn't moved a muscle—because he can't. His lips are parted, glistening with saliva. His eyes are wide—glassy. Eyelashes clumped together in thick spikes.

His hair is still wet from the water. Probably from sweat, too. I breathe in deeply, my eyes flashing at the whiff of ammonia. *Yeah...*

I swing my axe over my shoulder, letting it sit alongside my neck as I lean in. Close. Closer until I can feel Madison's heat on my lips. He's trembling, head veering as far right as he can get it.

The tendons beneath the thin layer of skin bulge, strained against the pressure. I let the spiked end of my lip ring drag over the flesh in the barest graze. My tongue darts across my painted lips. I'm foaming at the maw to get a taste of him.

Of that sweet, delectable fear oozing from his pores.

All for me. Because of me.

And I'd be a fool to deny myself such a sweet, little treat.

When my teeth scrape the tendon, Madison whimpers, head shaking rapidly, sending drops of salty wetness splattering across the side of my face. I swipe a few up with my tongue. My eyes roll back as my dick fully hardens, sending my blood ablaze.

Fuck, he's got me wrapped around his little finger.

Such a strange little thing, he is.

Not blurting the one word that would get him out of this...

It's almost like he's beggin' for it.

When the butt end of the handle bumps against his chest, he squirms away, tugging against the binds keeping him pinned. I pull back just enough to let my breath fan across his face.

I know he can smell the tobacco on my breath. Maybe even the trace hints of the mint I crushed between my teeth right after.

His air is just as hot. Just as yummy.

I let the axe drag down my chest until the curved blade digs into my trapezius with a sharp bite. My eyes nearly roll back at the willful pain. My cock bucks, derailing my train of thought.

I wanna scare my little treat.

But I wanna taste him, too.

My gaze drags down his stomach, bypassing the sharpness of his ribs, down to his tiny belly button, until I reach the elastic band of his boxers. The dark blue material clings to his legs, still wet from the water I doused him with. And the piss he couldn't keep inside.

I kinda wanna see if I can get him to do it again, but I don't think his bladder is full enough.

Maybe I could get a little trinkle...

But the soft firmness pushing against the flowing material around his thighs thwarts that idea in an instant. My head cocks to the side. Then lowers so I can get even closer.

My eyes narrow, then widen in surprise.

Oh, how fuckin' sweet...

"Well... well... well..." I *tsk,* flicking my tongue along my teeth, pressing hard against the sharpened points until the natural instinct to pull away kicks in—and then, I push even more.

"What's this, darlin'?" I use my free hand to palm his semi-erection. Madison jerks at the touch, squealing like a little pig. He bucks against the dolly, nearly tipping it over. My lips purse as my brows hike mid-forehead.

Mmm, he's got some strength in there after all.

Although, he's still here... he hasn't given up, so maybe that says a lot more.

My earpiece crackles as someone presses a button. I hear a few panted breaths followed by echoing static, and then Ravage's voice. "Two safe-worded. Just got them out." His breath makes the winded crackling worse as he blows in my ear, then it's cut off, leaving my ear canal ringing in the silence.

That means there are only two others still hanging on, along with my little treat, of course.

I nearly groan, almost succumbing to the urge to pout. I wanted to take my time with him. To explore every inch of him while he's at my mercy, but if history has told me anything, it's that I'm on the biggest ticking clock.

And each second that drags is another I'm wasting when I could already be tasting my treat.

With a clicking noise, I firm my grip and slam the toe of my boot against the metal plate Madison's feet are planted on. The dolly lurches forward. Madison careens, a scream ripping from his throat as the dolly teeters, sending his dick sliding through my gloved hand.

I watch through a half-lidded gaze, distorted by the blinding light flashing, as Madison tenses from head to toe. Every muscle, every limb—hell, probably even his organs—solidify like they're bathed in cement.

It only makes me hotter.

He shakes his head no. A continuous motion that must make him dizzy.

So foolish.

A small whimper I nearly miss croaks from deep within him. I press closer, sending the butt end of my axe bumping against his torso. His shoulders wrack with a sob, tears streaming, snot gurgling.

I sigh. "Your dick is hard, darlin'," I speak the truth into the static-charged air. My little treat doesn't budge. His head never stops shaking. Those sobs never cease for a moment, only change direction into something softer, more resigned the longer I stroke him through the thin, damp material. The only barrier between us.

The last piece to shred.

"Fear makes some people hard. All that adrenaline pumping into your system... the spikes from the all-consuming panic..." I drag my tongue across his cheek, growling at the rough scrape of invisible stubble.

"It's all about the chemistry, darlin'. Nothin' to be ashamed of."

I trace my spiked index finger just beneath the ribbed band hanging low around his hips. My eyes never stray from Madison's wrinkled lids as I press my hips forward, dragging my hard cock across his stomach. *Shit, he's so tiny...*

He sucks his in, pulling away from the contact. I cackle in amusement, not deterred in the slightest. I only press harder, ensuring he feels every inch of what he's done to me.

"Your fear turns me on, too."

His lips part, opening and closing like a fish out of water. "Is this p-part of it?" he stammers. My eyes light up at the sound of his voice, hoarse and cracked from endless screaming. "I re-read about sex-sexual c-contac-ct."

Ahh, the waiver.

I beam. "Nah, darlin'. Nothin' like that's ever happened. Until now. You're just too tasty to resist." Madison's eyes dart all over my face, pinging from my hair to my forehead, my mouth, down my neck to where my axe is still hanging.

A nightmare he wants.

C'mon, darlin'...

"Oh, Jesus," he whimpers, then the sound cuts off to nothing, but his lips still move like he's talking to himself.

"Give me what I want, Madison..."

He pants heavily—loudly. Screams ricochet somewhere in the motel. A distant vibration. My temples throb from the fuckin' strobe lights. I hate that it distorts my vision of my little treat so much, but maybe with the illusion, it'll be easier to make him give in.

Time's runnin' out.

"Give it to me." I let the tip of my finger graze his cockhead to prompt a response. His eyes fly open wide, nearly bulging from his skull. His throat bobs. His muscles strain, veins bulging beneath the skin in a pattern I'd love to trace with my tongue.

I flash my teeth. "Just nod your head."

A breath. His. Mine.

...He nods.

Chapter Eight

All Part of the Game

Madison

My gut is gnarled, twisted, and coiled with equal parts dread and trepidation and...

Oh, Jesus. Why did I nod? *Why did I nod?!*

Static's eyes gleam, his white irises glowing. Black-painted lips are stretched wide, showcasing two full rows of teeth that look like they could shred my flesh into tiny bits and pieces...

Tears pool. Drip. Splash as they fall somewhere below. Somewhere I can't see because I'm fucking trapped. Strapped and pinned to a rusted, metal dolly. The straps are thick, and they feel like leather—not that it even freaking matters.

Jesus, I can't think properly.

My head's spinning. My dick is hot. *So hot. And hard.* I'm hard, and the clown from *everyone's* nightmares knows it. He sees it, too. Feels it because he's touching me.

He's touching me... My head slams back against the metal with a *ting* that reverberates in my skull. His textured grip is insane. It burns. Stings, a little too, but the pressure...

My heart is banging against my sternum, knocking so loud I can hear it in my ears, rushing over the whistling of my breath in and out through my nostrils.

The pointed tip of his finger delves deeper, a long, drawn-out scratch from my glans, down my shaft. A path of searing heat that makes me buck.

Static cackles, and the sound shoots straight to my nape, where the hairs stand on end, and a chill slithers down my spine... where it spins around and pools at my groin, making me that much hotter.

I slam my eyes closed as my face burns more than ever before. In shame. Embarrassment for how my body is betraying me. How *good* it feels, even as my skin is crawling with the desire to just get the hell *out.*

But I can't think. All I can do is feel. What he's doing to me. How he's touching me. That I *like* it. The ache of fear mingling with the taste of pulsing pleasure.

It's all part of the game.

I can do this.

I can hold on.

"*Mmm,*" Static rumbles, a deep vibration directly against my chest. That damn axe of his digs into me. A dull ache deep in my tissue. Each hair fiber pricks on my head, standing straight out. I'm sure I look like I got jolted with electricity.

Because I did.

Static is his name, after all.

And he exudes the most potent, electrical charge I've ever felt in my life.

A line from his long fingers directly to my cock.

His hand works me over in fast, jerking motions, and my hips try to move of their own volition, trapped effectively by Static's own devices.

His fingers are so long, I can feel them overlapping around me, his sharp fingertips scraping my bare flesh with every downward stroke. Hell, on the upstroke, too.

It burns and aches and stings and... *oh... no.*

Something hard bumps against my lips. My eyes snap open. The wooden handle of his axe is pressed against my mouth. The blade is pointed low, so the angle is weird. "Suck on my axe, darlin'."

Gooseflesh takes over my entire body. Every inch of skin is alight with bumps. Sense of touch is heightened to the point of stinging bliss.

The pressure of the textured wood has my lips splitting for entry before I can think—because I can't.

My brain left the room—hell, it left the state minutes ago. Hours ago? What time is it?

"Shit," Static drawls, his accent thicker than ever as he draws the word out. I shudder as it presses deeper, making space inside the small cavity of my mouth. It slides over my teeth, my tongue. They make their own grooves in the wood.

Copper.

Potent metal lingers on my tongue.

I swallow it down, unable to hold back my whimper.

The red... the red was blood. I'm—I've—I've got someone's blood in my mouth.

"That's it, treat. That's real nice." His drawl confuses me while it's muddled with his sinister tone. Sharp and wild.

I try to shake my head, to clear the fog that's long since taken over, but I can't move.

Shit, I forgot I can't move.

I fight against the binds again. Static's hand moves faster.

I slump as my balls tingle, tightening and throbbing. Saliva pools in my mouth, increasing by the second. I try to swallow it down, but it creeps out between my stretched lips, dripping down the wooden handle. Onto my chest, down my stomach.

Static's hovering over me, towering. So tall and leery. I feel utterly and wholly consumed. Decimated and irrevocably discombobulated.

His white eyes snap up to my face. The sudden move makes me gasp, having that frightening gaze locked on me. It drops to my mouth, where the axe is still lodged very tight. My spit is warm but sticky. And it itches.

Static's hand leaves my dick to swipe up a bubble forming near the corner of my mouth. His finger pricks my skin as he drags it across my face before sucking my spit into his mouth, wrapping his scarily long tongue around the digit.

I gasp, choking on the spit that flies into the back of my throat.

The axe clatters to the floor, drawing a shriek from my throat as the blade dings against the wood, sending a deep, jolting vibration into the air. One I feel in my bones.

The clown drops out of sight. I blink through the flashes, disoriented. My head throbs, my temples pounding to the beat of my heart—which is going absolutely haywire.

Hands on my pelvis make me jerk. My head drops. Static is below me and... and *oh... Oh, Jesus...*

He shoves forward and buries his white and black painted face into my damp boxers. I feel the rush of air as he inhales. It lasts a long time. His shoulders raise, chest nearly bumping into my legs from how full his lungs get.

"You smell delectable, darlin'. Wonder if you taste just as good, too." His long fingers rip my boxers down my legs. The waistband is stretched tight, trapped around my upper thighs from the black strap crossed over both of my legs, a few inches above my knees.

My dick bobs in his face. The fog circulating the air is cool against my burning flesh. Static descends on me. The pulsing light makes each inch of movement appear distorted, frozen in time.

He moves. *Flash.* Leans forward. *Flash.* His tongue's out. *Flash.* It's on my dick. *Flash.*

Wet heat surrounds every inch of me. I gasp and cry out, hands fisting. Tugging, pulling against my restraints.

Sharp teeth scrape down my pathetically rock-hard erection. Nothing more than a tease, but I scream, regardless. At the threat, the pleasure.

Why does it feel so good...

What's happening?

His throat closes around my head and squeezes the glans with a tight constriction that makes my brain flash like the freaking pulsing lights dousing the room in a drugging pull.

His hands drag up my thighs, scraping over my leg hair still standing on end, moving around my hips to my ass, where he digs in deep to the muscle there. Pointed fingertips score my flesh, adding a fresh sting to the ache his mouth has put in my dick.

The ache to come. To release the boiling adrenaline coursing through my bloodstream.

All of it—every *ounce*—has congregated to my balls, where it sits heavy and tight and painful. But so *good and wrong and...* I need it.

The muscles in my legs flex, and my fingers clench, nails biting into my palms until my skin separates with a fresh wave of stinging air. I flex them outward, scraping them over the metal bar, gathering what's probably rust beneath the nails as I dig. Scrape. Bury.

Static's spiked, black hair tunnels in and out of my warped

vision as he moves over me, using his grip on my ass to pull himself closer. Deeper. His teeth are sharp with every swipe of his mouth.

They cut me, maim me, make me bleed. But then, his tongue is right there, wickedly long and wet, soothing the destruction of his fangs.

He pulls back. Air caresses my wet flesh, making me hiss at the loss of his warmth. My hips make a pathetic careening gesture, desperate for it again, even as my brain screams at me to *stop*.

That my very flesh is seconds away from being ripped off my body and devoured by the sinister clown with death in his eyes... or maybe it's the desire for carnage.

But my dick doesn't care. My body doesn't either.

The fear... like he said... makes me *hot*.

Oh, Jesus, I'm pathetic.

I'm nothing more than a whimpering, pleading mess for a freaking clown to put my dick back into his mouth.

What the hell happened to this day? Am I even alive? Did I die minutes after walking inside Mayhem?

"You're very much here, darlin', and at my mercy, just how I want ya."

Nope, okay. This is happening.

I'm just screwed in the head. Gone completely mental... It's the psychological torture they stated in the waiver.

Static made me his victim, and I fell right into his hands... or his mouth. His very sharp mouth. That feels way too good...

He buries his face in my crotch. I can feel his nose dragging over my flesh, the sharp plumes of air as he pants against me, inhaling every inch he touches.

Oh... my God.

"Such a little treat," he drawls, accent so thick and heavy. And then, his mouth is back on my cock, enveloping every inch with a heady swallow.

A swallow that is my ticket straight into hell, break lines cut, and gas pedal pinned to the floor.

CHAPTER NINE

THE TASTE OF HIM

STATIC

Madison's timid little whimpers are a hit straight to my brain—and my fuckin' dick. Which is harder than it's ever been. My little treat is... such a surprise.

The scrape of his fingers against the metal as he scrambles for purchase is music to my ears. I bob my head over his length, sheathing my teeth the best I can, but fuck, these fuckers were not made for suckin' a dick. No way, no how.

I know he feels 'em with every drag of my mouth, but it seems the sharp bite of pain only makes my little darlin' that much hotter.

Shit, he's amazin'.

The lingering scent of his urine wafts into my nose whenever I bury my nose close to his groin. I swallow around his cockhead, just to get as close as I can. He fills my throat. Not too big, leaning on the average side, but definitely the perfect size to fit inside my throat without suffocating me or triggering my gag reflex too harshly.

Every time I pull back to tongue the ridge just beneath his head, I bury my fingers deeper in his crack. My gloves keep my fingertips from feeling much more than hot, damp heat.

A heat I want nothing more than to feel against my bare skin, but there's no time.

Not yet, anyway.

But I'll make sure to get more with my little treat.

He and I are far from done.

His body is glistening, the white light only accentuating the gleam. He flashes in and out, like the shutter of a disposable camera.

Now that I think about it... I wish I would've brought one. To capture this moment in time... and to send as a little reminder to my treat if he decides he wants to try and forget this. Forget *me*.

Yeah... I chuckle around his dick, making it buck against the vibration. My little darlin' will *never* forget this.

Getting head from a clown is something no one would be able to stop thinking about.

I swallow greedily, relishing in the taste of him. Salty and musky. A little bitter.

Those hands of his keep scraping, the rest of his body bowing, resisting the binds keeping him secure. My eyes flash up to his left hand.

Before I can think of the consequences, I release the strap around his wrist, freeing just that hand. His fingers delve straight into my hair like they have a mind of their own. Like he *needs* to touch me.

He yanks my hair, ripping a few strands right out of my

fuckin' skull. I grunt. He tugs harder. Yanking, pulling me closer, further away. Like he can't make up his mind.

I shake my head, and his dick stabs the inside of my cheek. He hisses as my teeth dig in near his base.

I drag my mouth back down at the wave of static flooding my ear. My heart hammers against my ribs. My fingers dig into Madison's crease. I graze his hole...

"Oh, Jesus," he wails. My eyes roll up, watching tears roll down his face. Dripping. His blunt nails carve into my scalp, surely shredding the skin. I slurp on his dick, relishing in the twitch, in the pulse in his balls as my chin taps against them with every downward drag.

Mmm, I bet his cum is just as sweet.

The first pulsing spurt against the back of my throat brings equal parts wonder and dread. I pull him out of my throat, my eyes rolling back as Madison unloads in my mouth. Thick. Salty.

Painfully fuckin' sweet.

I keep sucking in heavy pulls, never wanting it to end. Madison is too good. Whimpering, tears still flowing through clumped eyelashes fanned across the planes of his cheekbones. Hand, fingers, clutching, gripping my skull. Keeping me pressed close. Pushing me away from the onslaught.

With a bated breath, I stand on surprisingly shaky legs, eyes lingering on the smears of my grease paint staining his skin. Marking him as mine.

My dick has a mind of its own, throbbing and aching inside my pants. And the sight of my little treat, the *taste* of him lingering on my tongue and in the back of my throat, only makes me teeter on the edge.

I grip his waistband and slowly drag his now mostly dry

boxers over his legs with a hiss, hating the sight of his package disappearing from sight.

With gritted teeth, I force myself to remember this *will* happen again.

I'll make sure of it.

Whether I show up in my darlin's nightmares or his dreams, he *will* come to see me again.

And if he doesn't...

I'll find him.

I've never been one to care about moral consequences—or even the legal ones.

Once he's covered, I hover above him, over him, filling his space with *me*. His arm lifts from his side, fingertips brushing over my arm, plucking at the striped fabric. A hesitant touch.

He moves up, tracing the worn, nearly shredded collar around my neck.

Staring through a half-lidded gaze, I unsnap the collar from my neck and drag it off. I trail the frilly end over his exposed abdomen, up his chest, before wrapping it around his neck and snapping it in place.

My head tilts to the side as I observe my treat. Collared by me, with *my own* collar...

Yeah, that's nice. *Really nice.*

I push against him, nearly knocking the dolly off balance. Madison's face is buried in my chest. Warm breath seeps through the fabric of my shirt. Resting my chin on the top of his head, I reach down and start undoing his binds.

One by one, the straps fall away until I'm forced to pull back to undo the ones pinning his ankles.

"Another safe worded. Two left." My earpiece crackles.

It's time to depart...

I eye Madison. From the top of his head to his shoes, bare everywhere except for his boxers and *my* collar.

Who knew I had such a sweet tooth?

I dip down, hunching over to press my lips to his ear. His eyes are wide as he watches me descend on him, limbs stiffening, even through the drugging haze of postcoital bliss—or maybe he's still too scared to feel it properly.

Maybe it's magnified tenfold...

Grazing a canine against his lobe, I rasp, "You better run, darlin'... 'Cause the others are comin' to get ya." I delve my fingers into the longer hair atop his head and crank his head around to slam our mouths together.

I swallow his choking gasp with greed, thrusting my tongue between his lips for more. Madison's wary at first, unmoving against me. But the moment my tongue slips against his, he groans too and falls pliant, like the perfect little victim.

Shit. Shit, yeah.

Hammering footsteps make me jolt. I rip my mouth away with a growl and shove Madison away. He trips from the sudden movement and clambers to the floor with a shriek.

Such a beautiful melody.

I can't wait to hear him scream for me again.

I flash my eyes and take a step forward. "They're comin'." And with immaculate timing, more feet hammer down the hall. A door opens with a bang, then there's a piercing scream.

Madison's eyes shoot wide. He stares at the door, chest heaving. He looks back at me. I lunge with a cackle, and he shrieks and shoots to his feet, scrambling toward the door.

I watch with longing as my treat flies out of the room, leaving the door hanging open on one hinge. I yank on my hair with a silent growl, breathing heavily through my nose.

Reveling in the scent of his piss lingering in the air, the last piece of him left—aside from the clothes I ripped off his body, which will certainly be coming home with me—I press the tiny button on the edge of my earpiece. "One of the last ones is out and on the way."

My eyes catch on the stain in the carpet below the dolly, and I grin.

Chapter Ten

"Red"

Madison

The floor beneath me wobbles and slants as I push my feet into it, sending myself reeling faster and faster. An echoed, hollow scream fills the air, louder and more piercing with each passing second. With each choking beat of my heart.

The room Static had me trapped in felt like a whole other world. At least, it did until he freaking shoved me right back into reality—literally.

I trip over my own feet and stumble into the wall. My palms slam down on the plaster, sending a plume billowing into the air. I choke on the particles, gasping. Sucking in lungfuls that burn and shred my esophagus. My fingers dig into my throat, squeezing the sides until the pressure of my Adam's apple being shoved backward makes me gag. Air finally fills my lungs to capacity so fast, more tears melt my eyes.

Doors line either side of the narrow hall. I veer to the left, toward what appears to be a window. I bang on the glass, hammering my clenched fists against the opaque glass. It rattles in its frame, shuddering and groaning from the pressure of my assault.

With strength I didn't realize I still had, I put my whole weight into it, shoving forward and slamming my hands against the window. I need to get out of here.

I—I can't breathe.

My skin's crawling with phantom legs, more than eight. Maybe ten—twenty. A hundred. All over every inch of exposed skin that burns in the rotten, musky air that smells of death, decay, and ruin.

Of horror and nightmares brought to life.

Hell on Earth because *Jesus*, that's what this has got to be. The devil tempts me, right? That's what the pastor at church growing up always said. That he'll bait his victims, tempt them, make them crave to give in to their darkest desires...

My eyes slam shut as the more than vivid... not *memories*, per se, because it just freaking happened, but the recollection of what that... clown did to me.

God. If I'm not already in Hell, I sure as heck have a one-way ticket there now.

Goodbye, pearly gates.

A door behind me creaks open. I jolt and suck in a breath at the same time I shove all of my weight against the window, making myself as flat and as small as possible.

A foot slides across the exposed wooden floor. A board creaks. A silent curse. Nails scratching against the plaster.

With my head angled to the side, my chin nearly touches my shoulder. I strain my eyeballs further past me, making out the shape of a body. "Lenny?!" I whisper yell, pulling my sweaty torso off the glass with a dragging *shnick*.

"Fuck!" His scream bellows out, echoing down the hall,

bouncing off the ceiling for four long, drawn-out, and far too freaking loud beats. His hand flies to his bare chest, which is slick with rivulets of... something.

I bring myself closer, unable to help my increased, rapid breaths. I haven't stopped panting since we got here. I'm about to pass out again any second. I can feel my brain screaming from not getting enough air to circulate.

One of his eyes is swollen shut. My gaze travels up—and that's when I scream.

Blood.

Dripping out of his forehead.

A lot of it.

Lenny slams into me, slick arms clutching mine. We both grunt at the point of impact. I stumble back, cursing again as my spine is jarred against the wooden frame of the door.

"Someone's behind me," he pants in my ear, a weak whisper that trembles. All the blood drains from my head. If Lenny wasn't pinning me in place, I would've collapsed.

My eyes shoot wide as something comes into view behind him.

Something... green. The stuff from literal freaking nightmares.

Oh, Jesus... there's so many of them.

I wail, unable to hold it back. Lenny shivers, his own weak sobs coming out heavily against me. His tears trigger more of my own as we cower together in pathetic heaps, waiting to be slaughtered.

Gnarled, exposed teeth flash just below another set of glowing eyes—this time green. The face is warped, like he's been melted or something, but I don't freaking know, and I don't care to, either. I shove against Lenny's big body, my fight or flight kicking in—and it always says *run. Get the heck* away.

"Red!" The word is screeched right into my ear, making my eardrum pop and explode. I bellow out in pain at the burst, followed by a pounding ring. I crumple to the ground, clutching my ear as sobs wrack me. That *Red* echoes. Deeper. Into my very core.

Red.

Red...

I could've freaking said *red* this whole time?! What the fuck? How could I forget that out of everything I read? Everything I was so meticulous and cautious about?

It's like the moment I stepped behind that black door, it all disappeared, and all I was left with was the instinct of survival —anyway, anyhow.

Even if that meant...

My head blanks out.

The presence of another body steps away, leaving me painfully cold. I shiver from my balled-up form on the floor. "Red," I croak, far too late.

"Let's go." A grunt. Then, my arm is snatched up with really long green and black fingers that... I shudder, eyes rolling back as my stomach convulses. I keep my eyes on the floor, unable to look at the monster tugging me along. Lenny's bare feet are in my peripheral, slapping against the debris-covered floor like he doesn't feel every uneven, splintering board. Or the loose screws and nails. Or the shredded carpet probably covered in rat droppings.

I catch sight of my own bare body and vomit right there.

I hunch over on a retch and upend the contents of my stomach—which isn't anything but good ol' watery stomach bile. Bright green and yellow splatters across the ground as it spews from my mouth. The smell seeps into the air.

Another grunt. "Surprised your queasy ass lasted so long."

Please don't look at me.

I clutch my stomach on a whimper and wipe the back of my hand over my mouth. Eyes pierce the back of my head as I push myself up, forcefully keeping my eyes off the freaking clown collar wrapped around my throat.

That feeling of being watched never leaves. It sinks into my spine, right at my nape, where it stays as Lenny and I are forcefully dragged down the hall and through a door that... isn't a freaking door because it's just a *wall*.

Just as I'm shoved through the opening, I glance back to find a pair of white eyes pinned on me and even whiter, sharp teeth splayed wide, black lips stretched, and that god-awful, wicked tongue flicking outward.

I shiver, then whimper as I'm cast into darkness.

COLLIN, Brianne, and Kane all sit in metal chairs in equal states of undress and disarray. When Lenny and I step into the room, light suddenly blooming around us, everyone's heads crank toward our entrance.

"Damn! Thought y'all were murdered or something," Collin says as we shuffle toward our own chairs. Lenny plops down next to Collin, leaving me to take a chair next to Kane. He eyes me warily. I keep my head down.

Can we not talk about murder right now...

A bottle of water enters my peripheral. I take it with a mumbled thanks and upend the entire thing, trying to wash the taste of acid out of my mouth—and the taste of Static's tongue...

"You lasted a long time," Kane tells me when I finally finish, capping the bottle with a crinkle. I blink warily at him, noticing the sweat still clinging to his forehead. His hair's in clumpy knots, and he has no shirt and only one shoe.

He's covered in some sort of...

"What's all over you?" I croak, wrinkling my nose. My voice is long gone.

"I have no idea, but whatever it is fucking stinks." I lean forward to take a whiff, but it slithers right up my nose, nearly making me gag. My eyes roll back as my stomach protests, and I scoot back.

"Yeah, I know. I was... drowned in the stuff."

"Like... in a tub?"

He nods shakily. He runs a hand through his gooped hair, making it clump even worse. His hand trembles as he brings it back into his lap.

"You guys lasted for nearly an hour. Practically no one else has done that."

I don't feel very accomplished.

"Can we go?" I ask. Lenny's still silent, which I don't think is very normal for him from the way I've seen him act since I moved in earlier, but I think we all have the right to be a little messed up right now.

I know I am.

Brianne and Collin both look absolutely wrecked, clothes hanging off their bodies. They're glistening with various liquids. I think Collin's even bleeding, coupled with some bruises.

"Yeah, let's." Kane stands on wobbly legs and walks across the small, dark room to rap his knuckles on the wall. The door jolts open, making me cry out in surprise. No one even bats an eye, which I'm grateful for.

"If you all would follow me."

We file behind, each step haggard and slow. My entire body aches, and each press of my feet against the floor makes my spine pulsate and throb, sending live wires of pain radiating outward.

We're brought to another room that looks nearly identical to the front office, where we signed our freaking souls away. Dark, ominous. *Hollowed.*

Our IDs are handed back to us quickly, which we all clutch in our hands awkwardly without any proper clothes. Which makes me glance down at myself. I'm the only one in this obvious state of undress.

"Um, can I get my clothes back?" I ask hesitantly, forcing myself to look up. Their eyes light up in amusement as they track over my naked body. Their gaze locks on the collar still donning my neck.

I don't know why I haven't taken it off yet.

I should take it off now.

I trace the sharp edge of my license as I wait.

"No, sorry. It's all in the waiver." They flutter their hand around to enunciate their words. My jaw drops open slightly, though I'm not really all that surprised.

That creepy clown probably kept them for himself.

I eye my dried, pissed-soaked boxers with chagrin. Kane bumps his shoulder into mine. "It's okay. I've got a hoodie in the car. And it's dark out right now." I nod my acceptance and turn away as we're ushered out of Mayhem.

Once the cool air stings my skin, I suck in a pleading, whimpering breath. It seems the others do the same because we all stop and shiver, staring up at the cloud-covered sky, making the inky darkness feel denser and heavier as it settles upon us like a weighted blanket.

A suffocating blanket made of coal and ashes. Of hell and devilry.

I peer over my shoulder, eyeing the darkened, decrepit motel with equal parts disdain, misery, and curiosity. The inside is nothing like I'd imagined. The layout, the... *people.*

The outside, though, is every bit the abandoned motel one would imagine. Shuttered windows, peeling paint, weathered wood. All wrapped in a bow of horror.

With a shiver, I right my gaze back down to the gravel, head hanging heavily between my shoulders. Kane limps on his one bare foot as we shuffle across the gravel parking lot back to the Pontiac that's a beacon of sanity we all desperately need.

We settle in our seats, each of us disturbingly quiet.

We're all alone. And we feel every second of it.

The chug of the engine and the vibration rumbling through the car as it starts does nothing to quell my unease. Even the crack of rocks beneath the tires as Collin pulls out of the parking spot doesn't help.

Kane hands me his hoodie without a word, and I silently pull it on, wrapping both ends completely around my midsection, not even bothering with the zipper. Keeping one arm around my midsection, strangely because it feels like I need *something* against me to keep me together, I drag my phone out of the compartment in the door, powering it on.

With a quick glance around the cab, I notice everyone else is already on theirs, screens dimly lit in the shadowy darkness.

Collin's eyes are strained on the road, headlights curving on the blacktop as he turns out of Mayhem Motel's parking lot and onto the highway. My head cranks, vying for one last glance at the broken, neon motel sign, then at the front door I willingly walked through.

A choice that I'm pretty sure changed me.

And maybe not for the better.

I feel wrecked, wholly and utterly drained. Like Static sucked every pulse of my life force from my veins—*through my dick*—leaving me in nothing but this useless skin suit.

The air I pull in feels heavy, thick with something I can't name, as we drive through Vitriol to jump back on the interstate.

Despondency. Regret.

Staggering pleasure and shocking acceptance.

My head thuds against the fogged-over glass, each breath pluming out increasing the uneven edge of the condensation against the glass. Just as my eyes fall shut, my phone vibrates in my hand.

I flip it over, peering at the dimmed screen with one eye cracked open.

A text message notification lines the screen. A photo.

I glance around the car, eyeing everyone warily, although I'm not sure why. Lenny's slumped over against the opposite window, eyes closed and shoulders moving with even breaths. Kane's crouched over his phone, thumb scrolling on the screen.

Collin's staring out the windshield, thumb tapping on the wheel to the beat of a song I think he said was by some band called Motionless In White. I'm pretty sure Brianne's near sleep too, her arm unmoving from where it rests against Collin's upper thigh.

The road stretching out in front of us is dark, the almost neon glow of the painted lines on the uneven asphalt the only break from the darkness. The occasional set of headlights pass, followed by the rush of wind whipping past, but that's it.

The two-minute reminder makes my phone buzz again. I drop my attention back to my screen and type in the numbers of my passcode with a shaky hand.

A small, red number sits just to the right of the green message icon. My thumb hovers over it, trembling as my breath comes out in stuttered pants. My heart rocks against my ribs.

I accidentally graze the screen with the tip of my finger on a shudder.

My heart, still beating in time with the chaos consuming my lungs, shoots into my throat, pressing right against my uvula as I stare down with wide, burning eyes. At the face that will haunt every dream to come.

Static stares at me with those gleaming white irises. His hair is still spiked straight up, in a bit of disarray from my fingers...

I gulp.

The metal in his face glints, even in the shadows the picture was taken in. Those pointed teeth are on full display with that long tongue of his scraping across a few on the top row.

I shiver, locked on his tongue for a long moment before I force my eyes to move downward.

His neck is bare without his collar. Long and slender with dark streaks of grease paint that are creased in the places he bends his neck.

But I'm back to looking at his mouth. His tongue. How long and big it is. How it felt in my own mouth at the brief, jarring kiss... The way it wrapped around my...

Oh, Jesus. Oh, no...

I stifle a groan and shove my hand against my lap, pressing against my length, hoping to impede the boner bound to pop up any minute.

The fear does not turn me on... It doesn't.

My phone vibrates. A bubble emerges.

I see you see me darlin

Oh, Jesus... the bubble must be blue... he can—

III be seein you soon too

That makes my throat cinch so tight, not even a drop of saliva could fit through the constriction. Pressure builds in my gut, making my stomach extend as it pushes outward. Then down.

To my balls, where they throb, heavy between my closed legs.

I whimper, hating the way my eyes keep lingering on that picture of him. It scares me... makes my skin crawl with desperation to *escape.* But his mouth... and those eyes... and his neck...

I finger the frayed, black collar still around my neck. My eyes pinch against the burn.

It felt as good as it did bad. As wrong as right.

What did he do to me? And why do I like it... Want more...

Sweet dreams my treat... Dream of me

With a heavy, clanking thud of my heart and a choking swallow, I lock my phone. But Static's face is still at the forefront of my mind. Where I know it'll stay.

Masking every dream. Every waking thought.

Like a wound I refuse to acknowledge... in hopes it'll get bigger.

Worse.

Until I'm consumed by the infection.

Plunged in the static.

Chapter Eleven
My Little Secret

Cedrick

I can taste him in the back of my throat—thick and salty and musky. *Absolutely perfect.*

I miss him already, and that's sayin' something—because I never miss anyone. I fuck and I move on, but there's somethin' about this boy that I just want to sink my teeth into and never let go...

My tongue flicks out against the sharp ends of my teeth, and I press into them, hissing as they pierce my flesh. But when that first bead of blood wells up and sinks into my taste buds, my eyes roll back, and my head falls between my shoulders. Cold air plumes around me, causing goosebumps to prickle down my arms. I shiver involuntarily, body rolling with the motion before I straighten and force myself to head back inside, flicking my cigarette butt to the ground.

Madison is gone.

But not for long.

"WHAT THE HELL'S got you so chipper?" Wesley asks when I step into the room to get changed for the night. I can't bite back the smirk that tweaks my lips, but I honestly don't even try.

"Was a good night," I drawl as I pull my shirt over my head. Graves whistles when my body comes into view, and I roll my eyes at him. It's the same thing every single time any of us gets undressed in front of him—the fucking slut. I quirk my brow at him as I drop my pants. "Shut up, you whore."

Graves pulls his full bottom lip in between his teeth as his eyes blatantly drag down my body. "Well—"

"Not a chance in hell," I tell him with a smirk, before blowing him a kiss and pulling on a pair of sweatpants over my boots. With my back turned to him, I grab a makeup wipe and go about removing the paint from my face. It takes a few, and I have to scrub pretty hard, but eventually, I get all the white and black off my face, leaving me clad in only my white eye contacts.

I stare at myself in my reflection, blinking once, then twice.

Someone I barely recognize stares back at me. His eyes are alight with something burning beneath the surface.

Something... *new.*

I pull my contacts out and put them in their container, followed by my teeth, and then blinking through the dryness. I look away from myself to grab my phone, pulling up mine and Madison's conversation again, just to taunt myself a little more, when I'm interrupted by Wesley's loud ass antics.

"Kierra! What're you doing back here?"

I freeze, locking my phone and shoving it in my pocket. I glance up as Kierra—our front desk girl—walks into the room, a sweatshirt hanging from her arm.

"Nothing really. Just thought I'd say goodnight and congrats to you guys before heading home." Her voice is loud but gentle, and it demands everyone's attention. We all murmur our thanks and goodbyes, and as she walks back out the door, she catches my gaze and lifts her dark brow. I feel my throat roll with a swallow, but she turns her back and continues out without a word.

I pull in a deep breath and grab my phone once more, bringing it to my chest like I can protect Madison's number just by holdin' it close.

"What's got you holding your phone like that?" Kaser asks as they saddle up next to me. I jerk out of my reverie and nearly drop my phone.

"Nothin'."

"Nothin'?" they mock me, accent just as thick. They lift their brow, lips pursed. "Or should I be sayin' who?"

My heart thuds heavily in my chest—and I don't fuckin' like it. "No," I snap, shoving my phone in my pocket and turning away from my best friend. I can feel their eyes staring into the back of my head, but I ignore them as I gather my shit in my backpack and sling it over my shoulder.

"I'm headed home," I mumble, not giving Kaser my eyes again.

"Mhm," they hum, eyes still glued to me.

Their observation makes me uncomfortable, but I decide to ignore it as I walk out of the room and away from everyone because what the fuck else am I going to do? Confront them? Tell them I broke a rule and got a client's number from the system for my own personal use? Lose my fucking job because of it?

I don't fuckin' think so.

Not that I think Kaser would snitch on me. They would never.

But this... *he*... is my little secret. One I plan to keep all to myself.

I STARE up at the darkened ceiling, at the roll of the lights across the flat surface, unable to sleep. It's been hours, and I can't get my little treat out of my head. He hasn't texted me back, and I *ache* for him to... but also, I'm glad he didn't.

It makes me wonder if he's dreamin' of me.

If my texts scared him enough to infiltrate his subconscious and now, as he lies there, his mind is filled of me and what I did to him. What I *will* do for him again.

I inhale deeply, eyelids fluttering closed as I practically *smell* Madison's urine all over again. It was subtle, but his fear was not. He was absolutely *trembling* with it, but he endured it all so beautifully.

I've never seen someone last so long, tolerate so much, and for what?

He could've used his safe word. So many people would have, but he didn't.

And I want to know why.

I need to...

My phone buzzes where it lies on my nightstand, illuminating the already-lit ceiling a bit more. My heart shoots into my throat as I roll to the side and scoop it up, but when I tap the screen and see it's only a text from Kaser telling me they're on their way home from a hook up, I feel my stomach drop.

I rub the ache in my chest as I open my thread with Madison. I scroll to the top—to the picture of me I sent him—and I grin. It's a creepy fuckin' picture. And I know it scared the hell out of him. I think I look odd without my collar, but thinkin' about him keeping it... *wearin' it...*

I can't stifle the groan that escapes me as I reach down into the waistband of my sweatpants and palm my twitching cock. All I've got are memories, but they're as fuckin' fresh as the taste of his piss and cum on my tongue.

I let my eyes roll back as I shove my pants down and spread my legs wider, stretching the band of my sweatpants tight around my upper thighs. My cock springs free of its confines, and I nearly groan in relief at the wave of fresh, humid air skittering over my body.

A fresh wave of goosebumps breaks out over my skin, and I relish in the burn as I slowly start to stoke myself to the memories of my sweet little treat's whimpers. His soft cries. His pathetic little mewls.

"Jesus fuck," I grunt, tightening my fist around my girth at the base, stifling the rapid approach of my orgasm. I blink open my eyes as I lie there and stare up at the ceiling, cock throbbing against my stomach. There's something about him that really does it for me.

And I'm gonna find out what it is.

But for now, I slowly start stroking myself all over again, breathing in the heavy, humid air that surrounds me as I slowly work myself up again, but it doesn't take long to get right back on the precipice. To taste the edge that's so close. I stop again with another heaving breath, feeling my skin tingle and buzz and relishing in it.

I push my tongue out between my lips, wetting them and imagining it's his. Shy and hesitant, trembling with fear as it probes against my mouth, searching for something unknown but desperately needed.

Because he needs it.

Needs me.

He just doesn't know it yet.

My eyes roll back as I tighten my hand around my shaft on the upstroke. I rub my thumb just under my head, then drag it up to my slit and back down, smearing the precum I'm oozing. It's with that newfound wetness that I let myself fall right the fuck over to the sound of Madison's screams ringing in my ears.

By the time my cock is done spurting and I'm lying spent on my bed, covered in cum that nearly reaches my chin, I finally notice that my bedroom door is open. I slowly flick my gaze over to Kaser, who's leaning against the doorjamb with their arms crossed over their chest, eyes half-lidded.

"Yes?" I croak, voice hoarse for some reason.

"You were being loud," is all they say, like that explains why they opened my door. Not that I care, really. It's not the first time and certainly won't be the last.

Kaser is the first person I experimented with. We learned everything with each other, and I feel no shame with them watching me, but it has been quite a while since they've initiated something.

I thought that road was gone between us.

"I thought you just got back from a hook up," I say, still catching my breath. I push up on my elbows, but I'm unaware of the cum still gleaming across my chest until Kaser's eyes drop to it. I smirk. "Like what you see?"

"You know I do." They run their tongue along the fronts of their teeth before stepping into the room. They leave the door wide open because it's just us here.

It's only ever been us.

"Whoever they were didn't satisfy you, did they, Kase?"

"They usually don't, Ricky." They also use their nickname for me, and it has my blood running hot all over again, but I know my dick won't get hard for at least another ten minutes. But that doesn't mean I can't satiate them in the meantime.

I lift a brow. "Why don't you come clean this mess off me then?" I gesture toward my chest with my chin and follow their eyes to the mess. Kaser licks their lips, and I know I've got them. "That's right, baby. You know you wanna eat it."

"It's been a long time," they rasp, and their words nearly get lost in the darkness that shrouds us, but I don't let it.

I can't.

Because through it all, it's always been us.

I reach up and rub my hand over their shaved head. They dip down and drop their face next to mine. Their stubble rubs against mine, and I groan at the roughness as I drag my tongue across their cheek.

"Take what you need, Kase. I'm here," I tell them as their breaths deepen in the hollow of my neck. They inhale shakily, and then, their tongue dips out to lap up the sweat that's trickling down. I toss my head back with a groan, relishing in the sensation of a hot, wet mouth on my body—even if it's not the one I want.

Kaser's breaths intensify the further down my body they get, their tongue lapping and slurping my cum greedily. Their lips suction around my nipple, and my back arches at the sharp sensation of teeth sinking into my flesh.

"Fuck," I hiss, and they hum contentedly. "Fuckin' brat," I murmur as I run my hands over their head.

"Mhm," they say, running the flat of their tongue over the ridges of my abs, scooping up the last of my cum. They lean back and let it drip from their mouth in an obscene display that makes my dick twitch.

"Jesus, Kase." I reach forward and rub my thumb along their tongue before pushing it back into their mouth. They roll the muscle around my digit and hum as they suck.

Pushing them onto their back, I caress the back of their head while they're sucking on my thumb, and with my other hand, I shove it in the front of their sweatpants to wrap my fingers around their throbbing cock.

Kase mewls against me, and *fuck,* I forgot how fuckin' soft they get like this.

It's a nice distraction.

I squeeze my eyes shut at the assault of my little treat, but I can't stop the influx of images ravaging me.

His soft cries, his pleading words.

Pathetic little mewls and desperate moans of pain.

Tears of undiluted fear streaming down his sweat-slick skin. Their salty essence on my tongue.

"Oh! Sh-shit—" Kaser pants heavily into the side of my neck, hips jerking as their release nears. I feel their cock spasming in my grip, so I tighten my hold and smooth my thumb over the head, smearing the oozing precum, which is what sets them off.

Cum fills my palm, soaking my arm, and covering me with warmth. Kase breathes heavily into me, lips pressed against my flesh as they pant. I turn my head to the side to catch my own breath, feeling something akin to shame while also being exhilarated because I just made my best friend come while thinking of someone else.

CHAPTER TWELVE

DANCED WITH THE DEVIL

MADISON

It's been over a week since I've seen him, and I can't get him out of my mind.

He haunts my dreams.

Shoot, who am I kidding? He haunts me even when I'm awake.

Everywhere I turn, I swear I see him. Smeared white and black face paint, hauntingly sharp teeth, and piercings glinting in the sunlight. The crazy, mismatched pattern of his tattered clothes billowing in the slight summer breeze...

I shiver even though it's still eighty degrees outside.

School starts tomorrow, and I can't sleep, so I'm on another walk to try to tire myself out—but it's not working. Maybe because I keep opening my phone to the text thread with his freaking face staring back at me... but I can't help it.

There's something that keeps calling me back. Something... haunting about him.

He... *touched* me. In a way no one ever has. And I can't forget it—as much as I'd like to.

"Static," I choke on his name as I round the corner, pulling myself further away from the lamppost and bathing myself in inky darkness. Static changed something in me—and I don't think it's for the better.

I don't feel better, anyway.

I feel all messed up inside. Confused and discombobulated.

This isn't how I wanted my freshman year at college to go. It was supposed to be easy—or well, *easier than this.*

I got the courage to move away from home—which took a strength I didn't even know I had, but I freaking did it. I'm here now, and I'm doing this all on my own. But then, I had to go and impress my new roommates, and now, everything's all messed up... or *I'm* all messed up.

I can't tell.

Either way, I wasn't supposed to spend this time thinking about a clown that scared me half to death... okay, *mostly* to death, if I'm being honest.

I still have nightmares of those flashing lights. Of monsters and sharp teeth. Of that bloody axe in my mouth and a hot, wet tongue on my—I suck in a breath as the memory assaults me all over again.

Dizziness overtakes me, and I have to stop and hold onto the edge of the brick building to keep myself steady.

"You all right?" Kane asks from the porch, and I blink through the haze covering my eyes. I didn't even realize I'd made it back home already.

"What?" I ask, staring up at him. "Oh," I say when it finally registers what he said. "Yeah, I'm good. Just got, uhm, lightheaded."

"Did you eat today?"

"No?" I ask, confused.

"Why not?" he inquires.

I pause for a moment as I slowly make my way up the stairs. The thick clouds in the sky are blocking the moonlight, making the night appear even darker than usual. When I reach the top step, I drop down onto it and let my head fall to the side, resting against the wooden beam there.

"I forgot," I tell him honestly, too tired to come up with another answer. I'd already messed up. There's no point in lying now.

"You forgot to eat?" Kane asks softly. I don't sense any judgment, but my skin prickles, regardless.

"Everyone forgets to eat sometimes," I snap back softly. It's rude—and I don't want to be rude—but my face heats with embarrassment, and I'm feeling shameful.

He throws his hands up in front of him in a placating gesture. "Hey, dude. I'm not judging you. I was just asking."

I let out a deep breath and let my eyes fall closed. A breeze blows past, and it feels good against my fevered skin. "I know. Sorry. I just don't feel well."

"I can see that," he says as he drops down on the steps beside me, hands resting on his stretched-out knees.

"Saying I look like crap?"

"Yes," Kane deadpans, and it makes me snort. He bumps his knee into mine, and I flush at the contact, however innocent. Good thing it's dark out and he can't tell how easily my face gives me away.

Blasted paleness and lack of bodily control.

It's quiet between us for a few minutes as we stare out into the night. The city is surprisingly quiet, only the sound of traffic in the distance to keep us company.

"Want me to make you something to eat?" Kane offers,

shattering the silence that's made a home between us. "Might help you feel better."

That makes me smile—a real, genuine smile for the first time in days. "You know, that actually..." I trail off when my phone buzzes in my pocket.

My stomach sinks.

No one that's not in this house has my number—except for my parents and *him.*

I swallow the lump that's lodged itself in my throat and slowly pull my phone out. The screen illuminates the darkness as I unlock it to find a text from that same number.

UNKNOWN:

Miss me yet darlin

Before I have time to process the first text, another comes through.

UNKNOWN:

Because I miss you

Oh, God.

Oh... my God.

My phone slips from between my fingers and clatters onto the step between my feet. My vision whites out.

"Hey—what—" I hear the scrape of my phone against wood, and I reach out blindly, taking it back from Kane and shoving it against my thudding chest, hoping that he didn't see a thing.

"Mads?" he inquires, his voice a soft wave through the rushing of blood through my ears.

"I gotta go," I squeak out, and before he can answer, I scramble to my feet and rush inside. I take the stairs two at a time until I'm in my room with the door locked behind me, back pressed against it and chest still heaving like I ran a marathon.

With my eyes scrunched shut, I slowly pull my phone away from my chest to stare down at the screen. It lights up, showing me my basic blue background and the time—11:27pm.

But I'm scared.

I know what's behind that lockscreen.

But what if it's not real?

What if I made it up?

That makes the next breath come a little easier. I'm so worked up and scared, my mind is conjuring things that aren't really there just to rile me up. I'm too tired. I've barely been sleeping, and my brain is playing tricks on me.

That's gotta be what this is.

With renewed confidence, I unlock my phone and promptly swallow my tongue. Because no.

I was wrong.

So very, *very* wrong.

Static is real.

And he won't leave me alone.

Why won't he leave me alone?

I want to cry. The tears burn the backs of my eyes, traveling down to my nose, and even making my chin wobble, but they don't fall. They just glass over my eyes until the screen in front of me distorts and eventually turns black once more.

Before I even realize what I'm doing, I'm texting him back, renewed fire burning in my veins.

ME:

You need to leave me alone.

It's marked as read instantly, and I nearly drop my phone in surprise. Knowing he's looking at the same thing I am at the same time does something uncomfortable to my stomach.

Three little dots appear for a moment before his next text swishes through.

UNKNOWN:

You dont want that do you

Brows furrowed, I type back:

Yes, I do.

UNKNOWN:

We shall see

I blink rapidly down at my phone.
We shall see?
What the heck is that supposed to mean?
My heart thunders in my chest as I reread those three words over and over again, regretting my decision in engaging with him more and more with each passing second.

Oh, God. What did I do?
I just danced with the devil, that's what.
And now, he knows he has me right where he wants me.

SLEEP DOESN'T COME AT ALL. I spend the entire night staring at the ceiling, the walls, and mostly, my phone where it lies charging on my nightstand, like the offending object it is.

I suppose I could get my number changed, but then, on the off chance something happened with Mother or Father, they wouldn't have my new number, and I need them to be able to get ahold of me. Not that they would after what I did, but if...

So, basically, I'm stuck.

I groan loudly and drag my hands down my face. Exhaustion is pulling heavily at me, but I still force myself to sit up. Sunlight is just beginning to peak through the gaps in the curtains, and I avoid the rays because of my throbbing temples as I grab a change of clothes and head to the shower.

Thankfully, no one else is up this early, so I'm able to scrub some of my sleepiness away, and by the time I'm out, I don't feel one hundred percent better, but I do feel more awake than before, so I'll take it.

"You look even worse than last night, and that's saying something," Kane says when I walk into the kitchen. I startle at the sound of his voice, a squeak-sort of noise escaping my throat. My hand flies to my chest where it leaps from my sternum, and in turn, Kane just chuckles.

"My bad. Forgot you startle easily."

"Forgot after just last night... or literally any moment since you've known me?" I deadpan, too tired.

"Apparently," he muses, flipping a pancake on the stove. "Want some?" he asks, gesturing to the pile he adds another flapjack to.

"Sure, thanks." I grab a dish and some food and take a seat. After soaking my pancake in syrup, I look up to find Kane already staring at me.

"Yes?" I ask with a mouth full of food, which I recognize is incredibly rude, but I also can't be bothered to care too much when I'm this hungry. I can't remember the last time I ate, and for the first time in quite a while, I actually *feel* hungry.

"Nothing. Just glad you're eating."

I hum noncommittedly.

"Good, yeah?" he asks once he sits down with his own plate and I'm onto my second.

"Mhm," I hum, taking another bite.

"Thanks." Kane grins. "It's my dad's recipe. Even the syrup."

"Wait." I pause between bites. "This is homemade, too?"

"Yeah," he chuckles.

"No wonder it's so good." My eyes nearly roll back as the sweetness assaults my senses. I was never allowed to have this much sugar, so I'm probably gonna be on a sugar high for the rest of the day, but it'll so be worth it because this stuff is incredible.

"I'm glad you like it, man."

"Thanks," I mumble, face heating.

"'Course." Kane smiles just as the others start piling into the kitchen.

"Yes!" Lenny shouts as he saunters in. "Kane's famous pancakes!"

"Dude, we're all right here. We can hear you," Collin mutters as he strides in right behind Lenny. He grabs his own food and then leaves without another word.

"He's not a morning person," Kane responds to my unanswered question. I nod my understanding and take my last bite before pushing my plate away. I swear my stomach has doubled in size, I'm so full.

The kitchen is full of rambunctious activity as Lenny and Kane fuck around with each other and banter back and forth, and I'm content just to watch them. Eventually though, time draws near, and I excuse myself back to my room.

I grab my things and sling my bag over my shoulder. I look down at my phone. I nearly don't grab it, but I know I'll need it, so I slip it into my pocket with unease before my exit.

The walk to class is refreshing. The cool summer air is nice against my freshly showered skin, and I relish in the dampness of it as I walk the few blocks to my first building of the day. Other students are milling about, and for the first time since I left home, I finally feel like I belong.

No one is looking at me twice. I'm just another classmate to them. And it feels so nice to be just like everybody else.

GOD, college is hard.

My brain *physically* hurts. And it was only the first day.

I don't know how I'm going to survive four years of this.

There's too much information, and I don't know where to store it all.

I stare blankly down at all my notebooks before opening my laptop, and I just start scribbling all the information I can remember until my hand is cramping and my brain doesn't feel quite so full.

And now, it's time to organize it all.

I flip through different folders and notebooks until each class is organized by their own color and corresponding notes. It takes me hours, but by the time I'm done, everything is effectively how it should be, and my brain feels less full than it did, so I call it a success.

I shove my schoolwork away from me, groaning as I stretch out my legs. I've been stuck in the same position for hours without realizing, and my entire body aches because of it.

A knock sounds at the door, and I jolt with surprise.

"Yes?"

"Just me," Kane says as he pushes my door open. He's got two plates of steaming food in his hands and a sheepish smile on his face. "Brought some food because you've been stuck in here for hours and I figured you might be hungry."

"Uh." My face flames. "Y-yeah. That's... that's great. Th-thank you." I stand and take one of the plates from him and greedily inhale the scent of cheesy chicken and rice. "Smells amazing."

"Thanks. My parents loved to cook, so I guess I kinda just took on that quality from them?" He poses it like a question as he sits at the foot of my bed. It's then he reaches into his hoodie pocket and pulls out two cans of Dr. Pepper and hands one to me.

I take it with a shy smile and a soft thanks that makes my face burn hotter than ever. Kane just nods his head and leans back against my bedframe and dives into his food without a word said, like this silence between us is comfortable.

But I guess maybe it is because I don't feel inclined to talk, really. It's nice to just eat and not feel like I'm forced to make conversation.

Plus, this food is really freaking good—and I tell Kane that, too.

He chuckles lightly, and it makes my heart flutter a bit.

"Thanks, Mads."

"Y-you-you're welcome," I stutter over the words, hating myself more than ever that I can't just spit things out like a normal person. My tongue always sticks to the roof of my mouth, like it's glued in place, and I have to chew my way around it just to speak.

"So, how was your first day?" Kane asks, fork scraping across the paper plate he's using.

I blow out a breath, thankful for this topic because it's easy enough.

"Long. And exhausting. I don't know what I expected, but I didn't think I'd be this tired—mentally, anyway. There's just a lot in my brain that I don't know what to do with," I tell him honestly, pushing a few grains of rice around with the prongs of my fork.

"Ah, yeah. I know exactly what you mean. But you'll get used to it. I know that sounds cliché, but you will. It just takes time."

I nod my understanding. "Thanks. I'm sure. It's just..."

"Not what you were thinking?" he finishes for me, and I nod.

"Yeah."

"It never is, buddy. It never is."

You're freaking telling me.

Chapter Thirteen

Right Fuckin' Here

Cedrick

My blood is boilin' in my veins.

I want to claw the very skin from my bones. Peel it back layer by layer until my meat is exposed to the damp, humid air of the night I'm shrouded in. And then, I want to sew it all back together with Madison trapped right inside so he's stuck against me—with me. With nowhere else to go.

He's talking to that fuckin' *boy. In his bed.*

They're eatin' together, and I can fuckin' see them. Laughing and talkin' without a care in the world.

I hate it.

I hate all of it.

He won't text me back, but he's sitting there with this... whoever he is. In his *bedroom.*

My fingers curl around the branch of the tree I've hoisted myself up in.

It's the biggest stroke of luck that my little treat's bedroom has a front row view to a tree not more than ten feet away—and hidden in the shadows at that.

I mean, if he looked hard enough, he'd see me, but I dressed in dark clothing for a reason. Not like that's outside the normal for me, but still.

I don't want him to see me just yet.

As the two of them finish up their meal, I pull out my phone and tap on my conversation with Madison. He hasn't texted me back since I told him I miss him, and I gotta admit, it stings a bit, but I expected it.

He's scared...

I scared him.

That brings a wicked smile to my face.

Fuck. I love him all small and scared.

But he's just gonna have to get used to it. That's all there is to it.

As him and the other boy leave the room, paper plates in hand, I lean back against the bark, relishing in the scrape against the back of my neck as I ponder what to do next.

Work tonight was exhilarating 'cause I'm still ridin' the high that is Madison Thomas Payne.

Such a pretty name for such a pretty boy.

It was kind of pathetic how easy it was to find him. But I have no regrets. Especially not now that I'm here, watching him. Only a pane of glass separating us.

But even I know it's not enough. Before long, I'll be running on fumes. I know I'll need to get my hands on him again... but how? He won't come back to Mayhem; that much is clear. And he won't even return my texts at this point.

I need him to need me just as badly... because what we shared was something I've never had with anyone else.

That lick of fuckin' fear and exhilaration. It was so tangible, I've never tasted anything like it. Equal parts terror and arousal, so sharp and twisted as it settled on my tongue and wrapped itself like a vice around my lungs.

I need it.

I'm chokin' without it.

And just then, my treat walks back into the room, and I know exactly what it is I have to do.

I pull out my phone and type the words I've wanted to since the moment I climbed into this tree.

ME:

Youre so close I can almost taste you again

MY EYES WIDEN as I watch my treat pleasure himself. The way his hand is frantically tugging at his cock, the shaking of his arm. His heaving chest and the sweat drippin' down his face.

He looks every bit of the fuckin' treat he is.

And my mouth fills with saliva.

I need to taste him.

I lean forward in the tree again, fingers inches away from the glass from where I've climbed down a thick branch. If Madison were to look outside, he'd see me easily. But he's so distracted by his own pleasure that he doesn't—and I'm thankful for that because I *need* to see this.

"What are you gonna do?" I muse to myself as I send

another message to him—this time a picture of my own cock straining through the material of my black pants.

When his phone buzzes where it lies on the floor, his hand falters in its movement, and for a moment, I don't think he's gonna stop, but then, he does. He reaches for his phone, cock bobbing in front of him, and my tongue flicks out to wet my lips at the sight of his shiny glans glistening in the yellow light of his bedroom.

He unlocks his phone and swallows when the message is marked as read. The movement in his chest picks up speed, and as he stares down at my clothed cock on his screen, he reaches down and grabs his own once more.

"Oh, how fun," I muse, lips curling upward with pleasant surprise. He never ceases to amaze me.

Madison touches himself in a frenzy of hurried movements, and I find myself frowning, wishing he'd slow down so I can better enjoy this moment before it's over.

ME:

Slow down

When his phone buzzes with my incoming text, he doesn't stop. If anything, his movements become faster, jerkier. He tosses his head back, and the tendons in his throat bulge under the strain. He twists his fist around the head, and then, he's shuddering as his cock erupts in bursts all over his floor.

His stomach contracts, body tensing through each wave, and his hand finally slows down until it eventually falls to his side. His head rolls to his other shoulder, then drops down to his chest, where he works to catch his breath, and despite him not listening to me, I've never seen such a magnificent show.

Of course, I wish it would've lasted longer. I want as much

time with my treat as I can get, but that... that was truly something else.

He is something else entirely.

His phone must've reminded him of my text because he jerks from his reverie, nearly dropping it to the floor. He holds it in front of his face, and because of the light illuminating his freshly flushed cheeks, I have the absolute pleasure of watching the blood drain from them.

Madison's eyes widen and dart around the room frantically. And then, his hands start to tremble and shake. I chuckle to myself as I slowly back up on the branch, putting myself back into the shadows, where he'll be less likely to see me as he starts freakin' out and searching his room.

He yanks his jeans up, and completely ignoring the cum soaking into the carpet, he hesitantly crawls onto the floor and peeks under the bed, heaving a sigh of relief each time he checks a space and finds it void of *me*.

Little does he know...

I'm right fuckin' here.

And I'm not goin' anywhere.

"Sweet dreams, my little treat," I whisper into the darkness, hoping the words float over to him and through the pane somehow, someway. "I'll be seeing you soon." I pull my pierced bottom lip between my teeth, only allowing myself to watch his panic for a moment longer before I climb down and start the trek back to my car that's parked a couple of blocks away.

My own dick is hard and throbbing inside my pants with its own heartbeat, but I ignore it in favor of replaying every single fuckin' moment of my treat's hand wrapped around his own cock—because *I* did that to him. Without even touching him.

My words alone scared him and turned him on so bad, he couldn't control himself.

Fuck. He's perfect.

I clench my hands into fists, relishing in the pointed tips of my gloves digging into my palms. The sharp bite is just what I need to get me back to my car without hazing out. But the second the door closes, my eyes glaze over, and I'm stuck staring through the windshield for an undetermined amount of time as flashes of Madison run through my mind like a movie, taking over my conscious mind for its own viewing pleasure—not that I'm complaining.

He's utterly amazing.

I just don't think I'll ever be able to get him to that place where he won't be such a scared little mouse...

Who knows.

Maybe.

I changed. And so did Kase.

But there's something heavy inside of Madison that I don't understand. Something... dark and twisted. And maybe, eventually, I can understand. But right now, when he's so scared and pulling away, there's no way he'll let me close enough to try to figure out what it is.

I just want him.

And I know he wants me.

But I don't know if he'll *let* himself want me.

That's the fuckin' problem.

"Where were you?" Kase asks as I walk through the front door. I slowly pull it closed behind me even though I've already been caught. For some reason, my heart is in my throat, and I can't swallow past the lump.

"Out," I tell them as I yank my hoodie over my head and drop it beside the shoes. It's soaked with sweat and needs washed, but that's tomorrow's problem.

"It's nearly one," Kaser says easily, but I know better.

They're pissed. And that's exactly why I'm not going to tell them where I was... or *who* I was with.

Things are a bit complicated now that we've resurrected this... *thing* between us. It's only ever been about sex, but I feel like I owe them something when, in reality, I probably don't. But they're my best friend. And I'm lying to them.

I'm utterly fascinated with this boy.

He's consuming my every waking thought, and I'm not telling Kaser about it.

Because I want to keep Madison all to myself.

"Ricky," they call out as I brush past them in the front hall.

"Yes?" I turn and quirk my brow. My face and neck are still covered with the thick grease paint from work. I can see Kase's curiosity in their eyes, and for a second, I worry I'm going to spill if they ask.

"What are you doing?" They reach out and drag their finger along my cheek, smearing the sweat-soaked paint.

"Whatever do ya mean?" I run my tongue along the fronts of my teeth, making Kase roll their eyes.

"You know what the fuck I'm talkin' about." They move back and cross their arms, leaning against the wall. Their muscles bulge around their biceps, and I rake my eyes down their body appreciatively.

"Can't say I do." I effectively end the conversation right

there. Madison is mine, and I refuse to share him with anyone —even my best friend in a simple conversation.

I turn my back on Kaser and walk toward the bathroom so I can take a fucking shower—and take care of the straining problem in my pants because at this point, it's beyond painful.

"Want some help with that?" Kase calls out, and I stop just before my hand wraps around the doorknob. I look down at my cock tenting the fabric of my pants, then back up at the white door in front of me.

They've moved closer. I can hear Kase's breath feet away, feel their body heat radiating toward me, *begging* to be touched. I can taste it in the air, but for the first time, the taste doesn't appeal to me.

Because it's not him.

Fuck.

"Not tonight, Kase," I tell them, turning my head slightly to the side so they can see the half-quirk of my lips. "I'm tired." And that's not a lie, but it's not the body kind of tired they probably think I mean.

I'm exhausted fighting this... this *thing* inside that's frothing at the maw to take another bite of my sweet little treat. I've had him so close I could almost taste him again, but then, he scurried away, lost in the wind yet again.

Now, *that's* exhausting me.

"Mhm. I'm sure you are."

"I wasn't at the club," I tell them honestly.

"I know. You wouldn't go in full gear," they say, nodding toward my clothes and probably the paint still on my skin, too. "But it makes me wonder what *you would* go in full gear for?"

"Give it a rest," I groan, smacking my head against the door before pushing away and stalking toward Kaser. I push them so deep into the wall, they barely even have room to suck air into their lungs. "Is this what you want, Kase?" I purr against their throat as I dip my head down. I reek of humid summer air and sweat, but I know they don't care. And frankly, neither do I.

"You want my hands on you?" I ask, trailing the tip of my tongue across the shell of their ear. "*Hmm?*"

"Yes," they breathe out, falling slack against the wall, against me. And I fucking revel in it.

It's not him, but it's someone.

And I'm probably a shitty fucking person for taking advantage of my best friend right now. Like this. But I don't care enough to stop myself from shoving my hand down the front of their pants and wrapping my fingers around their cock.

Chapter Fourteen
Slow Down

Madison

I'm going to be sick.
    I'm going to be sick.
    I'm going... to...
I throw my head over the side of the toilet just in time to spew the contents of my stomach, which is throbbing and convulsing to the beat of my erratic heart.

Static saw me.

I don't know how or where, but he did. *I know he did.*

But I fell right into his trap. I let my emotions override my brain, and now... now—"Oh, God." My stomach heaves again, and I retch over the toilet, though there's nothing left to empty.

A knock sounds at the door. "Hey, man. You, uh, all right?" Collin asks awkwardly.

"Y-yeah," I stutter, wiping my mouth with the back of my hand. "Just, you know."

"Okay, man. Take it easy," he says, and then, I hear his retreating footsteps, leaving me in ringing silence once more.

"Shoot," I gasp, falling back against the tub. I shiver when the cool porcelain seeps into my exposed skin, but I don't move.

I can't.

I'm frozen because there's Static's face in my mind's eye. Bright, white eyes, and crazed, sharp smile. Large hands covering every inch of my body, manipulating me how he wants me. Touching me and teasing me and taunting me. Pulling from me something deep and dark. Something I never would have touched otherwise, and now, I can't get it out of my freaking head.

As scared, as absolutely *terrified* as I am, I'm... curious, too. And I hate that. Because I don't want to be.

I don't want to wonder about the man that... did those things to me. That won't stop texting me strange things and making me... making me *do that.*

Again.

And he watched the whole darn thing...

I think.

There's no other explanation for him telling me to slow down. It doesn't make sense. But maybe I've got it all wrong. Maybe he just assumed I was a nervous wreck and was absolutely yanking myself past the point of pain—

I suck in a breath at the memory. Because it was *him* I was thinking of... and I think he knew that.

Because he was right.

Fear... turns me on.

"Oh, God," I groan loudly, rolling my head to the side where it thumps against the wall, then back again, repeating the motion over and over.

I've completely lost my mind. That's what's happened to me.

I've freaking lost it over a clown I met at a horror experience place.

It takes a few more minutes of rapid breathing before I'm able to breathe semi-properly again—and even then, I still feel queasy and faint. But I manage to stand on my feet without falling over. I splash cool water on my face and brush my teeth, and then, with a groan, I head to my bedroom in silence, head hanging heavy between my shoulders.

I'm weighed down by it all while equally feeling exhilarated.

Because I've never felt so alive... and that scares me.

DAYS PASS IN A PARANOID BLUR.

I swear everywhere I look, I can see his face, those *eyes*, staring back at me. But I know I don't. I *can't* be. Because he doesn't know where I am.

But he got my number... which means he could've easily gotten my address.

I shake my head resolutely, fighting against the onslaught of images from a few nights ago. *It's just my fear thinking*, I tell myself over and over. *There's nothing to be scared of.*

But even as I say that, I know it's a lie.

Static is the very thing to fear.

He's the product of my nightmares brought to life.

He's the devil incarnate my parents always warned me

about, and I'm falling right into his sinful trap. But I can't seem to stop. I don't know if I... *want* to stop.

Do I?

I know I don't want to be scared. I don't want this adrenaline pumping through my veins constantly. I don't want to worry about what's going to happen every time I turn my back or close my eyes. But the way he makes me feel—for that split second when my dick gets hard—it's unlike anything I've ever experienced in my life.

I drop my head down onto the table in front of me with a loud *thud*. A few *shhs* resound, but I ignore them.

What am I going to do?

I'm stuck in a hell loop. That's what this has to be—one viscous eternal hell I'm meant to find an escape from.

I just wonder what kind of damning thing I did to deserve this.

MY STOMACH SINKS the moment I feel my phone vibrate against my thigh. I must tense because Kane glances over at me from where we have our homework spread out between us. I may be a few years behind him and he's in school for vet tech, but we still study together, and he helps me where he can, which is nice.

"What's up?" he asks, quirking a dark brow.

I shrug as nonchalantly as I can. "Nothing."

"Bullshit. You look like you just swallowed a lemon."

"I do not," I argue, meeting his intense gaze, but I know it's fruitless.

Kane just stares back at me, waiting for my answer.

"Just got a text," I mumble beneath my breath, dipping my head down.

"What was that?"

"I said," I enunciate, "that I just got a text."

Kane's eyes narrow. He leans back and crosses his arms across his chest. The muscles bulge, and I would probably drool from how good he looks if I didn't feel like crap right now.

"What does a text have to do with you looking like that?" he asks, eyes concentrated on mine, darting back and forth. I keep looking away so he can't see into my soul and tell the lies that are planted there or any of that stuff. "Unless..."

"Unless what?" I blurt a little too quickly.

"Unless someone's bothering you." He sounds cold. I shiver.

I swallow. Feel the roll of my thickened throat as saliva makes its way through my esophagus. What do I even say to that?

Oh, yeah. The creepy clown from Mayhem Motel might possibly be stalking me, but I can't be sure because I've never seen him. But he has been texting me.

That would go over so well.

They'd call my parents, and I'd get locked up in an insane asylum.

Nope.

No, thanks.

I've gotta deal with this on my own.

Somehow... someway...

"Madison?" Kane says my name, prompting me out of my reverie. I shake my head, pulling myself back into the now. I dig my fingers into my eyes, rubbing the itchiness away.

"No," I tell him, instantly regretting the bitter lie as it leaves my tongue. "Everything's fine. Just tired."

"Okay..." he drawls slowly, not looking convinced.

"I haven't been sleeping well. My, uh." I feel my face get hot with embarrassment. He knows enough about them, I know I have no reason to be ashamed, but I still feel it, anyway. "My parents," I say, because that's all the explanation I need to do.

"Ah, I gotcha," Kane says lightly. He lifts his hand and pats my shoulder. His touch is warm and comforting, but I don't feel anything other than that, and it's kind of disappointing.

I want the buzz back in my skin. The tingling down my spine. The rush of blood pounding in my ears and the warmth of heat flooding my groin.

I want my head to pound so hard I can't think, and I want to breathe in everything that's wrong with me until I choke on it.

"Oh, God," I breathe out, choking on the air around me as I come back to the now. Kane is patting my back, and once I catch my breath, he starts rubbing in smoothing circles.

It feels good but not the kind of good I want.

Or apparently now *need.*

Thanks to him.

CHAPTER FIFTEEN
DEVOUR A FUCKING RAINBOW

CEDRICK

It's been too long without him.

He's stopped returnin' my texts. He's staying inside the house more often than not.

He's hidin' from me.

Whether he knows it or not.

The only time I get to see him is when he's walking to class—because he has no other choice. And I *hate* that I can't touch him. That he's so close, yet so far away. Sometimes mere feet, others across the courtyard. But he never sees me, no.

I keep myself hidden because the last thing I wanna do is spook my little mouse into disappearing completely. He's too skittish for anything extreme when he's not forced into it.

I just need to find a way to see him more because this... this is *not* enough.

My skin is tingling, burning, *achin'* with the desire to touch him again. To feel his sweat-slickened skin against mine as he writhes pathetically, whimpers escaping those ample lips that I can't wait to feel wrapped around my cock.

I need Madison.

Any way I can have him.

And I'll be damned if he's the reason I don't get 'em.

SCREAMS ECHO down the darkened hall, and I wipe sweat from my brow, smearing paint along the back of my glove. My victim got away from me, but I can't bring myself to care.

For the first time since I started scaring, my heart's just not in it. Because I can't stop thinking about Madison and how utterly perfect he was.

How everyone else pales in comparison.

It's pathetic, really.

"What the fuck is up with you?" Ligature bitches in my earpiece. "This is the third person tonight—"

Before Booker can even finish his sentence, I'm yanking my earpiece out of my ear and shaking my head to clear the ringing that now resounds. I shove it in my pocket and let out a thunderous growl.

"I know," I mutter to no one but myself. The ropes hangin' from the beams in the ceiling swing around me as I pace back and forth. I bury my hands in my hair and yank, tearing strands from my skull. But even the sting of that is not enough to redirect my thoughts back to the now.

All that's in the forefront of my mind is how pretty Madison looked strapped to that dolly. Small and weak and pathetic. And so, so precious.

He was... *is* the sweetest thing I've ever tasted.

And I want more.

I *need* more.

"I can see you pacing back and forth in there, *Static.*" Kierra's voice rolls through the speakers hidden in the corner of the room.

"Fuck off," I mutter as I continue my pacing. My sweaty hair is sticking up on all ends, teeth bared, and eyes crazed.

I probably look every bit the psycho I'm portraying.

"*Harrumph.*"

"What's got you looking like that?" Kierra's voice crackles on the speakers after a minute of silence, and I startle because I thought she'd left me alone.

"Nothing, Kierra."

"Well... another group is about to come in so you might want to get your shit together." And I just know the bitch is smirking as she stares at me through the screen the cameras display on.

"Yeah, yeah. I'm on it," I tell her as I square my shoulders, rollin' em back and straightening to my full six-foot three frame. Ropes smack me in the face as I do, but I easily swing them away, unbothered by them as I exit the room with little to no purpose but a job I still have to do.

I just need to get my shit together.

I need to get Madison out of my mind.

Clearly, he's not worth the trouble. He's too... *No.*

I shake my head vehemently. *I'm* too much for someone like him. The things I like, the things I want, could never match up to someone as pure as him.

It was just a one-time fluke, and I should probably start tryin' to get over this shit because it's affecting me way too much.

I mean, for fuck's sake, it has me dreading work, and I *love* my job. Who wouldn't?

Yeah.

I need to get over Madison Payne.

THAT'S EASIER SAID than done, especially when the boy continues to rob my every thought. Sleeping and awake.

He's a fucking thief, is what he is.

I stare up at my dark ceiling, blinking through the bleariness in my eyes of another night of missing sleep—because of *him*.

I dream of his soft cries and loud whimpers.

His snotty tears and choking gasps.

His pleas.

His beggin'.

His enchanting beauty as he stared up at me through those dark, clumped lashes, wishing for a reprieve he didn't really want because that was the best he'd ever felt in his entire life.

And *fuck*, when Madison lets go...

There's nothin' else like it.

"Fuck." I toss the blanket back with a growl and shove upward until the cool air of my fan is drifting over the bare skin of my torso, causing goosebumps to break out against my flesh.

I pull my pierced bottom lip in between my teeth and chew on the metal of the jewelry in it as I let my mind drift.

There's nothing else I can really do at four in the morning.

I guess I could go over to his place, but he'll be sleeping—with his curtains closed—so there's really no point in that.

He's getting smarter, the little shit head.

But as annoying as that is, I find it so amusing that he's going through the precautions he is to keep me out when he has no idea who or where I am. Or when.

For all he knows, I could be cuddled up under his bed this very second, listening to every sound of his breath. His heavy exhales with a slight snore at the end, I imagine. His soft intakes of breath, quieter than a mouse.

I think he'd twitch a bit in his sleep. Either from nightmares or just dreams in general. And I'd imagine they're vivid, too.

Just like he is.

He's the only splash of color I've had in this oil-stained world I live in, and I don't think I can give that up.

It's not false color like people see during an oil spill, when light reflects on it and they see hues of pigmentation.

No.

Madison is the whole goddamn rainbow put right in front of my very eyes.

And who wouldn't want to devour a fucking rainbow?

"You look like shit," Kase says when I walk into the kitchen at seven in the fuckin' morning.

"Thanks for that," I deadpan as I pull out a chair and drop down into it. I let my head fall into my hands to block some of the bright light from above. That's when I feel Kase's hand on my shoulder. I tense briefly at the contact, but then, I lean into it, letting my head rest against their side.

"Just sayin'. Not sleep well?" they ask as they run their fingers through my hair, and I groan at the warmth that tingles along my scalp and down the nape of my neck.

"No."

"Wanna talk about it?"

"No," I repeat, not opening my eyes.

"Fair enough," they chuckle. And it's the ease within it that I can tell right then and there that we'll be okay. That this... thing between us won't change anything—just like last time.

That it was a one and done. Or, well... a few times and done. Just to release some tension with someone we trust. Someone familiar.

Even though I know it, I still feel the burning need to ask, but I won't.

I'll live in the uncertainty until I get my answer eventually.

Until then...

I'll suffer in the unknown.

"So, since we don't have to work until later tonight, what are you gonna do today?" Kaser asks as they move around the table to the other side. They take a seat and sip coffee from their overly large mug. I hike a brow but don't say anything for a minute.

"I don't know," I finally reply after a while.

"Just wanna chill today?" they ask, and yeah. That does sound nice, but no. I wanna see my treat. I wanna talk to him.

But he's fuckin' refusin' me, and I'm about to lose my shit.

'Cause who was I kidding? I can't give him up.

My fingers tighten around my own coffee mug that Kaser poured for me. And for a moment, I fear it might crack, but thankfully, it doesn't.

The ceramic is hot to the touch, and the burn is enough to center me   for the moment.

Maybe I'll go into work and see if maintenance will let me view the video footage from when my treat came to visit me.

Oh, that would be lovely.

Watching him through a screen, unaware he's being recorded. For me to watch over and over and over until I'm satiated.

Oh.

My eyes light up as inspiration sparks.

My little mouse with his own little camera. Hidden.

Just for me.

Oh, *fuck.*

Yes.

Yessss…

My fingers tighten on the mug for a moment before I let go. I push back from the table so quickly, the liquid sloshes over the side and spills onto the surface. Kaser looks up at me, questions in their dark eyes, brows pulled together in confusion.

"Nah," I rush out, reveling in the adrenaline pumping through my veins again for the first time in days. "I need to run into town to get some shit."

"Want some company?"

"I'm good, thanks." I walk around the table and press a kiss to the top of their shaved head. Kaser leans into the touch, and for a moment, we're still. The world halts—even our breathing. For a perfect moment. And then, I'm moving away from them and out of the small kitchen in two long strides.

Time to find the perfect camera for a little mouse.

Who knew there were so many... devices to choose from?

A smirk curls my lips as I peruse the aisle again, skimming each camera with scrutiny until I come across one that I think might work perfectly.

It's small and square, connects directly to my phone, and doesn't have a range limit, so I can watch him from anywhere.

The only dilemma is the internet access it needs... but I can figure that out later.

This is the best thing I'm finding, and I don't want to waste any more time.

I grab the box and take it to the front to purchase. A chunk of change later, I'm walking out of the store with a newfound light in my eyes, visions of my treat already swimmin' through my head.

Fuck, I can only imagine how perfect he's gonna be.

The trip to Grosse Pointe takes half an hour too long, and by the time I make it to Madison's place, my blood is pumping heavy in my veins, and I swear my dick has never been harder.

The anticipation of this... *breaking into his house, his room.* Seeing it for the first time without him. Invading his privacy like this...

Fuck. I'm gonna come in my pants.

I park a few blocks away like I always do and grab the box. I spend the next twenty minutes getting it set up and synced to my phone so I can have the live feed. The internet issue I'm hoping I can solve while I'm inside... like them having it written down somewhere would be cool.

But before I know it, I'm out of the car and makin' my way to the house. The sidewalk is devoid of anyone, seeing as this is a campus town and everyone's most likely in class. Which bodes well for me, I hope.

I tuck my hands into my pockets and swing my head to the side to brush my hair away from my face. It's chilly enough out that my jewelry is cold, so I fidget with it on my way up their sidewalk to the front door.

My heart is hammering against my sternum.

I take a quick glance around, eyes wide as I turn my head.

There's no one around, but it almost feels like there's someone watching *me.*

It's eerie.

As I place my hand on my chest, I wonder if this is what *they* feel when they're being chased.

If so, this is fucking amazing.

I crack a smile as I reach for the front door, and—"My, oh, my. You college boys sure are stupid," I purr as I twist the handle the rest of the way and let myself inside.

I fully expected to have to force my way inside—and I wasn't above it, but this...

This just feels like fate.

Chapter Sixteen

I Need Madison

Cedrick

The moment I step inside, I let my eyes fall closed, and I inhale deeply as if I can smell Madison now. Just knowing this is where he resides is enough to make my dick twitch.

It's closer than I've ever been to his life outside of Mayhem since that night... and now, I have free reign.

My lips pull into a grin as my eyes widen at the realization that I'm alone.

I'm fucking alone. Inside Madison's house.

Fuck.

With a newfound grin, I take a few steps inside, the sound of my boots echoing in a dull thud across the carpet. I trail my gloved fingers along the rough, pale colored wall, enjoying the scrape the tips of my pointed gloves make before pulling away with a sigh.

I turn to face the room in front of me, surprised to find the room is large but somehow cozy. It makes my eyes narrow as I glance around the living room, inspecting for some discrepancies.

I notice furniture is mismatched and has definitely seen better days. The carpet is stained in a few spots. There are crumbs on the coffee table and a few glasses from the previous day—I'd assume—left behind, but other than that, the place is mostly clean.

I suppose that's good for Madison's sake... Because if he stays, I can see him as much as I desire, but that doesn't mean I have to fuckin' like him enjoying living here, surrounded by all these damn men all the time. *Especially that one that was in his room*—I cut myself off with a hiss as my pointed gloves dig into the soft inner flesh of my palms.

No.

No, no, no.

I don't like him at all.

He's a problem I'm gonna have to deal with.

I pull in a sharp breath and let my head fall back between my shoulders. I roll it around, listening to the cracks of bone as they pop from the movement. I stretch my shoulders out and flex the tendons in my neck until my muscles scream and my neck is aching.

It's only then that I let my shoulders drop and the air bleed out of me in a slow breath.

I'm here for one reason and one reason only.

To be able to see my little mouse.

With a newfound ease, I slowly make my way through the living room and into the kitchen, fingers trailing over the backs of chairs and scraping over grooves in the wood, creating a few new ones of my own. Nothing anyone would ever notice, but my own little mark.

I walk over to a pile of papers on the counter and flip

through them, noting the names on the front. There's mostly mail for a Kane Wilson, with a few junk things for a Lenny Mason and Collin Olbrich.

I mentally store those names for later when I come across a packet for the Wi-Fi information. My face breaks out in a grin because, *fuck*. Everythin' is just proving that this is exactly what was meant to be.

I flip through the instruction papers until I reach the back, where they luckily have the name and password written down.

What a bunch of fuckin' idiots.

Don't they know crazy people like me exist?

With glee, I take my phone out and snap a photo before connecting it to their internet. Then, I go about syncing the camera and making sure it's all good to go before placing the papers back where I found them and making my way up the stairs to my little prize's room.

I need no map to tell me where to go. I know exactly where it is.

Each step I take has my heart beating a little faster, a little heavier. The all-too-familiar rush of adrenaline pumps through my veins, and I crack my neck against the sensation as it slithers up my neck and causes goosebumps to break out over my covered arms.

Fuck. This is too good.

I can't believe I'm about to do this... Go this far just to see him.

But at this point, it's not even a choice.

I need Madison, and I'm gonna take 'im.

My heavy boots thud against the carpeted steps, causing them to creak with each step, and I relish in the noise as I make my way toward my mouse's bedroom door.

It's not hard to guess which one is his—it's the only

bedroom with a window that faces the east side of the house right by that huge, beautiful maple tree. Like my place inside it —*watching him*—was meant to be.

My fingers wrap around the knob with reverence, and the moment I push the door open, I let my eyes fall closed as his scent wafts over me in a cloud so thick, I choke. My hand flies to my crotch to press against my rapidly swelling cock from where it threatens to burst out of the confines of my pants just from his lingering scent *alone*.

Fuck, it's been too long.

I inhale deeply as I walk into his room and close the door behind me, determined to suffocate in his scent that smells slightly of lemons and laundry detergent. It's such a clean... *innocent* smell compared to the acrid scent of his sweat and piss, and it's throwing me because both feel so much like him, but how can I know that when I barely know him?

All I know is what his fear tastes like. What he looks like when he's at rock bottom and scared shitless. When he's on the precipice of pain and pleasure and about to teeter over.

Sure, that's more than most people ever see of someone. It exposes the most of someone, but it's also not everything.

It's not the little things.

And I think...

I think I wanna know the little things, too.

But he won't let me, so I've gotta do what I gotta do.

Force my little treat into it.

But it's okay because I know, in the end, he'll love it.

With a smirk, I glance around his room. It's a little bigger than it looks through the pane of glass I'm used to looking through, but that doesn't surprise me. I scope out his books, mostly nonfiction and religious—a worn maroon bible amongst them all—with some cheeky romance titles thrown in... and my collar. Sitting right there on his shelf. What a little surprise, my treat is.

I finger one of the spines and pull it out, noting a half-naked man on the cover. I raise a brow at the rows of abs on him before putting it back with a shake of my head and a smile curving my lips.

I pull my pierced lip between my teeth and tug on it as I explore more of Madison's room, namely his bedspread, which I reach down and hold up to my nose to smell.

He doesn't have a whole lot of belongings, but each thing I come across as I flick my gaze around feels so intimately him that it nearly makes my heart clench to see it and to know it's his.

My phone buzzes in my pocket, pulling me out of my reverie, and I drop his blanket back onto the bed.

KASE:

Are you actually gonna show up?

I look down at Kaser's text and feel my face go hot. For fuck's sake, it's already three o'clock. I need to be at Mayhem in thirty minutes, and I haven't even put the camera in place...

ME:

Im gonna be a bit late but Im comin

I text back quickly and then shove my phone in my pocket before reaching for the camera. With a newfound sense of urgency—because I know Madison will be home soon—I scan the room for the perfect place to hide this.

It's gotta be somewhere with a good view, but it has to remain hidden...

I narrow my eyes.

And then, I look up.

Chapter Seventeen

I Fall Victim to Him

Madison

I flop back on my pillows with a groan, my homework displayed out in front of me.

Why did I decide a psychology degree was the way to go? This shit is way too confusing, I don't understand—

A knock sounds at my open door.

"What's up?" I say, never taking my eyes off the ceiling. My fan rotates in slow circles, circulating the air and causing my papers to ruffle.

"We got pizza," Lenny says, and I turn my head to the side to glance at him. He's shirtless—because of course, he is—and I feel my face heat before I can even open my mouth to say a word.

Lenny, of course, notices, and smirks at my reaction.

"You're so innocent, it's cute."

"S-shut up-p," I stutter, and I hate it.

"Nope." He pops the "P", and straightens from the door-jamb. "Come down and eat. We've got plenty."

My stomach growls, and I swear I can smell the pizza sauce from here. Man, I love pizza…

"I should probably keep working…" I argue pathetically. "I've got too much work, and a lot of this I don't understand, so I have to study for it—"

"How about you come eat, and then, I'll see if I can help you after."

I stare up at Lenny, who's significantly taller than my five-foot seven frame. "You'd do that?"

"Sure. I'm dumb as shit when it comes to anything but business, but I'll try."

"Thanks, Lenny. I appreciate it."

"Sure thing, Mads. Come on." He holds his arm out, and I follow him down the stairs, where the scent of garlicy sauce and dough is strongest.

LATER THAT NIGHT, when Lenny and I are sitting on my bed, my phone vibrates beside me. I pick it up distractedly, eyes still mostly on the papers in front of me, and glance at the screen.

UNKNOWN:

You have a lot of people in your bed for
such an innocent boy

All the blood drains from my face in an instant as every single hair on my body stands on end. I straighten my spine as my phone slips from my fingers and drops onto the bed beside me. Blood rushes through my ears as my face burns hotter than ever before, and it takes a while for me to notice that Lenny is talking to me.

"Madison!"

"Y-ye-yeah?" I stutter, worse than ever before.

"What's wrong? Why do you look like that?"

I stare blankly at Lenny's concerned face in front of me. His brows are pinched, and his lips are downturned. His nose is wrinkled like he smelled something bad, and his eyes are widened.

"I... I think I-I need to-to lie down," I mutter after a moment, still staring blankly at him and hoping what I said makes sense.

"Okay..." he drawls slowly. "Are you sure?"

"Yeah. Yeah, just... tired, I think." My hands are trembling in front of me, and I press them against the tops of my thighs to help still them. But it only makes my legs vibrate instead.

Lenny pushes the papers off his lap and stands, but as he turns back to me, he says, "Madison, are you sure, dude? You don't look so good."

"S-s-ure. I am."

"Okay..." One brow hikes, but then, he turns his back and makes his way out of the room, leaving me alone in my panic, which is the last thing I want, but I can't have anyone witness me like this...

Another vibration.

"Oh, God," I choke out, scraping my nails down my throat as the bile burns its way up my esophagus.

And another.

Another.

And more.

"Shit," I blurt the swear word that rarely ever escapes my

mouth. My heart is in my throat, in my stomach, in my *eyes*, as it pounds and pounds and *pounds.*

I can't control the shaking of my hands as I reach for my phone when it goes off *again.*

My screen is full.

> UNKNOWN:
>
> Youre panicking
>
> I can see it ya know
>
> Its glorious
>
> I miss that taste
>
> Do you

"Do I?" I wheeze as I read it aloud. "Do I miss it? What is he even talking about?" I whine as I stare at the words in front of me, as I watch them blur as tears fill my eyes and splash down onto the screen.

Another text comes through, and I vow not to look. I scrunch my eyes shut and shake my head vehemently, but I can't... resist...

> UNKNOWN:
>
> The taste of your fear

But I didn't...

> UNKNOWN:
>
> Surely you tasted it too

My hand comes up to my mouth unwittingly, and I follow the path of my chapped bottom lip with the tips of my fingers, back and forth.

UNKNOWN:

Its so good isnt it

I shouldn't give in to his craziness. I know, but...

ME:

Why are you doing this?

How... How are you doing this?

I hit send before I can think any more of it.

Shit.

I can feel my heart in my throat, like it's about to leap right out of my chest.

What did I just do?

My eyes widen in panic.

I just engaged with a stalker. *Again.*

Madison, you absolute idiot.

UNKNOWN:

You know why Im doing this

As for how...

Thats the fun part

Oh. Oh, no.

I don't like that.

No. No fun part.

I'm shaking my head before I realize what I'm doing. And then, I stop when realization washes through me that he can probably see what I'm doing...

Oh, God.

"Oh, *my God!*" I shout, shooting to my feet. My stomach

falls to the floor simultaneously as I run to the window and slam it shut. I flip the lock and drag the dark blue curtains over it and take a few steps back, chest heaving. But my eyes remain locked on the window.

On the outline of the tree I know is just outside that window.

He wouldn't...

Would he?

Could he?

Holy shit...

I slowly sink to the floor and drop my head in my hands. I stare down at the pale carpet and grip the strands of my hair tightly into two fists. I keep them clenched as I start to rock back and forth.

Do I...

Do I have a...

A stalker?...

Am I really being stalked right now?

Is this really happening?

I don't know why, but I'm not surprised when my phone vibrates. I crawl to it blindly, and the text that comes through makes me run cold from my scalp all the way to the tips of my toes.

UNKNOWN:

Yes this is happening

And yes

Its cute when you talk to yourself

A ringing fills my ears as my face burns hot, and then, my eyes roll back as everything fades to black.

I come to, to the sound of a loud vibration against the side of my face.

"*Hmm*," I grunt softly as I slowly push myself into a sitting position. I scrub a hand down my face and reach for my phone, feeling resigned when I see **"Unknown"** flashing on the screen for none other than a call.

What the hell am I supposed to do with that?

He's calling me now?

"You're calling me now?" I repeat aloud since apparently, he can hear me, somehow, some way...

I don't want to think too hard about the particulars of that right now.

My phone stops, and his texts swooshes in.

UNKNOWN:

Yes

"Wow, r-really?" I deadpan, even through a stutter, which I would be proud of under any other circumstances.

UNKNOWN:

Answer the phone little mouse

I swallow the huge lump lodged in my throat. *Little mouse...*

Why does that sound so... threatening... and yet so alluring?

No. "No." I shake my head. "I will not fall for any of this... any of these games."

He's calling again.

I stare at it for so long, and then, my fingers move of their own volition, and I'm swiping.

"You already did, treat," is the first thing Static says to me, and the low timbre of his voice washes over me in a wave of goosebumps that actually *burn*.

"N-n-n—"

"Yes."

"I-I can't-t—Please—"

His dark chuckle resonates through the phone, and goose-flesh takes over my entire body.

"Can't... what? Can't talk to me? You're already doin' that, aren't ya?"

I can't respond. I can't even get my mouth to open without chattering too hard, my teeth clacking together, but that doesn't seem to be stopping Static.

"You're perfect like this... did you know that?" he drawls, and I can only listen with my phone glued to my ear. I'm frozen with a fear I can't explain I want.

"Your little body riddled and trembling, unable to control itself... Just as I remember it in that room. You remember that too, don't you, little mouse?"

Some small squeak escapes me, and Static chuckles darkly.

"Yeah, you remember. How could you forget? You keep my collar right there on your shelf as a little reminder of our time together, don't you?"

"W-wha-t-t?" I choke out, my words wet and snotty.

"You heard me, prize. I saw it. You can't lie to me. But it's okay... I left it for you. I'd rather you keep it and remember me."

My eyes dart to the very shelf he's talking about, and sure enough, there it is in all its black, tattered glory, where I stare at it from time to time. A reminder of the someone I became when I was in that room. The someone I'm not sure I ever want to be again.

But Static...

He brings this out in me, and I can't seem to stop it...

No matter how crazy it is.

"Okay... I don't—don't kn-know what's going on o-or how y-you know t-this stuff, but you need to l-leave me alone." I pull in a huge breath at the end because it feels like I'm suffocating.

"I think you know, but you don't want to, do you?"

"What?" I ask, shaking my head as confused tears spring to my eyes and start to drip out.

"You don't really want to know. You'd rather stay in the dark because the known is too scary for you." There's a long pause where all I can hear is the sound of his breaths through the receiver. They cause more goosebumps to prickle across my skin. "Isn't it, Madison?"

I swallow the lump that's formed in my throat at the harsh truth of his words.

"Tell me the truth," he demands, and I fall victim to him.

"Yes."

"Good boy."

My face flushes hot, and I swallow heavily. "Oh, God."

Static chuckles darkly. "God has nothing to do with this, my prize. It's all you and me and our time together. Are you excited for more?" He leaves the question open-ended, but I don't know how to answer that.

What am I even supposed to say?

The truth is too hard to admit—because even I can't say it to myself—whatever it is... But I don't think I can lie either because he'll see right through it and call me out on it.

Either way, I'm screwed.

My breathing kicks up in the panic that ensues. Black dots dance in front of my eyes, and I think I'm going to pass out again. My palms grow clammy, and my hands start to shake uncontrollably. Static is speaking to me, but I can't hear a word he's saying over the loud ringing in my ears.

"Maaadiiiisooonnn," my name is cooed so softly, I almost don't hear it, but the heavy, breathy way it's spoken causes chills to slither down my spine and settle at the base. I shiver uncontrollably as the tingles work their way back up and into my skull.

"That's it, mouse. Listen to me. Breathe."

And for some reason... *I do.*

I pull in a breath. And another.

And more. Until each one comes a bit easier and the room around me flashes back into vision and I can see my bed, messy and scattered with papers, my door, shut, the carpet below my feet, soft and well-used and stained in a few spots.

I reach out and run my hand along the fibers to soothe myself as I listen to the sound of Static's rhythmic breathing because for some reason, it's the only thing that's bringing me back.

"That's a good boy. You're doing so well. Just keep breathing. You've got this."

He's talking me through it so well, tears prick my eyes, and I nearly let them fall, but I *can't,* so I scrunch my eyes closed and let my head thud against the carpet with a dull *thunk.*

A deep breath, and then, on an exhale, "Don't look so discouraged, little mouse."

"How?" I croak into the floor, beyond masking my agony at this point. It's obvious he can see me, but I need to know how.

"That's the beauty, isn't it? Wanting to know... *needing to know...*"

"Bastard!" I cry as I shoot into a sitting position. I scramble for my phone and slam my finger on the end button. Static's unknown contact disappears, and I should probably be able to breathe a little easier at that, but I can't.

Probably because I know he's still watching me. Somehow. Someway...

Opening my eyes wide, I glance around the room, suddenly feeling more exposed than I ever have been. I eat in here, hang out in here, get... get *dressed* in here. I even... oh, God. I've even...

My face flushes at the memory of me touching myself the other night to the thought of none other than the man who's literally stalking me.

What a nightmare come to life—literally.

And I don't know what to do about it.

Static seems harmless enough... just someone who wants to play games. But I'm not sure I wanna play back.

And I don't think he's the kind that will take no for an answer.

Chapter Eighteen

This Sounds Serious

Cedrick

I'm nearly half an hour late to Mayhem, and everyone is *pissed*—not that I can blame them.

I've never been late before, and we've never had to delay opening, but I guess there's a first for everything.

They're all starin' at me when I come into the dressing room. I drop my head as I walk toward my vanity and plop down in the seat to start on my makeup. At this point, I've got it down-pat, so it should only take me five minutes, give or take—which I make sure to say aloud to everyone who's already ready and waiting... and staring at me with annoyance.

"Yes, I know. I'm fuckin' sorry," I mutter, my accent thicker than ever when I'm irritated. And as frustrated as I am with everyone being rude to me right now, I can't regret my decision to do what I did to Madison.

He's worth every bit of it.

I can still hear his voice in my head. His stuttering whimpers and desperate pleas. His resolute determination and abject ignorance.

He's absolutely perfect—and he never fails to keep on surprising me.

The way he passed out, eyes rolling into the back of his head, a bit of drool hanging from his thick, beautiful lips...

Fuck, he's perfect...

I reach down and adjust my cock, but of course, as I do, Wesley notices and whistles loudly. Or, well, whistles as best he can through the fake teeth he's wearing.

"Fuck off," I mutter, rolling my eyes as I swipe the rest of the black paint around my eyes, smearing it a bit at the corners so it looks messier before painting my lips and doing the same.

My phone buzzes with a notification just as I finish up, so I toss my brush on the table to check it. It's a motion alert for Madison's room. I glance around the room for a second before opening it up to take a quick peak at my treat before I go out for the night.

I find him sitting on his bed, legs curled up in front of him with his arms wrapped around them. He's got his chin resting on his knees, hair flopped across his forehead from where it hangs down slightly, and his right leg is shaking in the same rhythm as his hand.

He still has papers scattered across his bed, but they appear to be in the same place as earlier—like he hasn't done a damn thing since our call. And that makes me feel giddy—the control I have over him already.

"The fuck's got you so distracted today?" Kaser says as they come up behind me. I jerk and nearly drop my phone.

"Nothing," I mutter and lock it. I shove it into the drawer before reaching for my contacts to put those in before gluing my teeth on.

"Mhm," they hum, eyeing me through the mirror. I refuse to catch their gaze because I don't like lying to them, and this feels a little too much like lying, even though it's technically just an omission.

But I want Madison all to myself.

I don't want to share him, and frankly, I don't think I should have to.

"You seem to be in a whole other world," Kase says after a minute, propping their hip against my vanity.

"I'm just a bit distracted," I mumble as I finish with the teeth glue. I swipe my tongue over the front of my teeth, over the points at the ends, pressing hard against them until I feel the sting.

"No, shit, man. I'm asking why."

I pull back from the mirror with a frown. "What do ya mean, why?"

Kaser scoffs. "You're joking, right? You haven't been yourself lately. You're late for work, which you never are, and that's crazy to even think about because you love scarin' mother fuckers more than anyone," they finish with a huff, their accent thicker than it's been in a long time, which tells me exactly what I need to know—I'm getting off track here, and everyone can see it.

But what else am I supposed to do?

I need Madison...

I pull in a deep breath and let it out slowly before pushing to my full height in front of Kaser. I turn to face them. "Look. It's just..." I pause, trailing off as I try to come up with some excuse that makes sense.

"Who are they?" they ask, and I freeze.

"What?"

"Who. Are. They?" they ask again, enunciating each word

deliberately, never taking their eyes off me. And that's when I realize I'm fuckin' stupid to ever think I could hide from Kase.

"I don't know if I should tell you," I tell them honestly, dropping my head slightly.

"You're fucking joking—"

"All right, everyone! Time to get out there and scare some bitches!" Kierra comes through the door with a booming voice and a beaming smile, shattering the conversation between me and Kaser.

Their eyes narrow as they pull their latex mask over their face. "This conversation isn't over."

I can't help it. I roll my eyes and smile.

"Wouldn't fuckin' dream of it, baby."

"Fuck you." And then, they turn around and disappear through the door, following behind everyone else. I wait an extra minute to gather myself, waiting until I hear resounding screams, and then, I pull in a breath, force a grin on my face, and get my ass out there and hope this brings some sort of rightness back to my life.

"COME OUT, come out, wherever you are..." I taunt the newest group in a sing-song voice, scraping the blade of my axe on the floor as I walk so it creates the most grating noise that sends goosebumps erupting.

A small whimper escapes, and I stop and cock my head. I know they can see me, so I give them a show.

"Oh... *Tsk. Tsk. Tsk.*" I click my tongue. "That was a bad move..." I drawl as I near a girl cowering in the corner. My face splits into a grin the closer I get, and when I round it and the sound of her whimpers and cries increase tenfold, I let out a loud cackle that makes her scream brutally—and I haven't even touched her yet.

"Gotcha."

"Fuck!" she screams and tries to scramble away from me, but I reach out and clasp her ankle, keeping her pinned in place.

"No! Please, please, let me go!" she wails and drops to the floor in a useless pile of limbs. She's trembling, and I've barely touched her. I curl my nose. *Pathetic.*

They're all so pathetic compared to him.

My sweet, darling treat was absolutely perfect...

I need to get him back here.

Oh, *yes.* I smile to myself.

I need Madison back here so we can play again.

Fuck.

"Static, what the fuck are you doing? You just let her get away!" someone yells in my ear, and I blink through the haze to find the space in front of me empty.

"Well, damn," I click my tongue before pressing my finger to my ear and saying, "She wasn't good enough for me. Maybe you'll have a better stab at her." And then, I'm sliding to the ground with my head dropped back between my shoulders as I let myself daydream about chasing Madison through these halls all over again—only this time, it would be real.

There would be no game between us.

Just me and him and the fight for survival...

"Shit," I mutter as I reach down and adjust myself. Just the thought alone is enough to have my blood boiling in my veins.

The only problem is getting him here...

But maybe... just maybe...

The sound of footsteps resound through the room, and I lift my head to find a man standing in front of me, chest heaving, sweat pouring from his face in rivulets.

"What the..." he mumbles, and then, we make eye contact, and he freezes. "Oh... Sh-shit..." He slowly takes a step back, eyes wide, jaw slack. All the while, I just stare at him, head cocked to the side in amusement as he scares the fuck out of himself all on his own.

I'm not doin' a damn thing but sittin' here, but it seems to be doin' more than enough.

"Where ya goin'?" I ask as he steps over the threshold.

"Nowhere." He holds his hands up in front of him in a placating gesture, and I can't help but to throw my head back and laugh. Then, I slowly get to my feet, never taking my eyes off him. Maybe this is what I need. A new victim to release on.

He's no Madison. And I don't want him to be... but he'll do.

"Hey, now," I drawl slowly as he backs out of the room, tripping over the fraying carpet. "Come back."

"No... No way, man." He's shaking his head back and forth so fast, it reminds me of a dog out of water.

"Pathetic..." I muse softly, head cocked to the side ocne more as I slowly make my way toward him, my long strides eating up the short distance between us quickly. "You're all so slow," I murmur as I close the space and grab his upper arms. He yelps and tries to jerk away, but I'm stronger and hold on tight.

"He wasn't slow, though," I tell this stranger because who else is there to tell? "He was perfect. You all just pale in comparison," I spit between clenched teeth as I back him against the wall with my forearm pressed against his throat. He lets out a pathetic little squeak, and even though it's dark, I know his face is turning red.

"Wh-what're you talking about?" he gasps, and I laugh. I throw my head back and let it out. A full body, shaking laugh that vibrates through me before it settles like a warm buzz beneath my flesh.

"*Hmm*," I drawl, trailing my finger down his wet cheek. "Exactly." And then, I snap my teeth, and he screams, and it's...

It's ugly.

"So... who is it?" Kaser asks when I walk through the door later that night. I throw my head back with a groan, not even bothering to hide how annoyed I am. "Don't start that shit with me, Ced. You walked into this."

"How exactly did I do that?" I ask as I peel my boots off and leave them by the door before walkin' into the kitchen and making myself a strong Crown and coke.

"By lyin' to me."

I whirl around, glass in hand. I hold it aloft. "I did *not* lie to you."

"Well, you didn't fuckin' tell me the truth, now did ya?"

I turn back around to finish making my drink. After I've mixed it, I lean back against the counter to face Kaser and let myself have their wrath. I knew this conversation would happen eventually; I just figured there would actually be something between me and Madison first so I wouldn't seem like such a...

Freak.

I force the lump in my throat down with a large swallow of my drink, hissing slightly at the burn as it works its way through me.

"I didn't know what to say," I tell them truthfully because there's no point in withholding the truth any longer. Kase knows all my shit, so might as well lay it out there and hope they don't fuckin' call the cops on me or some shit.

"Start from the beginning," they say as they take a seat at the table, arms crossed over their chest, their own drink in front of them. I swallow another gulp for some liquid courage and open my mouth.

"It started that night at Mayhem... the night I met Madison."

"Madison? Who the fuck is Madison?"

"I'm getting to that, aren't I?" I snap, molars locked together.

"Fine. Shit, you're tense about this," they snark.

"Well, I don't exactly feel great telling you."

Kaser's face falls, and I immediately feel guilty. "Why?" they ask softly, and I sigh loudly.

"Because I've done some shit I probably shouldn't have done, but I can't take it back. Or..." I trail off and curl my upper lip in. "Won't take back, I guess is more accurate. And I don't want *common sense* talked into me because I know this is the way it has to be between us."

"Cedrick, you're rambling. What the fuck are you talking about?"

"Madison was a client at Mayhem. He was one of my victims, and... fuck, Kase, he was absolutely perfect. I can't even describe to you how beautiful he was. The way he cried. The way his eyes scrunched when he—" I cut myself off before

I can give too much away, but by the look on Kaser's face, they already know.

Shit.

"Damn. You went *there* with this guy? Really?"

"Yes."

"And..."

"And it wasn't enough," I tell them bluntly, waiting to see if they get the hint. And because it's Kaser and they're smart as fuck, of course, they do.

"Ricky, you didn't."

"I did."

"That's..."

"I know."

"You can't just—"

"I *know!* But it's already done. Too late to go back now."

"You can stop," they insist, but I'm already shaking my head.

"I can't."

"Cedrick..."

"I *can't,* okay. I can't explain it, but he's just... There's just somethin' about him that drives me up the fuckin' wall, and I *need* him, okay?" For some reason, my chest is heaving, and my eyes sting. I chug the rest of my drink before I can say anything more.

"This sounds serious."

"It is... I think."

"Does he know that?" they ask, and I can't help but snort.

"No."

Kaser's brows draw inward. "And why not?"

"Because he's kind of terrified of me still," I admit in a mumble.

"Why." Not a question but a demand.

"Because I've kinda been stalking him for the last few weeks," I let all the words out in a rush and then curl my lips inward after I've finished as I wait for Kaser to reprimand me.

"Cedrick," they say after a minute of just staring at me, "you stupid mother fucker."

I blow out a breath. "I know."

"What the hell did you think was gonna happen? That he was just gonna suddenly *not* be scared of you?"

I shrug. "I kinda like that he's scared of me," I admit with a half-grin.

Kaser rolls their eyes, but I catch their own lips twitching. "Of course, you do. But stalking someone isn't the way—"

"He won't talk to me any other way," I argue.

"How do you know that?"

I narrow my eyes. "I just do."

"Did you even try?"

"Fuck you," I snap, then try to take another gulp of my drink before realizing, with a frown, that I've already finished it off.

"Don't get snippy with me, buddy. I'm just pointing out the obvious, which you clearly can't see because you're too close."

"I'm not too close. But he won't want anything to do with me if I'm not Static," I snap the truth I've been trying to avoid thinking about ever since that night.

Kase's face softens, and I hate it. "Why do you think that?"

"Because I know it's the fuckin' truth, okay? He only wanted what was covered in makeup and tattered clothes. And that's fine. I can give that to him. It's easy to be him because sometimes, I feel like I'm Static more than I am Cedrick."

"But you're both."

"He doesn't want both."

"But you don't know that, Ced. You haven't even tried."

"And I'm not gonna fuckin' risk losin' him over it, either. I know he wants Static, so that's what I'm stickin' with."

"Risk losing him..." They repeat my words softly, and I wince. For fuck's sake.

"Pretend I didn't say that," I snap.

"I can't."

"Yes, you can."

"Cedrick, this sounds serious for you."

"It is," I admit.

"But is it serious for him?"

"Is having a stalker serious for someone?" I snark and immediately regret it.

"Cedrick!"

"FUCK!" I shove away from the counter with a growl. My fingers delve into my hair, and I yank on the strands until I feel the sting in my scalp.

"You were serious about that?"

"Obviously! I'm not fuckin' lying to you."

"Anymore."

"Okay, fine. *Anymore.*"

"This is so fucked, dude," they say, dragging their hand over their shaved head.

"You're telling me," I mutter.

And like the Gods have a sense of humor, my phone vibrates at that exact moment. I pull it out of my pocket without thinking about it. It's a motion alert notification for Madison. I open it to view, smiling softly when he comes up on my screen.

He's walking sleepily from his bed to the door, which he leaves open to use the bathroom, I'm assuming. He's gone for a couple of minutes, and then, he shuffles back in, one eye cracked open, black shorts and a white t-shirt on his small build, and I just want to rip them off of him.

I clench my fingers around my phone before locking it and putting it back in my pocket—and it's not until I meet Kaser's eyes that I realize what I've just done.

"Please tell me that wasn't what I think it was," they say, voice quiet but stern.

I purse my lips. "Depends on what you think it was."

"I'm worried you were just staring at that boy on your phone."

"And if I was?" I hike my brow.

"Cedrick..." Kaser blows out a breath. "Jesus fucking Christ."

"Yeah, I know."

"No, I don't think you do. You can get in serious fucking trouble for this, dude."

"Yes, I know," I repeat dryly.

"Do you? Do you really?"

"Ya. I just don't care."

"Oh. *Ohh,* that's just great. You don't care that you could go to fucking jail. *Again,* I might add."

"It was *one time!*" I argue.

"Yeah. But this is much more fucking serious than fifth degree theft as a kid, Ced!"

"I know."

Kaser drops their head back with a long, drawn-out sigh. "Jesus, this is fucked."

"Yep."

"*You're* fucked."

"Mhm."

"You're not helping, either. You know that, right?"

"Right."

"Oh, fuck you."

"I mean, if you're in the mood..." I drawl with a smirk, which makes Kase roll their eyes.

"No, I'm good. Now I know why it didn't last as long this time. You've had someone else on your mind." They sound kinda sad when they say it, and I rush to fix it.

"Kase, that wasn't—"

"No, I know. I know you'd never do that. But I get it, too."

I drop my head a little, feeling defeated and exhausted because I don't know what to do. "I'm sorry."

"I know. I love you too," they snark. And all feels right for the moment.

"You're my best friend, you know."

"Yeah, 'cause no one else is crazy enough to be."

"That ain't no shit," I bite back with a grin and stride over to the table to wrap them in my arms, feeling a sense of warmth I haven't felt in a while. I press a kiss to the top of their shaved head.

This is all a mess, and I might be fucking it all up—but at least I have Kaser to help me through it.

I just wish I would've talked to them sooner.

Chapter Nineteen

Deal

Madison

I stare down at my phone screen, lip pulled between my teeth. I'm biting it so hard, I taste blood, but I can't stop. My heart is pounding in my chest so hard, I can feel it in my ear drums.

Have I? Have I missed him?

It's been an entire week of *nothing* from him. I thought he'd given up... maybe *forgotten* about me or something.

But no.

Here he is.

And I think I might be excited about it.

Shit.

I swallow down the saliva pooling on my tongue and nearly choke on it as another text comes through.

UNKNOWN:

I want to bite your lip like that

Would you let me

Please tell me you would

Oh... *Oh, God...*

He can see me...

My heart rate kicks up—as does my breathing—and I slowly lift my chin and look around my room. My curtains are pulled back to let the daylight in, and that's where I focus my gaze. I narrow my eyes as I stand, even as the chug of my heart threatens to choke me.

Phone in hand, I press call and hold it to my ear as I slowly make my way toward the glass pane separating me from my nightmare.

The line clicks.

Silence.

And then, a breath that makes me *shiver.*

"Hello, little mouse."

"What do you want?" I croak, clearing my throat at the end to try and sound braver than I feel.

"You," is all he says.

I blink once. Twice. Pull my lip back between my teeth as I contemplate his answer. "Why?"

"Because you're perfect."

I can't help the unattractive snort that escapes me. "You don't even know me."

"I know enough. But fair. Tell me about you, Madison. Tell me things I should know."

The hand I've pressed against the glass of the window shakes slightly as I stare out at the tree in front of me.

Is he sitting in this tree? Looking at me as I look at him?

What would I do if he was?

"Why should I? I don't know you," I say. "And you're stalking me," I add breathily as an afterthought.

"Stalking, huh?" Static says, accent thick enough to make goosebumps burn their way down my arms. "Is that what you call tryin' to get to know someone?"

"Is this what *you* call trying to get to know someone?" I repeat incredulously.

"Yes."

"What a way of doing it," I mutter, shaking my head, but my lips twitch of their own volition.

"I wanna know you, Madison. All your good and bad, deep and dark. Give it to me." Static's voice is low and gravelly, and it makes me shiver.

I have no idea who this man really is, but... I think I want that too.

Someone to know me... *the real me.*

I swallow thickly.

"This is crazy... You're my..." I clench my fingers tight around my phone and squeeze my eyes shut, trying to find some grasp of common sense because the words he is saying sound way too good to be true—and I'm falling for it.

"You're my stalker," I finish with a heaving breath, chest aching from the strain.

"*Mmm,*" he hums, and I shiver.

The line is silent for a few minutes as we just listen to the sound of each other's breathing.

And then he says, "I'm your stalker, your nightmare. You're my rapture, my most delicious treat, and *I miss you...*"

I break out into a full body shiver that's so violent, I nearly drop my phone.

"Come to me, my mouse. Come play with me again. One last time."

"W-what?" I stutter, unsure I heard him correctly.

"You heard me, darlin'."

"Static…"

"*Yeeessss,*" he hisses low and slow in my ear. "Say it again."

I swallow. "S-sta-static." It's a mere whisper, but it's good enough for him, it seems.

"Fuck. That's a good boy. You're so good when you want to be, aren't you? Which is all the time, I bet. You look like you always wanna be good, but you can't help but be a little selfish sometimes, isn't that right?" I move away from the window and yank the curtains closed, my face flushing hot at the rush of truth coming from Static's lips.

"You wanna put yourself first and give yourself everything you want while you listen so prettily… *Mmm,* yes, I can see it now."

"P-please st-stop…" I beg him, hand over my burning face, but it's no use. My dick is getting hard, and I'm pretty sure he knows it.

"Why, darlin'? You love it, don't you?"

"No," I argue fruitlessly.

"Show me," he demands softly, and I whimper.

"*Mmm,* yeah. Do that again, treat."

I choke back a sob as I reach into the waistband of my sweatpants and wrap my fingers around my now straining erection. It feels so good to touch it, I can't help but gasp at the immediate contact.

"Good boy, Madison. That's so good of you. Now, I want you to wrap your fingers around yourself and stroke. Hard and fast. I want you to come for me, and I want it to *hurt.*"

"Wh-what?" I ask on a stutter, unsure I heard him correctly, even as my fingers move to obey.

"You heard me, darlin'. Now, do it. And turn a little to the left so I can have a better view."

I obey Static on instinct, turning and wrapping my fingers around myself tightly. My phone is clenched in my fingers so hard they ache, but I welcome the burn as I start to stroke myself mindlessly, head tossed back between my shoulders, eyes hazy as I stare at the wall in front of me.

My mouth falls slack as I listen to the heavy sound of Static's breath in my ear increase in speed.

"A-are you..."

"*Mmm...* You're so good. C'mon, darlin', faster. Let's come together."

"Together?" I squeak, equally surprised and turned on at the turn of events.

"Yes. I can feel it. So close. C'mon, yes." And that's when I learn one thing about Static that no one else does.

When he's about to come, his accent gets so thick, it's barely understandable.

"Fuck, that's it, treat. Come for me."

"Oh, God, Static!"

"Say my name, darlin'. *Fuck.*"

Heat bursts from my groin, and a hot wetness soaks the inside of my pants. I stroke myself through the aftershocks until I'm trembling and my knees feel weak.

"Damn, you're so good," Static says breathily through the line, and I startle, having nearly forgotten everything that just occurred.

My eyes widen, and ice fills my veins. "I... I can't..."

"Darlin'—"

"I'm sorry." And I hang up, tossing my phone on the bed before dropping face first onto it with a groan.

What the hell is wrong with me?

What *was* that?

Even with my face covered, I can feel the room spinning and my stomach clenching with the need to vomit. My clothes stick to the front of me uncomfortably, and I itch to take them off, but *I can't move.*

Blood rushes in my ears, and the sound of my heart thumping fills my head until it's the only thing I can feel. I roll over onto my back with a gasping breath to stare up at the spinning ceiling, not seeing anything but dark spots as they dance in front of my eyes.

What did I just do?

And...

And why did I like it so much?

God, help me, I'm so messed up.

STATIC HAS TEXTED me numerous times over the last few days, and I've managed to ignore every single one.

I'm honestly not sure how when I clearly show no signs of self-control, but I've been trying to surround myself with my roommates constantly, so I have an excuse not to look at my phone. And then, by the time I go to bed, I'm so exhausted, I just pass out.

It seems to be working so far.

"So, what's up with you, man?"

Or I thought it was.

"What do you mean?"

"It's not like we don't mind the company," Lenny says, shaking his head with a laugh as he plays *GTA* on the T.V. "But you've been hanging around more than ever before so…"

"So, what's up?" Collin interrupts, and my face turns red. I didn't know I was being so transparent.

"Oh, give him a break," Kane says, slapping me on the shoulder as he takes a seat beside me, his own take-out container in hand. We got Indian food tonight, which I've never had before, but I freaking *love* chicken tikka masala.

"I just, I, uh…" I trail off, uncertain of how to explain myself.

"You don't have to say anything," Kane assures me before taking a bite of his food. It smells spicy.

"I-I feel like I do. I've just. Well. You all know I've never done this before, and I guess I'm still just trying to… I don't know, find my way? Figure out what's best? I didn't want to be too anti-social, but homework is too consuming. But if I'm being too much, p-please just let m-me know—"

"Nonsense!" Lenny says, throwing his hand in the air to clap mine. "We love havin' you around, little dude."

"Gee, thanks," I mutter, face flushing bright red at the ridiculous nickname.

"For fuck's sake, Len, leave him alone."

"Sorry, sorry."

"Yeah, whatever." Kane rolls his eyes, but he's smiling, and I feel myself smiling, too—until my phone starts buzzing.

My smile falls, but I ignore the ringing until it becomes impossible because everyone else starts to notice it as well.

"Yo, who's callin' you? They're persistent."

"Probably just my mom," I mutter, face flushing with the lie.

"I didn't think you were talking to them," Kane says, casually calling me out.

"I don't, but she's just... well..."

"*Hmm*, yeah, I get that," he says with a soft smile just as the vibration ceases for the second time. I breathe a little easier thinking it's finally over—until it starts all over.

I nearly groan aloud.

"Might wanna get that—must be important," he says, never taking his eyes off me.

"Must be," I murmur in return. "I'll be right back." And then, I push to my feet but don't pull my phone out of my pocket until I've locked myself in the bathroom on the main floor and have the sink water running to muffle some of the conversation about to occur.

"What do you want?" I snap.

"My mouse is feisty tonight. I love it," Static drawls lazily, and I hate the way my body breaks out in chills.

"There's nothing to—" I start to argue before I stop, realizing it's pointless with him. With a sigh, I start again, calmer this time. "What do you want, Static?"

"Ohh, I like this side of you, darlin'. You sound so good... What's gotten into you?"

My molars lock together in irritation. "I'm just tired of the games. Tired in general. So, if you could please just answer my question."

There's a long pause. Long enough I think he's hung up, but when I pull the phone from my ear, I notice it's still connected. He starts talking before it's back against my ear.

"You love the games, my little prize. Because you want to be won."

I blow out a breath of irritation. "What does that even mean?"

"Soon," is all he says. Then, "I have a proposition for you."

"A proposition," I deadpan.

"Yes."

"And what would that be?" I don't even know why I'm indulging in my *stalker's* fantasies right now. This is absolutely crazy... but curiosity killed the cat, as they say...

There's a long pause again, where all I can hear is Static's unsteady breathing. It makes me feel better knowing he's feeling just as unsettled as I am. "Come see me at Mayhem again."

My blood runs cold. "What?"

"I want you at Mayhem again. Back where we first met. I want the chase, the catch, the *time with you*... Will you give that to me?"

"Why the hell would I do that? I don't even know you!" I don't realize I'm shouting until there's a knock on the door. "Hold on. Just a sec," I tell whoever knocked before turning around and spitting into the phone. "I don't know you, you freaking *psycho*. And you expect me to just make myself that vulnerable *again?* You're out of your mind!"

"So... if you knew me a bit better, you'd consider it?"

"Well, it would certainly make it less terrifying!" I shout. I mean, who does this man think he is? The gall.

"Deal."

What.

"Wait, what?"

"I'll tell you about myself, and in exchange, you come back to Mayhem for me."

"That's what you want?"

"Yes."

"You don't want... like... anything else from me..." I trail off, eyes squinting as I process his words.

"I want everything, darlin'. But if you give me Mayhem again, I'll take it."

"And you'll leave me alone after," I clarify.

"If that's what you want," he drawls lowly.

"Oh, it's what I want." I solidify the deal before I can even think about it.

"Then, it's settled."

"All right."

A deep chuckle resounds through the line, and it's the cockiness of it that makes me spit the words out without thinking.

"Wanna start now?"

Chapter Twenty

Quid Pro Quo

Cedrick

My lips curve into a smile as I stretch out in my chair, legs extended in front of me. "Oh, my little mouse wants to play now?"

A hitch of breath. "Why not? Get it out of the way faster so we can both move on."

"*Hmm.* Sure," I hum.

"O-okay. Uh, um..."

"Did you actually have something in mind?"

"I'm making this up as I go. Cut me some slack!" he snaps, and I can't help but grin. He gets so feisty sometimes, and I don't think he even realizes it.

After a long pause, he finally asks, softer than I thought he could, "What's your name?"

My blood runs cold.

"Excuse me?"

"It's only fair," he reasons. "You know mine. I want to know yours."

"I don't—"

"That wasn't the deal, *Static*," he reminds me. "Questions and answers for Mayhem, remember? So, if that's what you want..."

Damn, my little prize is good.

I run my tongue along the fronts of my teeth as I spin back and forth in my chair, contemplating how I want to play this.

I could lie, and he'd never know, but the thought of lying to him feels... *wrong* somehow. And even if this doesn't last, I don't want that between us.

Fuck it.

"Cedrick," I spit the truth of my name between us and hope it doesn't cost me everything.

"Cedrick..." he repeats, and my dick twitches hearing it spill from his lips.

"*Fuck, darlin'.*"

"What?"

I shake my head, trying to clear the onslaught of thoughts barging into my head at just that one fucking word falling from his lips has brought upon me.

"You're just perfect," I try to explain, but that makes me sound crazier, so I pinch my lips shut and leave it be.

"So... your name's Cedrick."

"Yes."

"That's not a lie, is it? Because I don't think lies count."

I huff a laugh. "No, little mouse. I thought about lying to you, but I don't want that between us. It's the truth—and I promise everything I tell you will be the truth."

"How can I trust that?"

I *tsk*. "You'll just have to. Just like I'll have to trust that me giving you this means you'll come to Mayhem."

A pause. "Quid pro quo."

I smirk. "Precisely."

"Fine. I'll call you later. I'm busy with my friends right now, so quit calling me every three seconds."

I chuckle darkly. He's so cute when he tries to be bossy. "All right, Madison."

"Okay, bye."

There's a resounding click, and then, the line goes dead. I throw my head back with a cackle, delighted at this turn of events, despite what I've revealed about myself.

If I have to get vulnerable with him to get him back, then that's what I'll do.

I'll do anything to win my little prize.

"Does he have you lookin'" at your phone like that?" Kaser asks later that night as I sit in my chair, pathetically waiting for Madison to call me back.

I think he's waiting so long on purpose... just to be a brat. But I don't mind. If he wants to have this little bit of control, I'll let him.

"Who else?" I mutter as I watch my darlin' pace back and forth across his room, wearing a path in the carpet as he stares down at the phone in his hand. His jeans are loose around his hips, gaping perfectly with every step, and my mouth is watering to touch him there, to trace that path of smooth, tanned skin with my tongue.

"You're fucking obsessed, Ricky."

"I fuckin' know, *Kase*," I mock them back, using the same tone of sarcasm.

But the thing is... they're not wrong.

I am obsessed with Madison. Wholly and entirely, sickeningly obsessed with him. I want to devour him. I want to consume him.

I want to feel him. Taste him.

I want to know him. His fears and desires. What drives him and what keeps him awake at night. I want to know what it is that makes him want to live.

I need everything.

But if all I get is Mayhem...

Well.

I'll take it.

"What the hell is that look for?"

"What?" I startle, looking away from my phone to glance up at Kaser. "What look?"

"You look like you're about to do something stupid."

"Aren't I always?" I drawl, hiking a brow.

"Yes, but this is different," they snort. "What are you going to do, Ced?"

And then, my phone rings.

My heart shoots into my throat, and I feel myself smile manically.

"Something I'm going to regret, I'm sure," I answer them absentmindedly as I swipe answer on the call and put it to my ear. "Hello, darlin',"

Kaser raises their brow but doesn't say a word as they stare at me for a few moments longer as Madison responds.

"Okay, I think I'm ready."

"Is that so?"

Kaser nods and then closes my door, which I'm grateful for. I spin around in my computer chair to face my computer and type in the password.

"Yes."

"Had to steel yourself for it?"

"Y-yes."

"Good."

"You want me to be afraid?"

"Fear is healthy. And I think we've already established how good fear makes us feel... so I'm all for it, darlin'."

"Oh," he squeaks, and I chuckle as I type in the password for the website and log in to the webcam so I can load it on my computer.

I want to see Madison as I talk to him.

"So, did you have anything in mind?" I ask as I watch him sit on the side of his bed. His legs are crossed, head bowed in front of him, light brown hair hanging slightly. He's picking at a thread in his jeans, unraveling it and twisting it around his finger, over and over again as we sit in silence.

I don't break it.

I can't.

Because I revel in it.

Madison takes a deep breath, and then, he says, "Have you been stalking me?"

I've been expecting this question, so it doesn't surprise me. I chuckle darkly and smirk at my screen as he lifts his head and squints his eyes at the sound.

"Yes."

He rears back. "Y-yes? Just yes? Th-that's it?"

"That's what you asked me."

"So, I have to get specific if I want details."

I shrug even though he can't see me.

He sighs loudly. "Fine. How have you been stalking me, *Cedrick?*"

My eyes roll back as my name rolls off his tongue. What I would give to hear it in person...

"Fuck, darlin', you have no idea what that *does* to me."

I watch his throat roll with a swallow. "W-what does that do to-to you?"

My lips splay wide. "Which one do you want me to answer first, little mouse?"

He releases an irritated huff, and I chuckle, deciding to give him some mercy. "I got your number and address from your form at Mayhem, which I'm sure you already figured out. As for how I've been *seeing* you... There's a lovely tree right outside your window—"

"I knew it!" he shouts, interrupting me, shooting up from his bed, eyes wide, and mouth agape, and I smile. *My treat.*

"Smart, darlin'."

"Don't patronize me."

"I wouldn't dare."

"Good."

Let's go for gold.

"But there's also a camera in your room."

All the blood leaves Madison's face. He sways on his feet before falling back onto his bed shakily. His eyes are wide and appear glassy as he stares in front of him.

It goes silent for several minutes, and I fear I've broken him.

"Madison... Madison."

"I'm..." He clears his throat. "I'm here."

"Good. I thought I lost you there for a second."

"No... so, uh, um. What you're... you can see me right now?"

"Yes."

"What am I doing?" he asks, voice trembling as he slowly lifts his hand and holds up his middle finger.

"Well, treat, I think even if I couldn't see you, I'd be able to guess that you're giving me the finger."

He drops his hand immediately. "Holy shit."

"Yes."

"You can really see me."

"Yes," I answer, softer.

"Like... really, really see me."

"Yes, Madison," I repeat again because I can sense his rising panic.

"This is actually insane. You know that right? Like this is crazy. All of this." He twists his fingers together, and my brows tug. I don't like the direction this conversation is headed.

"How do'ya mean?"

"You're... Oh, God. You're my... You're my like *actual* stalker, and I'm *talking to you!* I'm engaging with you, and I... oh, no, no, no..."

My heart kicks with his words, ready for what he was about to say before he trailed off.

I lean forward, gripping the arms of my chair. "And you what, Madison? What were you going to say?"

"And I actually want it!" he wails, throwing himself back on his bed with a cry. The blanket poofs up around him, hiding his face from sight for a moment, and my breath catches in my throat.

Fuck, he doesn't realize how perfect for me he is.

I let him have his crisis for a moment as I process his words and how, for the first time in my life, someone has made *me* feel... *warm...*

He wants me.

He fuckin' wants me.

"Darlin'," I say after a few minutes of haggard breathing.

"What?" he snaps snottily.

"It's okay."

"It's okay?" he repeats incredulously. "It's okay? What about any of this is okay?"

"I just meant—"

"I know what you meant, *Static*," he sneers my name like a curse, and I wince. "You meant it's okay because you get what you want out of this, and in the end, I'll be left all fucked up *again!*"

I take a breath as I process his words... and the fact he said *fuck.*

I swallow because I hate them.

"What do you mean, again?"

Madison takes a deep breath. "It doesn't matter."

"It does to me."

"Why?"

"Because it does. I... I want to know you."

"Because it fills your stalker-y fantasies," he snarks.

"No," I argue. "Because it's the truth."

He blinks once. Twice. Utters a soft, "Oh."

I try again, "Please?"

"Wow. A stalker saying please."

"I think most people would be surprised at how feisty you are."

"Maybe." But then, he chuckles, and the sound warms my blood.

"My parents are super religious, and, well, they-they're not... *kind,* I guess you could say." He's fidgeting with his fingers, and it makes me smile softly. "I grew up really sheltered, which I know now, and it took a lot for me to get out of there and be where I'm at now. So, of course, it's only ironic that I end up back under the power of someone."

I clench my fists, hating the words I'm about to say. Words he didn't ask for, but ones I'm about to give him, regardless. "You're not under my power, Madison," I tell him in a painful whisper. "If anything, I'm under yours."

Silence descends.

And then, it shatters.

"W-what? That doesn't... I don't..." he stumbles over his words, head shaking between his shoulders, and I can't help the small smile that curves my lips. Or the small jolt in my chest at the sight.

Damn.

He's cute.

"It's all about power, Madison. And it's all yours, I promise you."

"I don't understand!" he shouts. "How is it mine when you're the one doing all of this!"

I swallow sadly. "You'll see."

He huffs a breath like he doesn't believe me. "Sure, I will."

"You look cute when you're frustrated," I say to not only break the tension but to steer the conversation in a different direction.

"Oh, God. I... I forgot already! How did I forget..." he seems to mutter to himself before he stands with his hand on his hip, head cocked to the side as he looks around his room. "Where is it?"

Shit.

"Where's what?" I ask, feigning ignorance.

"The damn camera, Cedrick. I want to know where it's at."

"Do I have to answer that?" I ask as I blow out a breath.

Madison's brows furrow, and his lips purse. "Yes."

"Fuck. I just love watching you, little mouse..."

"I know! Now, tell me!"

Damn it all to hell.

"It's attached to the light fixture," I mutter, hating this truth game more than ever before. I'm giving him *so much* and can only hope he gives me the same in return...

"You... that's right in the middle! You can see everything!" he accuses me, and I smirk even though he can't see me.

"I know..." I trail off.

"Oh, God... That means you've... you've seen..." he's stuttering so bad, I just want to kiss his lips to still them.

"That I've seen... what, darlin'? That I've seen the way you wrap those fingers around your cock and pleasure yourself? That I've seen the way you like to make yourself feel good? That I now know how to do it myself for when we see each other again? The answer is yes. And I fucking loved every second of it because you're *perfect.* Your body is perfect, your cock is perfect, and those noises you make... *Fuck.* Those are incredible. I can't wait to hear them in my ear again."

Madison's face is bright red, and it looks like he's about to swallow his tongue.

"Don't look so surprised, my treat. It's not like I haven't tasted you already."

"Shit," he hisses, and I love it because I know he so rarely swears. "I don't need the reminder."

"You don't?" I tease. "Think about it enough already?"

"Yes," he admits easily, and I grin. Oh, that's just perfect.

My treat is incredible.

"Are you thinking about it right now?" I ask lowly, leaning in closer to the screen.

"Y-yes..." he stutters, and my heart soars.

Gotcha.

Chapter Twenty-One

Give Me a Prize

Madison

My dick is rock hard, and I hate it... but I can't help how good it feels, despite the situation.

I'm terrified because I know he's watching me, but I... I think I like that he's watching me. I don't know. I'm so confused, I don't know what to do.

"Quit thinking, little mouse. Just listen to the sound of my voice."

"Easier said than done," I mutter, face flushing as I fall back on my bed to stare up at the ceiling.

"Close your eyes."

And I do.

"Good boy. Now, I want you to reach down and undo the button of your jeans. Yes. Just like that."

I let out a slow, deep breath and allow myself to follow the command of Cedrick's voice. It's calm and soft and exactly what I need. It makes my mind go a little fuzzy as I flick the button open and push the zipper down.

"Now, I want you to touch yourself. Just do what feels good."

"I... I can't..." I stutter, fingers freezing right at the entrance of my boxers. I'm trembling with the desire, but I just...

"Yes," he tells me. "You can. You want to know why?"

"Why?"

"Because I'm telling you to."

"Oh, God." I tremble. And with tears pricking my eyes, I shove my hand inside and wrap my fingers around my dick. The sensation is euphoric, and I toss my head back with a groan as I start stroking myself in a frenzy.

I can't seem to control it, but the moment I start, I can't stop. My blood burns hotter than ever before, and my arm moves of its own volition.

Breaths puff from my lips in heavy pants, warming my face and making me feel faint, but then...

"Oh..."

Then, I feel it.

"That's it... Show me, my treat. Give me a prize for all my hard work."

And it's with Cedrick's encouraging words that I shove my boxers down my legs just as cum erupts from my dick and splatters up my bare abdomen.

"Oh, *fuck...* Look at you..."

"You-you're looking at me," I pant, eyes scrunched shut through the euphoria, and Cedrick chuckles darkly in my ear, sending a wave of goosebumps down my arms.

"Yes, the fuck I am. And you look good enough to eat."

"Oh... oh, shit..." I mutter, face flushing. "I just..."

"Yes, darlin'. *Mmm, mmm. Yes, you did.*"

I'm panting into the phone, and I know he can hear it, but I can't help it. I remove my hand from my dick but accidentally end up swiping my fingers through the mess on my stomach.

"Have you ever tasted yourself, my treat?"

"W-what?" My face gets hotter than ever before.

"You heard me."

"No. No, of course not." But I swallow in a gulp loud enough for Cedrick to hear... or maybe, he sees it.

"Of course not?" he mocks me, accent thick. "What's that supposed to mean, darlin'? You don't wanna know what your cum tastes like?"

I nearly swallow my tongue. "I—"

"C'mon, treat. Eat it for me. Tell me what it tastes like. I miss it so much." And then, he groans, and my mind goes all staticky, and before I realize what I'm doing, I'm bringing my fingers to my lips and sucking on them.

My release is cooled now, but it doesn't taste bad. It's...

"Tell me," he demands.

And I do.

I pull my fingers out with a wet pop and a heaving breath. "It's kinda... tangy, I guess? But sort of sweet and salty. I don't really know how to describe it, but it... it doesn't..." *Oh, God... this is so embarrassing...*

There's a creak through the line. "It doesn't taste bad, does it, darlin'?"

I swallow the thickness in my throat. "No."

"Good. Eat some more. Clean it all up for me."

And so, I do. I swipe my fingers through the mess and eat and suck on my cum while Cedrick listens and watches through the camera above, and I... I *like it...*

I'm so messed up.

But right now, I just don't care.

By the time I've finished, my chest is heaving, and exhaustion has settled in my bones. I curl up on my side, phone still pressed against my ear and listen to the sound of Cedrick's breathing as I slowly drift off into darkness.

When I wake to the sun's rays streaming through the gaps in my curtains, I'm naked and disoriented, and my phone is wedged against my neck. I roll away with a groan, blindly reaching for my phone.

The last thing I remember is…

Oh, God.

I freaking fell asleep. On the phone with him.

What is happening to me?

I click the button on my phone, but it doesn't do anything, and that's when I realize it must've died at some point in the middle of the night. With a huff, I reach for the charger and plug it in before curling beneath the blankets and falling back into a peaceful abyss.

Bang! Bang! Bang!

"You're not dead in there, are you, Mads?"

"Huh?" I shoot up, blankets pooling around my waist as I'm jarred from my slumber. The banging sounds again, and I wince. "What?" I shout, louder this time so whoever it is will freaking stop.

"Yo, it's one in the afternoon. You never sleep this late. Just wanted to make sure you weren't dead or somethin'." *Lenny.*

"No, I'm okay!" I shout back and run my fingers through my disheveled hair. My phone vibrates on my stand next to me, drawing my attention. "Was just up late studying!"

"It was a Friday night, dude!" Lenny responds with a laugh. "But glad you're good. We'll see ya later tonight then?"

"Yeah, thanks!"

The moment I hear his retreating footsteps, I roll onto my side and reach for my phone, my heart rate kicking up because I already know what—or *who*—I'm going to find on it.

UNKNOWN:

Good morning darlin

You mustve worn yourself out 😉

My face flushes at his most recent text, and I shake my head, despite my lips curving into a smile as I stare down at his... well.

I suppose I should make him a contact in my phone at this point.

I add him, and feeling cheeky, I use the photo he first sent me as his contact photo. Once that's done, I go back to our thread and text him back.

ME:

You wore me out. I've never slept this late before.

It's like he was just sitting around waiting for my response because my text gets read immediately, and for some reason, that makes my heart flutter.

CEDRICK:

Id love to wear you out in all sorts of ways

Oh, Jesus Christ, he really just gets right to it, doesn't he? Tugging my bottom lip between my teeth, I type back.

ME:

I think I might like that.

CEDRICK:

Ohhhh dont tease me my treat. I dont have
any self control especially when it comes
to you

Ill ruin ya

I swallow.

ME:

Maybe I want to be ruined.

Madison, what in God's name are you thinking?
Are you insane?
Oh, Gods, I must be.

But this is the most alive I've ever felt. Cedrick is... he's fun. He makes me feel alive and vibrant and like... like there's actually life worth living. That there's more than the word of God and the rules set forth within it.

That living can be more than just a devotion to one thing... You can worship many...

And I think I want to worship Cedrick.

I think I want to kneel at his big, thick, black boots. I want to run my fingers over the buckles and the zipper, feel the smooth texture against the sweat of my palms. I want to bend before him and run my tongue along the seams, soaking it with a part of me.

I'm going to lave his leather until it's shining in my spit and his self-control snaps and he has no choice but to take me and tie me up and use me however he pleases... just like he did at Mayhem.

I blink the daydream away.

Holy shit.
Is that what I want?
Do I want Mayhem again, too?
My phone buzzes, and I startle.

CEDRICK:

Dont tempt me little mouse. Ill eat you alive

ME:

Why me?

I'm turning this conversation around, and it's not like I exactly want to, but a part of me wants to get to know him, at least a little bit, before I give him all of me.

It takes him a few minutes to respond, but when he does, I'm surprised by the length of it.

CEDRICK:

Why not you? Youre absolutely perfect to me Madison. Everything about you since the moment I laid eyes on you has drawn me in and Ill admit Im obsessed. But at this point I think its more than that. I crave you. I crave to see you, to touch you, to know you.

My breath is stuck in my throat as my heart hammers away in my chest. That's way more than I ever expected from him... and it's... it's a lot.

But maybe a lot is a good thing?

I don't know.

I don't know how to do any of this.

CEDRICK:

I crossed a line didnt I

And for some reason, that makes my heart clench.

I hurry to text back.

ME:

No, no. I just… don't know what to say to that.

CEDRICK:

Because I freaked you out

I knew I shouldnt have said that

ME:

You didn't freak me out.

I'm just… processing.

CEDRICK:

Can you process a little faster

I bark out a laugh, and in my mind's eye, I can just picture that leery smile twisting Static's face. It makes me shiver.

CEDRICK:

You look beautiful right now

I flush from head to toe as I read those words over and over. I hunch over on the bed, hiding my face from view.

ME:

I should find that camera and take it out.

CEDRICK:

Why when you love that its there

Shit… Do I?
I think I do…
I swallow thickly, heart starting to race all over again.

ME:

You can see me, but I can't see you.

How's that fair?

CEDRICK:

Do you want to see me?

I pause, tapping my finger along the side of my phone as I contemplate what I really want, but who am I kidding? *Of course,* I want to see him.

ME:

Yes.

CEDRICK:

Say please

ME:

Pretty please.

CEDRICK:

Oh I got a pretty too lucky me

And then, a photo comes through, and the breath escapes my lungs because... *holy shit... it's...*

It's him.

It's Cedrick.

Barefaced and deadpan, staring straight at me, through me, *into me.* Just like he did that night but this time, through a photo.

God, it's unreal how he does that.

His eyes are the darkest green I've ever seen. I shiver as goosebumps burn their way down my spine.

His face is chiseled with a dusting of stubble, and dark hair hangs across his forehead in spiky tendrils. His ears are stretched, and he has pointy silver jewelry in his lips and nose, just like I remember feeling when he was—

I suck in a sharp breath at the memory of his mouth on me. So hungry and demanding and knowing.

He already knows me better than I know myself, and if that's not crazy, I don't know what is.

I tug my bottom lip between my teeth. I can't tear my eyes away from Cedrick.

He's... well, he's beautiful.

How he can go from a terrifying clown to this handsome man is absolutely crazy, but... he does.

CEDRICK:

Did I scare you off

You hate my face dont you

Fuck

I find his panic so endearing, it makes me grin from ear to ear. This side of Cedrick is unlike anything I ever imagined, but it's... it's sweet.

ME:

Your face is handsome. Thank you for showing me.

CEDRICK:

Handsome huh? Never been called that before

My brows tug together.

ME:

Really?

CEDRICK:

Really

ME:

That's sad.

CEDRICK:

There are lots of things that are sad and
thats not one of em

There are worse things lol

What are you doin

I miss you

I blink at the rapid flip in conversation, how he goes from self-deprecating to moving the conversation to me, but I let him because obviously, he doesn't want to talk about it.

ME:

You already know what I'm doing...

CEDRICK:

Doesnt mean I dont want you to tell me

ME:

I'm sitting here talking to you because
apparently I don't have anything better to
do with my day.

CEDRICK:

Im that special huh

ME:

Apparently stalkers get special privileges.

CEDRICK:

Not just any stalker I hope

ME:

Just the good ones.

CEDRICK:

Im a good boy yay me

My face flushes seeing Cedrick call himself a good boy. It reminds me of when he called me one... of how much I liked it...

CEDRICK:

You like good boy dont you darlin

ME:

No.

CEDRICK:

Liar

I see you

I see when you lie

Its cute

When you get all red

I wanna kiss the blush

And then bite it

Oh, God. I swallow and tug my bottom lip between my teeth as I glance up at the light fixture, where I know Cedrick is looking at this exact moment. And for some reason I can't explain, I push to my feet and walk to the center of the room, just below where I'm sure it must be.

I reach up on my tiptoes and blow the camera a kiss before walking out of my room, leaving my phone behind as I find my roommates to spend the rest of the afternoon with them— away from my stalker and his sweet-talking words that are quickly becoming way too much.

It's easy to talk to him... and that's a problem.

The next night on the phone, I find myself revealing things that I never would have otherwise. And it's nothing of pertinence either. It's small, stupid things like my favorite color—green—or my favorite food—pizza.

"Pizza?" he parrots, and I flush.

"I don't know." I twist my fingers. "I just really like it."

"No, it's cute," he drawls, and I flush.

"It is not! It's just food!"

"If you say so, treat. So, tell me more about you."

I gulp, hating the heat in my face. "Isn't this supposed to be you telling me things? Why am I sharing things with you?"

There's a pause. And then, he says, "Because you want someone to know you, Madison. And I want to be that person."

I stop breathing for three beats of my heart, and then, I choke on an inhale. "Oh."

"Oh?" he parrots. "Was that too much?"

"Too much? N-no, I just..."

"My favorite color is black," Cedrick blurts. "My favorite food is mashed potatoes, and my mom is an alcoholic. Fireball is her drink of choice, but really, she's not picky. She'll drink what's cheap if she doesn't have the money—and she usually doesn't. It's why I left with Kaser—why we moved up here. Well, that, and because their mom, Lillian, died. But that was a whole other thing, and that was so hard on both of us—"

"Cedrick..." I breathe.

He seems to finally take his own breath. "Yes?"

"Why are you telling me these things?"

There's a long pause, and then, he says, "I want you to know me, too."

"Oh. O-okay. Thank you for telling me that," I tell him earnestly, feeling much better knowing something so deep about him. My fingers hurt from wringing them together so much, but it's the only thing I have at the moment, and it's better than nothing. This is new territory, and I should be terrified revealing this much about myself to this man—the man who has blatantly been stalking me—but something is telling me to take the leap.

"Okay... so my parents are like, super religious, right? I know I already told you that. And they think the way you'd think they would, too—very conservative and strict. It's why I left... I just couldn't take it anymore. But not only that, I don't think I would've made it out alive if I would have stayed... just with who they are and how they think. It wouldn't have worked. Not only that, but as I started to grow up, I realized I thought and felt way differently than them, and things started to shift pretty quickly.

"Leaving was hard—probably the hardest thing I've ever had to do—but I did it." I take a deep, solidifying breath and let it fill my lungs for a moment. "I did it. And now, here I am. I'm in school, I have awesome roommates, which I don't know how I got lucky on that front, but I did. And I'm... I think..." I take a shaky breath. "I think I'm okay. That this is okay."

I don't mean to say that. But I do. And I regret it, but it's too late.

"This is okay?" Cedrick asks, and I gulp.

"I don't..."

"It's okay, little mouse. We'll take this as fast or as slow as you want it."

"We will?" I ask tepidly.

"Whatever you want, darlin'."

"Thank you..." It feels weird to thank my stalker, but it also feels right.

This feels right.

And I think I'm tired of fighting it.

It's nearly midnight, and Cedrick and I are talking on the phone *again,* just like we have every night for the last two weeks.

"You wanna what?" Cedrick asks, and I flush hotter as I pull the phone away from my face and run my fingers through my long hair. It's grown out over these last few weeks, and it's in my face as it hangs over.

"Never mind," I mutter, regretting bringing it up already. Maybe it's too early for that. Maybe he's not ready for this. I'm not sure I even am...

I don't know what I was thinking.

"No, no. Tell me again."

"No," I mutter, feeling embarrassed. I stare at the wall in front of me, hating that he can see me like this but loving it just the same.

"Yes."

"No, Cedrick," I argue, wanting to just end this conversation. It was stupid. I don't know what was going through my head...

"Madison," he demands, and I still. "Ask me again."

I gulp. Choke on the beat of my heart. "D-do you want to m-meet somewhere?" I ask again, feeling even less sure of myself this time around.

I'm not even sure I meant to say it before. It kind of just came out, but now that I've said it, I think I mean it.

I do want to see him... but do I want him to see me again?

"B-but it has t-to be-be somewhere public," I add the addendum quickly.

"Yes," he agrees easily, and I balk. *Just like that?*

"R-really?"

"Madison..." he drawls, and I shiver despite my nerves. "I've been dying to see you again. I'll do whatever you want me to do."

I glance around my room, knowing he's watching me at this moment and reveling in it. *It makes me feel powerful.* "Anything?"

"Yes," he agrees easily, and I feel myself smile.

"Wear your eyeliner."

Chapter Twenty-Two

Can Serial Killers Be Good Guys?

Cedrick

I'm still reeling from the endless conversations with Madison.

It's been two weeks since I told him my name, and I swear, we talk more and more every day.

I've learned that Madison is more than just a soft, shy boy with a stutter.

I know that his parents have traumatized him with their religious bullshit, and that's why he got out when he did—which I can't even imagine how hard that must've been for him. He's startin' all over on his own, and I admire that about him—and it's also something we have in common.

He enjoys spending time with his roommates, but he really puts most of his focus on his schoolwork because he wants to do well. He's worried he's not as smart as everyone else because it doesn't come as naturally to him, but I don't think he has anything to worry about.

Anyone that has the kind of dedication that Madison does will succeed in anything they want to do.

But more than that, he's... *fuck.* He's pretty fuckin' fierce, too.

And I admire him.

I've also revealed more about myself to him than I have to anyone aside from Kaser—and the only reason why Kase knows as much as they do is because we grew up together.

I've told him about Ma. Told him her name is Scarlet. How hard it was to leave her behind. But after Lillian, Kaser's Ma, died, it was made easier because I was always closer to her. And the fact she's an alcoholic solidified that choice.

Not that it made me love her any less because that's not true, but when you love someone with a disease like that... you have to learn to separate yourself somehow... some way, and I just had to get out.

Ma would get sober for a few weeks here and there, but she'd always go back to Fireball, and I was losing my mind with fear and worry over what was going to happen. If she'd come home, and if she did, would she even wake up.

Those fears haven't gone away since I've left, but I've been able to distance myself for my own sanity... or whatever I have left of it.

And Madison... my sweet darlin'... he was so perfect when I talked about Ma.

Somethin' I never thought I'd do with someone. Somethin' I didn't think I... *I could.* But he just makes it feel so easy to open up.

I want him to know me, as fucked up as I am.

And he still hasn't run away.

So, maybe I'm not as messed up as I thought.

Shaking my head, I walk through the doors of the club, only to find my favorite bartender behind the bar.

"*Wowww*, long time, no see," Ethan drawls, and I'd wince if I was ashamed, but I'm not. He knew what he was getting into with me.

"Been busy," I tell him as I saddle up to the counter.

"What can I get you?" he asks, and I don't miss the way his eyes rake up and down my body. Normally, that would make me feel hot all over, but tonight, it does nothing for me other than make me smirk.

"Corona with lime."

"Drinkin' light tonight?"

"Need to keep a clear head."

"Expecting someone?" He slides the glass across the bar, and I take it with a stilted smile.

"Something of the sort."

I don't tell him Madison is supposed to meet me here in approximately thirty minutes, and I'm actually nervous to the point I feel vomit sitting at the base of my throat.

I honestly don't know how we got here, but apparently, my little mouse wanted to meet—his idea—in a public place, and this is the only place my dumbass could think of.

My old fuck spot was probably not the best idea, but I know this place intimately, and it's not too far from where either of us live, so it's doable.

But now that I'm here, I'm getting a sinking feeling that maybe I should've chosen somewhere else... literally anywhere else. But it's too late now.

"Thanks," I tell Ethan as I tilt my head back and swallow a few glugs before wandering around the darkened room to find an empty booth.

After a few minutes of wandering around, I do find a small

table off to the side near the back of the room, which isn't quite as private as I wanted, but it'll have to do. I take a seat on the high-top chair and clamp both hands around my cool, damp glass and wait, heart pounding in my throat.

Time passes like molasses, but eventually, the clock reaches nine, and I know he'll be here any minute.

"C-Cedrick?" comes a soft, stuttering voice to my right, and my head jerks toward it.

"Fuck. *Madison,*" I greet him, eyes lighting up at the sight of him. He's dressed in dark blue jeans and a white t-shirt. His dark mousy hair is swept away from his face, but when he drops his chin to his chest, a tendril falls in front of his eyes, and I ache to sweep it away.

"H-hi." He clears his throat and stands up a bit straighter, like he's steeling himself. "Hi," he says again, more confidently, and my heart clenches tightly.

This boy.

Fuck me.

"Hi, darlin'."

"Oh," he squeaks, cheeks flushin' red, and I can't help but grin at the sight. He's so incredibly beautiful, I almost forgot how ethereal he is in person. "You wore it," he says, referring to my makeup, and I just smirk in response.

"Cameras just don't do you justice," I tell him bluntly as I look him up and down. "Well, take a seat. Don't just stand there all night." I lift my arm toward the chair in front of me and gesture for him to sit. Madison, still flushed, swallows thickly and shuffles over to the chair and lifts himself into it.

"You can't j-just say things-things like th-that," he mutters, eyes pinned to the table.

I'm trapped in his snare.

"Like what?" I ask, dazed.

"Like that cameras don't do me justice," he mutters. "It makes you sound crazy or something."

I lift a brow at him and smirk. "But you already know I'm crazy, so what's it matter what I say?"

"Other people might hear you."

"So?"

"So?" he repeats, voice raising a few octaves.

"You think I care what other people think, little mouse?"

"Oh, God." He flushes brightly all over again, face shining from the force of his blush, and I fuckin' revel in it.

I lean forward and reach toward his face. My finger traces down his cheek, following the warm path his blood is flowing. "Beautiful."

Madison scoffs.

"I mean it," I reiterate, "you are beautiful, Madison."

"Th-thank you."

"You're welcome."

"Why am I here?" he seems to ask himself after a moment, finally pulling away from my touch, and I mourn the loss instantly. I take my hand back and fold it in front of me before taking a swig of my beer.

Even though he didn't ask me, I answer him, anyway. "Because you want to be. This is all about what you want, darlin'. Remember that."

"Yeah, but..."

"But... what?"

"I don't know what I want," he confesses softly, and I smile.

"Don't you?"

"I—" he cuts himself off and purses his lips. "I don't know," he finally settles on.

"Well, I know what I want—and that just so happens to be you."

"But... why? I don't understand..." He seems to chew over his words for a minute before he settles on, "Why me, Cedrick?"

My eyes roll back hearing my name roll off his tongue so easily. "Ya, darlin'. I really like that, shit."

Madison's brows tug together. "Like what?"

I huff in amusement. "Nothin'. So, why you, *hmm*?"

"Yeah..."

"The better question is, why me?"

That seems to throw him for a loop. "What?"

"Why do you want me, Madison?" What I don't say aloud, what I don't even think on, is the fact my heart is hammering loud enough to feel it in my brain. Or that my breathing is changing the rise and fall of my chest, and I just hope it's not noticeable enough to Madison.

"Why do *I*..." he trails off, like he never expected such a question, eyes falling to the dark table between us, and my heart clenches painfully in my chest at the realization that he hasn't really thought about this. He hasn't thought through this, or about this, or anything.

It's all been a game to him.

"Because you made me see what's been right in front of me."

"What?" I'm not sure I heard him correctly.

"Clean your ears out, Cedrick."

"Fuck, you're a brat. Do you really mean that?" I ask. The thumping in my chest gets heavier, and I think I feel the telltale signs of my nose starting to burn.

I don't even know what he means by that specifically, but it

means something to him, which means it's important, and...
fuck.

I'm important to him.

Could I really be?...

"If there's one thing you should know about me, it's that I don't say things I don't mean. Everything that comes out of my mouth, I promise you, I have thought through a million different ways and have contemplated the consequences and actions of every possible outcome.

"So, to answer your question..." he trails off and finally raises his head to meet my eyes. "Yes."

"Yes," I repeat, and goddamn if that *yes* doesn't feel like a fucking proposal from the way it makes me leap.

This boy makes me utterly fucking foolish, and I feel absolutely crazy inside.

I want nothing more than to wrap him in my arms and consume him from the inside out, but I have a feeling that's going to have to wait a bit longer.

But what if I just...

I reach across the table and run the tips of my fingers over the back of his hand. He startles, eyes shooting wide at the contact, but he doesn't move away, and that makes me feel *alive.*

I grow bolder by the second, and the next thing I do is wrap my fingers around the side of his hand and pull it across the table so it's closer. I flip his hand and trace the lines of his palms back and forth until I see the prickle of gooseflesh along his arm.

Madison's breath catches in his throat, and I want nothing more than to swallow the sound.

"What—what are you doing?"

"Just touchin' you."

"Why?"

"Why not? You're here, and I want to, and I can, so…"

"Who said you could?" Madison snarks, and I smirk.

I glance up at him through my lashes. "Do you not want me to?"

"I didn't say that. But it's probably not smart for me to have met my stalker, let alone let him touch me."

I bark out a laugh, head falling back. I garner the attention of a few patrons, but I don't give a shit. My treat is funny.

"Ahh, little mouse, you *forget*. I've already been *all over you*. This is just a little tour on the other side of the wall."

"Oh," he squeaks, and that beautiful flush returns, and my smirk grows into a full-blown smile that makes my cheeks ache. My heart clenches tightly in my chest, and I swear I can feel the muscle twisting.

I don't know what this sensation is, but I think I fucking hate it.

It makes me feel out of control with all the stupid shit it's been making me do.

Like revealing my name and my face. And meeting Madison at the club… and *fuck*.

I'm gone for him.

And I don't think he has any idea.

Someone like me… someone impulsive and irrational and quick to strike with the desire for instant gratification…

I'm not the type of person to fall for someone. I can't be.

I need people now.

I don't wait.

But I've been waiting.

For him.

For weeks.

Just watching and waiting.

And here we are.

Holy shit.

"Cedrick?" I hear his voice, but it's his touch that shatters my reverie. The lightest graze of his finger alongside mine, and I'm blinking through the haze and focusing back on his blue eyes in the dark light of the club.

The lights are reflecting off his tan skin in hues of yellow and blue and green, and I've never seen someone look so beautiful.

"You're staring," he tells me, and I nod, not even bothering to deny it.

"I am."

"Why?"

"You're perfect."

"No one's perfect."

"I'm pretty sure you are," I tell him bluntly.

"Trust me, I'm far from it."

"Why do you say that?"

"There are things you still don't know."

"Then tell me, little mouse."

"We barely know each other," he argues, and I want to bite his tongue.

"Can't really use that argument anymore," I rebuke.

He sighs heavily and rolls his head between his shoulders. It's quiet between us for a minute, but I notice he still doesn't pull his hand away.

"I didn't come here alone," he tells me after a while, and I lift a brow but don't say anything, waiting for him to elaborate. "My roommate Kane is with me. He's over at the bar." Madison's face is pink, and I want to lick the path of his flush.

"Okay."

"You're not mad?"

"No," I tell him honestly. "I get why you didn't come alone. You're smart."

"'Cause you could be a serial killer or something," he explains.

I smirk. "Yes, I definitely could be."

"Like Dexter."

"You've seen Dexter?" I ask him, surprised.

He nods. "I've been watching it with my roommates."

"But isn't Dexter like, the good guy?"

"Can serial killers be good guys?" he asks incredulously.

"Of course, they can!" I argue. "He literally kills awful people."

Madison squints, and his adorable little nose scrunches up. "Yeah... but he ends up killing some good people, too."

"Okay, but not like, because he wanted to!" I will defend Dexter with my life, okay!

"If you say so..." he says, eyeing me, but I see the smirk playing on his lips, and I know we're okay. That this is okay.

"So..." I drawl. "About serial killers..."

Chapter Twenty-Three
You're the Only One

Madison

"You talking about serial killers doesn't make you seem any less creepy. I hope you know that."

"Oh, I know." He grins, and my heart stutters at the sight.

Cedrick is... God. He's *handsome*. His picture didn't really do him justice. And when he smiles...

Something happens to my heart inside my chest. It's like it turns inside out and thumps harder than it ever has before.

As nervous as I am to be here with him, to talk to him like this, it also feels as easy and natural as breathing. Being with him has been since the moment we met, and I guess, maybe a part of me was worried that something would change that, but also that *nothing* would have changed that. And I didn't know what to do, either way.

But I'm here now and...

I think I'm happy. I am.

My phone buzzes in my pocket, and I pull it out, for some

reason fully expecting it to be Cedrick, even though he's right in front of me.

"What's got you lookin' so disappointed?"

"What?" I mutter as I read through Kane's text. "Oh, nothing. It's just Kane."

Earlier That Day

I rap my knuckles on Kane's door after I've finished my homework.

"What's up?"

I wring my fingers together as I step over the threshold, the words stuck in my throat. I know what I need, what I want, but the prospect of asking for help is more daunting than I thought it could be.

"Mads?" Kane asks, and I jerk from my reverie.

"R-right, sorry."

"Don't be sorry, man. What's up? You don't look so hot."

"No, I... I'm fine. I-I just had—have a question." *There. You finally spit it out.*

Kinda.

He spins back and forth in his chair, hands resting over his stomach, face in an easy smile. "Sure."

"Would you... *Ugh.* Can you come with me on a date tonight because I'm scared to meet him in person." The words come out in a rapid rush of word vomit, and at first, I'm not sure Kane even heard me right, but then, his brows draw together in concern.

"You're scared?"

"What? Oh. No, no, not like that—"

"Oh, so is this like an online thing?"

And at that, I don't really know what to say. I can't exactly tell him *no, I'm meeting Static the clown from Mayhem Motel. The same one who scared the piss out of me and then sucked my soul from my body. No big deal.*

Yeah. No...

I'll let him think what he wants.

I just shrug and let him make up his own mind, not comfortable lying but not able to tell the truth either.

"Well, sure, man. I'll come with you. Anything you need."

I breathe out a breath of relief, eyelids fluttering as I lean back against the doorjamb. *I won't be alone.*

At least, there's that.

"Thank you, Kane. Means a lot."

"Of course. Come get me when you're leaving, okay?"

"Sounds good!" I tell him as I back out of the room, feeling so much better about tonight.

I'm seeing Cedrick, and I won't have to face him all alone.

Everything is working out...

Like it really is meant to be.

"Your roommate," Cedrick deadpans, bringing me back to the now.

"Yeah," I blink down at my phone. "He was just checking in."

"Uh huh. And how is this going, then?" Cedrick sounds short, and I don't know why.

"I don't know," I respond verbally as I type. "Haven't made up my mind yet."

KANE:

How are you feeling about it?

ME:

It's going really well. Thank you again for coming.

KANE:

Of course. Meeting people online can be scary, but I'm glad it's going well.

He can't take his eyes off you.

I flush reading Kane's texts and flip my phone over on the table. My eyes dart over across the darkened club to where I know he is, and we meet each other's gaze for a moment—long enough for me to catch his smirk—and then, I'm back to staring at the tabletop, feeling overheated.

"I don't like that he's made you blush like that."

"What?" I ask Cedrick, distracted. I focus my gaze on him, only to find him staring intently at me. His eyes appear dark as they stare right through me, and I fight back a shiver that crawls down my spine.

"Him." He jerks his head. I squint, confused, until my line of sight takes me to Kane across the room.

"Oh," I breathe.

"Oh," Cedrick mimics.

"Are-are you j-jealous?" I stammer, unsure if I should even be asking.

"Yes."

I blink once. Twice. "Oh."

Cedrick's brow lifts. "Not expecting that, little mouse?"

"No—not really."

"Why not?" he asks.

"I don't know... I guess just because I expect you to lie to me."

That makes him frown. "I haven't lied to you once," he says stiffly.

"Okay."

"I mean it, Madison."

"Okay, Cedrick."

"I wouldn't do that."

"Okay..." I repeat again, softer this time as I reach across the table and grab his hand. It feels strange to initiate contact between us, but I like how long his fingers are and how strong they feel against mine. They're calloused and rough but still sort of soft in a way as he trails the tips of his fingers over mine.

I shiver.

"This is crazy," I murmur after a while of silent touching.

"Probably."

"Not probably. It is."

"Yeah." His accent is thicker than ever, and it nearly makes my eyes roll back. He glances back over at the dance floor, and a smile flickers over his lips, eyes looking a bit crazed. "Do you wanna dance with me?"

"What?" I squeak, unsure I heard him correctly.

"You heard me, little mouse. Come dance with me." He reaches for my hand, and I fall into him like a trap.

I stand on unsteady legs and place my palm in his, letting

Cedrick tug me out onto the dance floor. It's not very crowded, but there are enough bodies that we kind of get lost in the swarm.

He pulls me close and places his hands tightly on my hips, his thumbs brushing just under the hem of my t-shirt.

My breath catches at the sensation, and I stand there awkwardly, unsure what to do with my own arms. I've never danced a day in my life apart from formal ones at church, where I was forced to dance with my mother.

And I'm pretty sure that's not the kind of dancing Cedrick expects at the moment.

He dips his head down to whisper against my ear, "Put your hands wherever you feel comfortable."

"I don't know how to dance."

"It's okay. We'll just sway then."

"I'll look stupid," I complain, face heating with embarrassment as I finally move my arms to wrap them around Cedrick's neck. It's the only place I could think to put them, but with the height difference between us, it probably looks stupid.

"Impossible," he rasps against me, breath hot enough to send shivers down my spine, and the next thing I know, Cedrick's guiding my hips back and forth. Nothing too strenuous, just a gentle rocking motion to the beat of whatever song is playing around us.

I feel myself smiling as I lean into it a bit, feeling my body loosen up a little with each passing minute.

"That's it, darlin'. Just like that," Cedrick praises me, his fingers biting into my skin as my hips rotate faster. He takes a step closer, putting our groins in touching distance, and I gasp when I feel his hard length against my crotch.

My gaze darts up to meet his knowing one, and he smirks, shooting me a wink. "See? You're a natural."

"This is crazy," I breathe, still surprised I'm really doing this.

I'm dancing with my stalker in a club.

What the hell?

"Crazy feels good, doesn't it?"

I take a deep, sobering breath, 'cause *it kinda does.*

But the clarity of my breath brings me back to the now, and while I don't pull away fully, I do put a little distance between us. Cedrick loosens his grip on my waist and looks down at me with concern.

"C-can I ask you something?"

"Of course."

I swallow. *Here goes nothing.* "Why do you want me at Mayhem again?"

It's the burning question I've had since the moment he brought it up, and I really wanna know *why.*

Like truly why.

"That's a loaded question, my treat," Cedrick drawls over the thump of the music.

"Is it?" I ask, taking a step back from him to cross my arms over my chest, and wait. Cedrick senses the shift and pulls back slightly as well, but not enough for there to be any great space between us.

I let him stew in silence as the club's music thumps around us, but it doesn't take long for it to become overbearing.

"I'm not sure how to answer that," he finally responds, looking down at me through his lashes. Our eyes meet, and my breath catches in my throat. I get caught in his snare for far too long before I realize someone is standing next to us.

"Oh," I squeak when my eyes catch on Kane.

"You told me to come get you when it's eleven."

"Is it really?" I ask. He holds his phone in front of me to show me that yes, it is, in fact, eleven o'clock.

"I..." I glance over at Cedrick, who's glaring daggers at Kane. "I've gotta go."

"Why?" he asks, never looking away from him.

"I have an early class tomorrow," I say as a way of explanation.

"'Course. Wouldn't want you to be tired," he drawls, and to anyone else, it probably sounds sarcastic—if Kane's scoff is anything to go by—but I know he's being genuine.

"Thank you," I whisper as I reach for his hand, jarring him from his one-sided staring competition. It jolts him out of it, and his eyes find mine once more.

"You really have to go?"

"You'll see me soon," I say with a smile.

"Tonight," Cedrick says with easy determination.

"Shh!" I hiss, eyes shooting wide as they dart over to Kane, who has stepped back a couple paces to let us say our goodbyes with some privacy.

"Why? You know you like it, my treat."

"Anyway..." I swallow thickly. "I really do have to go. Thank you... for meeting with me and everything. I'll... I will text you?" I phrase it like a question, confused as to where we go from here.

I take a step back to walk away, and Cedrick stands to his full height, having apparently been slouching to accommodate me. My head cranks back to look up at him, and I gulp.

Holy shit.

"Madison..." he drawls softly, and I whimper. "May I kiss you?"

"You... You're asking to-to kiss me?" I balk.

"'Course." He nods sincerely. And it's his nervous little throat bob that does me in.

"Yes," I say without thinking, and the next thing I know, Cedrick's mouth is on mine, and every thought I've ever had is wiped away with the swipe of his tongue across my lips.

He tastes faintly of lime and beer as he enters my mouth, and I gasp breathlessly when he reaches up and wraps his long fingers around the back of my head to pin me in place as he devours my mouth.

His tongue is wet and soft but demanding as it plunders my mouth, seeking solace inside me, and I open wide, unsure what to do as he takes control over me and does what he wants —but he doesn't seem to mind my lack of response other than mewls and moans because that seems to be all I'm capable of doing.

A throat clearing jars me, and I jerk back, eyes shooting open wide. Cedrick pins me in place with his teeth attached to my bottom lip, which he slowly releases as he pulls away. My groin is hot—and only grows hotter the slower he moves—but eventually, we're separated, and I'm left with an aching erection and a thundering heart.

"*Don't* fucking do that again," Cedrick says, still not taking his eyes off me, and for a moment I think he's talking to me, but then, Kane responds.

"Mads asked me to get him out of here by eleven, and you have been making out for five minutes."

"And?" Cedrick drawls. "He's a big boy."

"That's not what—"

"I don't give a fuck—"

"Okayyy... that's enough of that." I ease my way into the conversation by taking a step back from Cedrick and taking one step closer to Kane. "He's right, Ce—uh, he's, uh, right. I need to go home. For class. Tomorrow. Thank you. For tonight." I flush hotly. "I'll talk to you tomorrow." And with only a quick glance at Cedrick's bright, dark green eyes reflecting the lights of the club, I turn my back to him and walk out with Kane before I can change my mind and stay the night with my stalker.

Because that would be a bad idea...

Wouldn't it?

It definitely would...

I think.

The ride back to the house is tense, but I don't mind it much because my mind is swirling with what happened between Cedrick and me.

We danced, and I... I kissed him. Or, well, he kissed me. And it was truly something else.

It... it felt different than it did at Mayhem.

Mayhem was...

It was two pieces of us that we had hidden away come together, and tonight was the other halves finally meeting into a whole.

It sounds crazy, I know it does, but Cedrick... I really like him.

I know he's crazy and has gone about knowing me in an insane way, but I don't think I could've known him any other way. I couldn't have let myself. Not with the way I was raised, I don't think.

It was beaten into me over and over: Men don't lie with men. It's a sin.

And when Static made that choice for me, he made me see that there is no sin in what you desire because how could God create someone like me, if that's not what he wanted?

If he didn't want me to like men, then why do I?

Does God have that power to choose, or do we?

And if that's the question, then does God even exist? Is there even a higher power?

My thoughts swirl at a million miles a minute as Kane takes us back to the house, and it's not until we're parked in front of it and he's tapping my arm that I realize we've stopped.

"You look like you're a million miles away right now."

"Yeah," I answer, still kind of dazed.

"You all right? He didn't hurt you or anything, did he?" Kane asks, and I kind of want to cry. I got so lucky moving here, finding these people.

I couldn't have asked for a better life, even if the people who created me believe I'm throwing it all away.

"No," I rasp. "No," I repeat again with more *oomph*. "I promise I'm good. Just... having a bit of an existential crises, I think."

"About?" Kane asks, dark brow lifted in the shadows of the car.

"Religion."

It's quiet for a beat. "Oh."

I huff a humorless laugh. "Yeah."

"Do you wanna talk about it? I'm gonna be honest with you, I really don't know a lot about religious stuff. I didn't grow up like that and never really got into it, but you can talk to me, and I'll listen."

"I know... thanks. It's not really anything. More so just... Does God make gay people, or is being gay a sin?"

Kane blinks, then bursts into laughter for a solid minute before it slowly dies down. "Woah, dude. Holy shit. You just went super deep there."

I smile sheepishly and tug on my fingers. "I know. Sorry. Forget I—"

"No. I don't think being gay is a sin. And I don't believe in any god. Just my personal opinion. I can see that you do, so I'm sorry, but that's something I can't answer for you. But how can loving anyone in any capacity ever be wrong?"

His words are spoken so softly into the air between us that I lose the ability to breathe. My nose prickles with the onslaught of tears, and I choke on them as they burn their way out of my eyes.

"Oh, man. Shit. I'm sorry. I didn't mean to make you cry." Kane pats my shoulder to try to comfort me, and I'm mortified that the guy I had a crush on when I first moved in is seeing me cry like this, but it's good, too, because I don't feel that way anymore. And I haven't for quite a while.

The only boy that's been on my mind has been Static... *Cedrick.* And I don't want that to change.

ME:

Were you jealous?

I SEND the text the next night before I can think twice about it.

I've been thinking about Cedrick's reaction to Kane all day today, so much so I could barely focus in class, and I just need to know.

It's nearly nine by the time I get around to it, and I bet Cedrick is working, so I don't expect a response.

I waste time doing what little homework I can and cleaning up my room, making a show of it, if I'm being honest. I even skip dinner because I don't want him to miss a thing. But eventually, midnight rolls around and exhaustion settles heavily in my bones, and I fall against my pillows face first and let the darkness take me.

Buzz buzz.

Buzz buzz.

"*Hmm*?" I mutter, lifting my head slightly.

Buzz buzz.

Buzz buzz.

I reach out for my phone that's across my bed and smile groggily when I see Cedrick's name on the screen.

"*Mmm*, 'ello."

He chuckles, and it makes me shiver. "You sound tired, darlin'."

"I am. You woke me."

"Sorry. You want me to talk to you later?"

"No!" I rush out. "Talk to me now." I'm pouting, but I don't care. "Missed you."

"Ohh, someone's gonna regret this call when they wake up."

"M'awake right now."

"Sure you are, treat."

"What're you doin'?"

"Just got off of work and wanted to hear your voice."

"*Mmm*, that's so sweet. You're so sweet," I mumble into the line, burying my face into the warm pillow.

"What was that, darlin'? You're mumblin'."

"I said, you're sweet." He laughs again, and I think I can hear wind whipping in the receiver. "Where're you?"

"I'm at Mayhem. I've stepped outside to talk to you." There's an inhale, like he's smoking a cigarette or something, but I don't want to ask. I don't think I care enough.

"Scare anyone to death tonight?" I ask, heart clenching when thoughts of him touching someone the way he touched me rise to the surface. It actually makes my sleepy eyes pop open, and I force myself to sit up and run my fingers through my hair.

I drop my head into my hands with a sigh.

"Nope, haven't managed that one yet."

"That's good."

"What happened? You got weird."

"Didn't."

"Your breathing changed."

"Oh, so you can tell how I am by my breathing?"

"Yes, darlin'. What happened?"

"It's too early... or too late to talk about this," I mutter, scrunching my eyes shut and rubbing the sleep from them.

"Madison." He says my name like a demand, and I'm enchanted to answer to it.

"Yes."

"Tell me."

I blow my breath out in a punch, as well as the words. "I don't like thinking about you touching other people the way you touched me at Mayhem, okay? So, I'd rather just not talk about it."

It's quiet for three beats of my heart.

And then, Cedrick says, "Oh, my treat. You have no idea, do you?"

"No idea about what?" I snap, feeling vulnerable and irritated about it.

"You're the only one."

My heart stops. "What?"

Chapter Twenty-Four

Since Me

Cedrick

How can my little treat possibly not know by now?

"You're the only one."

There's a sharp intake of breath, followed by a long pause. "What?"

I take a drag of my cigarette, needing the pull of nicotine for this conversation, "Madison... you're the only one I've ever touched that way at Mayhem... I know it says in the contract, but I've never felt the desire, nor have I ever wanted to do that with anyone there before." Swallowing the lump in my throat, I continue on.

"It wasn't just a first for you, my treat."

"It-it wasn't?"

"No." Another inhale, this one deep enough to burn my lungs.

"Are you smoking?" Madison asks, and I startle.

"Uh..."

"Cedrick."

"Yes?" I phrase it like a question, unsure about his tone.

"That's so bad for you!" he chastises me, and I snort.

"That ain't no shit, darlin'."

He huffs. "Then why are you doing it?"

"Vices, darlin'. Vices."

"That's just an excuse," he argues, and I feel a smile tug my painted lips.

"That it is."

Silence descends between us, and I'm grateful for Madison's avoidance of conversation. Whether he meant to or not, I wasn't ready to talk about it, but I also said I would never lie to him...

You win some, you lose some, I suppose.

"So, work was good?" Madison asks, sounding far more awake than he did a few minutes ago.

"Yes. Always is."

"You love your job, don't you?" he asks softly.

"Ya. Never done anythin' that felt so right before. I got lucky."

"So, scaring the piss out of people feels right to you?" he deadpans, and I lift a brow, even though he can't see it.

"Darlin'..." I drawl before inhaling the last bit of my cigarette, then flick the butt across the gravel parking lot. "I think you know how much I *love* the smell of piss."

"Oh," he squeaks. "Right. I..."

"Yeah, treat. I remember."

"No-I-I know, I just..."

"I know."

"Feels like-like another life."

I inhale deeply and stare up at the crystal-clear sky. The stars are out and bright tonight. I find the big dipper easily and trace each star back and forth as I listen to Madison breathing in my ear.

"Is that a bad thing?"

"Just so much has changed in such little time."

"*Mmm.*"

"You don't agree?" he asks timidly.

I shake my head and drag my fingers through my hair, tugging it away from my sweat-dried face. "It's not that I don't agree. I just feel a bit different, is all."

"How do you mean?"

I chuckle darkly as I lean back against the building, the paint peeling off in flakes around my feet. "I've always been a do first, think later typa person. But I know you're the exact opposite of that."

"I..." I hear his swallow. "I am." He sounds confused, poor thing.

"So, we think about things differently, but that doesn't mean I don't see your point of view."

There's a pause, and then, "You know, you're very reasonable for a stalker."

I bark out a laugh at his whit. "Thanks, darlin'. I try to be."

The creak of the back door opening pulls me from my moment with my treat. I lean forward to meet Booker's gaze. "Yo, Ricky, you gonna come join us at some point?" he asks loudly.

"Yeah, yeah, I'll be there in a minute."

"Tell them you'll fuck 'em later!"

"Oh!" Madison squeaks, and my eyes narrow as Booker snickers and dips back inside, his stitched-up tuxedo still in place.

"Ignore him. They're all rude fucks," I speak into the line.

"No, it's okay. You get back to... whatever it is you were

doing…" he trails off, and I reach up to trace my bare neck. It still feels strange to perform without my collar, but I love knowing that it's sitting on Madison's shelf.

"Can you see it?" I ask him.

"See what?"

"My collar."

"Oh. Uh, um. Y-yes."

"Good. Put it on."

"W-what?"

"You heard me, darlin'. Put. It. On." I tuck my phone against my shoulder and blow out a steady breath into the receiver. "I'm waiting."

"Okay, okay." Madison's breathing has picked up considerably. I hear static over the line, and then, it's muffled as he drops the phone onto the bed, I'm assuming. Footsteps thud far away, then draw closer. He swipes the phone back up, and I smile when his breathing is close again.

"Did you do it?" I ask.

"Yes." His voice is small and meek. *Nervous.*

"Good boy." And I just know he shudders. "Send me a picture."

The sight of Madison Payne wearing my collar will never not make my mind blank out and my cock impossibly hard. Without thinking about it, I hit the camera button and watch the phone ring for a video call—a line we haven't crossed yet.

It rings for a few long moments, but then, it says connecting, and my heart thuds heavily.

"My treat," I breathe when Madison's face fills my screen, collar wrapped so beautifully around his neck, and I nearly choke from how perfect he looks.

"Oh," he squeaks, and my brows bunch at his reaction—

until I catch my own mirrored image and realize I'm Static. I forgot.

"Is this too much for you?" I ask him, finger tracing one of the spikes in my lip.

"N-no. No, it's... it's okay. It's still you. Just... wasn't expecting it, I guess."

"If it's too much..."

"Cedrick, it's fine."

"*Hmm*," I hum. "I'm not used to people calling me Cedrick when I look like this."

"You're still him, aren't you?" he asks, seemingly genuinely curious.

"I am... but when I'm him, I also become someone else. Static is... he's this part of me, and Mayhem is my release."

Madison smiles softly. "You need it."

I swallow thickly. "I do."

"I get it."

"Do you?"

He pauses like he's really thinking about it. "Well, not entirely, but I think I understand what you mean. I... um." He bites his bottom lip. "I'm trying to understand."

And that right there...

That's the moment I know I love Madison.

It hits me like a punch in the gut.

I suck in a breath so sharp, it's painful, and I nearly drop my phone.

"Cedrick, are you okay? What happened?" I hear Madison's worried voice over the line, and all I can do is focus on it while I breathe through the pain of the reality of loving someone.

Fuck.

This can't be happening.

I never wanted...

I just needed...

Fuck.

"Yeah. Yeah, m'good."

"What happened?" he asks again, and I'm shaking my head even though he can't see me from where my phone hangs at my side. "Cedrick, I'm worried."

"Just..." *Don't lie.* "My heart is burnin'."

"Heartburn? Shit. Yeah, that does suck. I'm sorry." And he does sound genuinely sorry. But that's not what I meant. I meant my heart literally feels like it's on fuckin' *fire*. But if he wants to assume heartburn, I'm gonna let him because there ain't no way in hell I'm correctin' him.

Not now.

Not ever.

I can't.

It'll scare him away for good.

Madison can't handle me at my fullest, and he sure as shit can't handle *this* kinda truth.

I slowly bring the phone back up to my face and give Madison the best smile I can, but it's more like a grimace than anything else.

"Oh, yeah, you look like you're in pain. I'm sorry."

"Don't be. It's all right, darlin'."

My realization is still burning hot in my chest, and it's making it hard to focus on anything other than that, but I need to stop thinkin' about it before I literally choke.

"Your question," I say after a moment. Madison's eyebrows draw together in confusion.

"Question?" he parrots.

"Your text. About if I was jealous."

"Oh." His face turns a beautiful shade of pink, even in the

darkness of his room, and I revel in it. *Yes.* This is what I need. Power over him, not the other way around.

"Yes."

"Yes?"

"The answer is yes."

"But-but why?"

"Because you find him attractive," I tell him bluntly, hating the words as I speak them into existence.

"What?" he squawks, and I can see the denial on the tip of his tongue.

"Don't deny it, darlin'. It's okay. Just don't lie to me, please."

Madison pulls in a deep breath, then lets it out slowly. "Okay... yes. I did find him attractive when I first moved in, but I haven't acted on those feelings, and I haven't even felt anything since—" he cuts himself off sharply, and I feel a sly grin spread across my painted face.

"Since..." I drawl, teasing him, knowing what's coming next.

"Since you," he finishes in a mumble, and I let the grin overtake my face, cracking and splitting the paint.

"Since me."

"Yes, okay. Are you happy now?"

"Very."

"You look full of yourself," he mutters, and I can't bite back a laugh.

"I always am."

It's quiet between us for a few moments, and I relish in the sound of our mutual breathing in what I wish was a shared space between us.

"Cedrick..." The silence feels tense for some reason.

"Madison..." I whisper.

"I'll come back to Mayhem for you."

My entire world stops spinning. "What?"

"I will. I just... gimme a little time. But I will, okay?"

"Darlin', are you sure?" I ask because as much as I want this, and even though we agreed on it, I... I don't want to lose him.

"Yes." He sounds breathless, and I feel over the moon.

"Anything you need," I reassure him.

"Thank you. Good-goodnight, Cedrick."

"Goodnight, my treat." And with a smile, I watch Madison's face disappear, feeling lighter than I have in so long.

I'm finally going to have both pieces of myself back in one place, and I absolutely cannot wait... except I can because I have no other choice but to.

Madison needs time and space, and I will give that to him...

I just hope he doesn't take too long because I am gettin' antsy already.

"Damn, what took you so long?" Booker asks when I finally step inside. It smells like booze and cigarettes, and I roll my eyes into the back of my head.

"None ya business."

"*Oooh*," Wesley chimes from somewhere to my right, and without looking in his direction, I flip him the bird.

"Someone's feisty tonight," Kaser drawls thickly, and I shrug as I walk up beside them and grab myself a beer.

"Not," I disagree. "Just not in the mood."

"Ricky? Not in the mood to party?" Graves chimes in on my left, and I raise my brow when he waggles his.

"No, G. Not tonight."

"Damn," he mutters, and I laugh quietly before taking a long pull of my beer.

It's gonna be a long night because I do have a question to ask Kierra, but it's gonna have to wait 'til they're all a little more fucked up and possibly won't remember why I'm asking to begin with.

"You look like you're thinking hard about something," Kaser says after a minute, and I shrug the suggestive words off.

"No more than the usual."

"It's Kian's birthday, man, and you're in a totally different world."

"Yeah, it's my birthday, and you're in a totally different world." We both turn toward the sound of Kian's voice as it comes up behind us. He's dressed in all black from head to toe —from his hair to his eyes, down to his cloak and his shoes. His teeth are pointed and sharp, covered in fake blood, and his face and neck are covered in highlighted black streaks and fake veins. Every bit the demon he is.

"Happy birthday, man," I tell him as he saddles up beside me.

"Thanks. Why're you trying to ruin it?"

I burst out laughing. Leave it to Kian to be blunt as hell. It's one thing I love about him—he doesn't fuck around, ever.

"Not trying to."

"You never do," he says, but he's smirking, and I know we're good.

"So..." I drawl. "How's it feel to be twenty-four?"

"Terrible. I'm old and decrepit," he deadpans, and Kaser

bursts into laughter. I follow suit, and soon, the three of us curl into each other laughing so hard, we can't breathe.

"It really does feel that way sometimes, doesn't it?" I say on a breathless exhale.

"Like you've got room to talk. You're only twenty-two."

"Almost twenty-three."

"In a month," Kaser argues.

"In a month," I confirm, taking a swig out of my bottle.

"Anyway, it's my birthday, so let's quit talking about Ced, hm? He gets enough attention with his new beau."

"Hey!" I squawk. I don't want nor need that kind of attention, and that has everyone in the room looking over at me.

"I'm just sayin'!"

"Well, don't. I don't—" But then, I cut myself off because that would be a lie, and I don't do that.

Shit.

"See?" he teases, and I look to Kaser for help, but they're just grinning ear to ear and smirking at me over their blue solo cup. A lot of fuckin' help they are.

Best friend, my ass.

"Anyway..." I try to change the conversation. "Have anything memorable happen tonight?" I ask Kian as he takes a drink from his cup.

"Oh, something memorable always happens, but there were these two girls that started crying the moment they saw me..." he starts, and I grin, knowing I've got him distracted.

Over an hour later and everyone is thoroughly wasted—and to be honest, I'm not far behind. I drank way more than I should have, but I had to keep up with everyone else, and when a bottle of rum got brought into rotation and someone mentioned pickle back shots, well...

Who am I to say no?

And so now, here I sit next to Kierra on the reception couch, watching the room sway slightly as she giggles next to me, nursing her drink in her hand.

"Hey, Kierra," I lean in to ask her in a too-loud whisper.

"Hey, Ced," she whisper-yells back, then giggles, eyes scrunching shut.

"I wanted to ask you something."

Her eyebrow lifts comically high as she cracks open one eye to stare at me.

"I thought you were gay?" she deadpans, and I snort.

"Don't worry, I am. As gay as they come. It's not about that."

"Oh, good. Because me, too." And then, she giggles.

"I wanted to ask you when Mayhem was closed next. I... can't remember," I trail off, feigning nonchalance.

"Don't you ever look at the schedule, Ced? It's posted in the dressing room."

"It is?" I ask, mouth falling slack. *How have I never noticed?*

"Yes, you idiot. It always has been. The next closing day is in a week and a half. We'll be closed Sunday and Monday for cleaning and some light fixing. Just checking lights and safety stuff."

"Oh," I nod. "Is that both days, or...?"

"Just Monday," she hums. "Cause Sunday, we finally get a day off."

"Yeah." I lean back against the couch and let my eyes fall closed. "Finally."

"What do you mean? You guys get days off every once in a while. There's no one else to run the front if I need a sick day." And she sounds so sad when she says it.

"What about Johnny? He doesn't come in?" Johnny's the new owner, but we rarely ever see him, if I'm being honest.

"He does, but I always feel like such a bother when I have to ask him, so I always just try to avoid it."

"Kierra, you're going to burn yourself out if you keep doing that," I try to reason with her, but she just shrugs.

"It is what it is." And then, she tips back her drink and finishes it in a few swallows and stands on her two feet shakily. "Woah, I'm drunk."

"I'd say," I laugh as I stand beside her to help keep her steady. I'm drunk myself but probably a lot more sober than she is at the moment.

At least I can stand.

"Thanks, Ced."

"Of course. Maybe you should crash."

"I think I'm gonna."

I take a look around the room and notice most of everyone else is spread out on the mismatched furniture, either sleeping or nearly there, still donning their costumes from Mayhem. It makes me yawn with my own sleepy breath, and I drop back down on the sofa.

"C'mere, Kierra. There's nowhere else to sleep."

She glances around the room, then looks down at me before shrugging and plopping down. "All right, thanks." And then, she leans her shoulder on mine and closes her eyes as she turns her face into my painted neck.

"*Mmm*, you smell good."

I chuckle. "Thank you." And then, with sleep-ridden eyes, I pull my phone out of my pocket to text my little mouse goodnight and let him know he's on my mind before I drift off into oblivion.

Chapter Twenty-Five

Tonight's the Night

MADISON

Tonight's the night.

I'm ready for him.

Or... I'm as ready as I could ever be, I guess.

My palms are sweaty, and I keep rubbing them against my jeans to no avail. The perspiration is constant; it's leaking from every pore... which is probably the least attractive thing about me, but there's nothing I can do about it.

"What's got you lookin' so pale?" Brianne, Collin's girlfriend, asks when I step into the kitchen around eleven in the morning.

I startle at the sound of her voice. "Oh!"

"Sorry." She holds up her hands. "Didn't mean to scare you."

"No, you're okay. Just a bit tired today."

"You look sick," she says bluntly, and I almost laugh, but it comes out as more of a choking cough.

"Y-yeah."

I walk past her at the table to pull the apple juice out of the fridge. I pour myself some, and when I put it back, I notice we're no longer alone.

"Mornin, Mads," Collin says.

"Good morning."

"You all right, buddy? You're looking a little peaky."

"That's what I said!" Brianne adds, and I purse my lips.

What is up with everyone analyzing me today, of all days?

"Yes, I'm fine. Just tired."

"Okay…"

I want to be irritated with the inquisition, but it's actually nice to know that people care about me and my well-being, despite it being a bit of an inconvenience at the moment.

I've never had that before.

"So, what are you gonna do on this fine Sunday?" Collin asks, and I shift on my feet. I don't want to lie, but I can't exactly tell them I'm going back to Mayhem either.

"Just going to go visit a friend." It's not a lie, anyway.

Brianne and Collin exchange a look as I lean against the counter sipping my apple juice. I look between them, brows furrowed, before they look back at me with matching grins.

"A friend, huh?" Brianne asks, her voice raising a few octaves, and I flush from head to toe.

I didn't realize that sounded so suggestive, but now that I think about it…

Shit.

"Oh. Uh, um… It-it's not like that."

"Sure, it isn't," Collin teases me, and I flush even hotter.

"It's not. He's just a friend—"

"*He!*"

My jaw snaps shut.

Did I just mess up by saying that? Are they... They're not homophobic, are they?

Oh, God.

Oh, God...

A hand clamps around my shoulder. "Calm down, little dude. It's okay."

"I... I'm—I'm sorry," I choke out, feeling like I'm dying.

I was wrong. So wrong...

"What?" Collin asks, sounding incredulous. "For what? Don't be, man. I'm stoked you're gay. I just had no idea!"

I blink rapidly. "Wait... what?"

"Hell yeah! Kane's the only one of us that swings that way —but he likes... how'd he put it... every and all? I don't remember, but anyway, he'd love to know he's not the only one in the house. You should tell him." He rubs my shoulder affectionately, and my heart thuds heavily in my chest. "Maybe you won't feel so alone."

And I don't know how he knows, but my chest fills with a warmth I've never felt in my life as tears burn my eyes.

"Th-thanks," is all I'm able to choke out, but it seems to be good enough for him because he gives me a soft smile and another squeeze.

"He's in his room if you wanna talk."

"Y-yeah. I think... I think I'll do that." My heart is thudding wildly in my chest, and the sweat that was pouring from me has increased tenfold, but I want this.

I think I even need it.

To share this part of me with someone.

Without finishing my apple juice, I set the cup in the sink and make my way up the stairs to Kane's room. His door is open, so I just knock on the frame a bit timidly. He glances up, and when he sees it's me, he smiles, and my own nervous façade cracks a bit.

"Hey, Mads. What's up?"

I take a deep, shuddering breath and let my eyes fall closed for a minute. *You can do this. It's just a few words. And he'll relate.*

"I was wondering if you had a minute to talk?"

Kane's brows draw together with concern, but he nods and pushes back in his computer chair to open his arms up. "Of course. Come on in. What's going on?" he asks when I take a seat on his bed. I pull my knees up to my chest and rest my chin on them to stare down at the floor as I try to think of a way to say this.

"I've never really said this out loud before," I finally start.

It's scary... but kind of exhilarating?

"Okay... Mads, are you okay?"

"I'm gay," I blurt and promptly turn as red as a tomato.

"Oh." Kane chuckles and runs his fingers through his hair. "Cool, man. Me, too."

"Uh, y-yeah... Collin kinda already told me and suggested I... maybe tell you? I don't know. I didn't mean to come out to him. I've never really come out to anyone before. My parents were really religious, and that's a whole thing in and of itself, and I have some trauma there, but I'm not like, in the closet or anything, it's just not something I thought I would ever do, but now I'm here, and things are good—"

"Madison," Kane interrupts me, and I take a deep, panting breath.

"Y-yeah?"

"Did you forget I came with you on a date with a man?" he asks, eyebrow quirked and a small smile on his lips, and if my face wasn't hot before, it sure as hell is now.

"Oh. Uh, y-yeah. I, um, I kinda did, actually…"

Kane chuckles and shakes his head. "It's all right. I mean, I didn't assume the way you identified, but when you made out with him, I kinda figured you liked men."

Holy shit, I made out with Cedrick in front of him.

How could I forget something like that?

"I am *so* sorry about that," I rush out. "I don't know what came over me, but that's so incredibly rude—"

"Mads, chill. It's all good, man, really. I'm glad to see you out living your life and having a good time."

"Oh… thank you." I blush furiously. "Speaking of… I'm kinda… going out with him again tonight…?"

Kane lifts a dark brow. "Is that a question?"

"No." I shake my head. "No, I am."

"Well, good on you then! Do you need back up again or…"

I smile sheepishly. "No, that's okay. I feel good about being alone with him. I really appreciate you being there last time."

"Of course. Any time."

"All right, well, I guess I better go get ready…" I stand from his bed and stretch my legs.

"What time are you leaving?"

"Oh, about six? That's when I'm heading out."

"You sure you don't need a ride?"

I promptly turn white as a ghost. "Oh, no, that's okay."

Kane's eyes narrow slightly, but then, he shrugs. "If you're sure."

"I am. Thank you though."

"Of course. Do let me know if you need a ride home or anything, I'm happy to help."

I pause right by his open door and turn back around to smile at him. "Thank you, Kane, really. I appreciate you."

"Of course, Madison. Have fun tonight."

"If that's what you wanna call it..." I mutter under my breath as I walk down the hall toward my bedroom, heart racing in my chest as the hours tick down closer to when I finally meet my stalker back where it all began.

MY NERVES ARE SHOT the second the decrepit motel comes into view.

It's as terrifying as I remember, and for a moment, I think, *why the hell am I doing this?*

And then, I look down at my phone, see Cedrick's face staring back at me, and I remember everything we've been through these last few months—albeit not all of it was roses and rainbows.

I mean... the man did stalk me, but...

I'm kind of over that, I think? Maybe? I'm not sure.

All I do know is that I don't really care anymore—if I ever did.

I keep thinking about Cedrick and how he made me feel at that club, on that dance floor. How each text, each phone conversation has been a highlight to every single day. I look forward to speaking to him, to learning about him and his life. Who he is and who he's been.

I love telling him about myself and my past because I know he won't care or judge. And it's... nice, to know that with certainty—that someone just wants me for me. Not for the money or the power my parents have. Not because of my last name or where I came from, but because I'm just Madison Thomas Payne and Cedrick Hades Vinton decided he likes me.

I roll the car to a stop right in front of the doors, and my breath catches in my throat.

I reach up and touch the collar around my neck—*Static's collar*—and tug on the frayed edges. Their roughness brings me a sense of calm as I step out of the car and into the darkness of the evening, watching the gravel dust settle back down around my tires.

I pull my phone from my pocket and open my text thread with Cedrick.

ME:

I'm here.

My heart is pounding in my throat. I really can't believe I'm doing this.

I never wanted to come here to begin with, but now, I'm here voluntarily.

It's crazy how much can change in just a few months... how much *someone* can change me.

My phone buzzes, and I glance down, choking on my own heartbeat as I read the words before me.

CEDRICK:

Ever play hide n seek darlin

Cause youre about to

A loud bang sounds from somewhere inside the building, and a scream erupts from my throat, eyelids shooting open wide.

CEDRICK:

Run

I don't think twice. I shove my phone back in my pocket

and take off across the gravel parking lot—but instead of running away, I run toward the danger. Closer to where I know he's waiting for me.

My breath is stuck in my lungs, and I pull in deep lungfuls of air with each panting gasp, to no avail. I'm choking on air as I reach for the doorknob and find it open. I run into the darkness without thinking about where I'm going—only that I need to try and find a place to hide, but it's freaking dark, and I can't see a thing.

Unfortunately, Static knows this place like the back of his hand, so no matter where I go, he'll be able to find me with ease.

I need to... make this difficult for him. I need *him* to chase *me* to know if this is worth it, that *maybe...*

I shake my head rapidly, making myself temporarily dizzy from the force.

No.

That's not what this is about.

This is about... Static and Madison's reunion. Nothing more.

It can't be.

I can't be.

I ram into a wall with a painful grunt. "Shit," I groan, all the air pulled from my lungs. My hands reach out and clamp onto the splintered wood, which I hold onto for dear life as I work to catch my breath.

"You're too slow, my treat," Static's voice sing-songs somewhere in the distance, and I shiver as goosebumps wrack my body.

I should've worn a sweatshirt instead of just jeans and a t-shirt.

"I'm not too slow. You're just crazy," I mutter to myself as I push away from the wall to start running again.

I squint my eyes in the dark as I scramble down a narrow hallway lined with doors. This part looks familiar, I think, but I can't remember for sure because the last time I was here, things were... a bit hazy, to say the least.

But I trudge on, feeling my way along the wall, hissing as paint and splinters chip their way inside my skin but never stopping, regardless.

I'll be damned if I let Static get me.

I'm not going to be so easy to catch this time.

Footsteps resound, and I suck in a breath. My fingers wrap around a doorknob, and I slowly turn it until the door creaks, and then, I step inside and slowly close it behind me, wincing when it creaks ever so slightly.

I back away from the door, step by step, and I watch with abject horror as the lights on the other side begin to flash like a strobe light. Smoke begins to curl beneath the door and enter the room, and I hold my breath for reasons unknown as I go to push myself up against the wall, but ram into something else instead.

I trip over it and fall flat on my ass, but my eyes never stray from the door as a shadow moves in front of it. I gasp silently and throw my hand over my mouth and nose to cover the sound of my breathing as I scramble backward to cower in the corner and look as small as possible.

"Come out, come out, wherever you are..." I hear Static drawl, and I nearly cry. The tears burn my retinas. He sounds so different, and I don't know if I like this anymore.

The sharp scrape of something sounds against the wall with every step, and I choke back the vomit that crawls its way up my throat—images of his bloody axe filling my head.

"Maaadiiiisonnnn," he sings. "Where are you, darlin'?"

"No. *Nonono,*" I murmur over and over as I curl in on myself, pulling my legs to my chest and wrapping my arms around them to pull myself even tighter. "This isn't happening. This isn't happening," I chant.

What is wrong with me? Why did I agree to do this?

I'm choking on the beat of my own heart when the sound finally fades, and I'm left in ringing silence.

The smoke is still pouring in, and I can't see anything because of the damn light, but I don't hear Static, and that's a good thing...

Right?...

I stand up, albeit very unsteadily, and wobble over to the door, head cocked to the right to listen for any sounds, but I can't hear a thing. Just eerie stillness.

I wait for a few more minutes anyway to make sure he's gone before I slowly pull the door open and step out.

The light is disorienting, and it disfigures the entire hallway, making the floor look slanted. I nearly trip when I take a step, so I'm forced to close my eyes to move, still stuck in utter darkness.

Feeling queasy all over again, I go in the opposite direction I saw Static moving in, hoping to get as far from him as possible. I run my fingers along the splintered wall, feeling each sliver that ends up in my skin like an omen to my stupidity.

I don't know why I thought this time would be different...

When I finally feel the edge of the wall, I open my eyes and realize I've made it to a fork. I can either go forward or move left.

And if that doesn't feel like the most apt thing I've ever experienced in my life.

Move forward—toward the clown that's chasing me or choose left... the side the devil usually sits on.

Well, shit.

Either way, I'm screwed, aren't I?

And just like that, a laugh bubbles up in my chest, loud and boisterous, and once it starts, I can't stop it. It wracks through my body so hard, it hurts—and that's when I hear it.

The heavy *thud, thud, thud.*

It's a sound I recognize.

Shitshitshit.

It's Static.

What do I do, what do I do? I'm panicking, and I know I am. My mind is racing a million miles a minute, but I hear the heavy thud of his boots, so I know he's coming, and I need to make a decision *now*—

"Clown it is..." I mutter as I start forward down the hall. "Always the damn clown."

The hallway opens up into a large room, but I can't tell what it is because it's still dark as all hell in here. I stumble into a wall and smack my face.

"*Oomph.*"

The brunt of the impact knocks the breath from my lungs, and I lose my balance. I stumble to the floor. Blink. Lights are flashing. Smoke is curling—wrapping around my neck like Static's hand once did.

I reach up and copy the motion, needing to distance myself from the memory, but before my fingers wrap around, they're ripped away.

"Too slow, darlin'..." His voice drawls heavily in my ear.

"O-oh, no..." I whimper.

Static chuckles, and I *burn.*

Chapter Twenty-Six

Good Boy

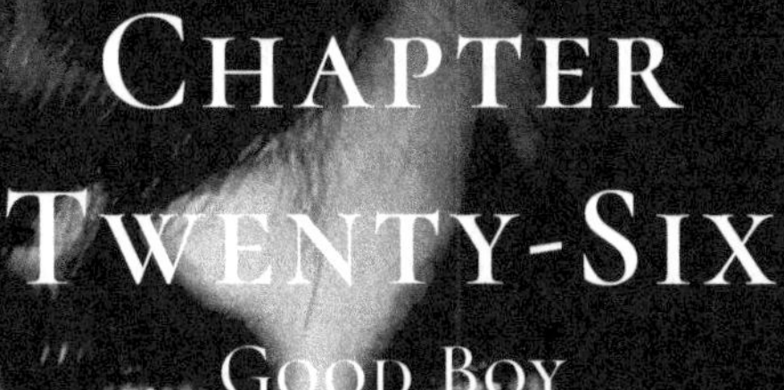

Static

My little mouse looks so scared, and I've never been more excited.

He's dressed in dark jeans and a faded green t-shirt that fits his slim, soft form perfectly. His eyes are wide as he stares at Mayhem with apprehension. I swear I can see his throat bob with a gulp as he closes the door to the car he drove, taillights reflecting in the fading light of the sunset.

"Here we go," I murmur as I run my gloved finger along the edge of the computer screen. I decided to keep the security cameras up and running tonight, just so I can keep an eye out for my treat, and I'm so glad I did.

He looks absolutely perfect through a lens.

I watch Madison pull his phone out and send a text—which makes my own phone go off in my pocket. I pull it out and smirk.

DARLIN:

I'm here.

He's so precious, it squeezes my heart. He probably doesn't think I can see him, but I can. I do.

And I know what he's going to do.

ME:

Ever play hide n seek

Cause youre about to

And then, I throw my axe across the room, so it thuds against the wall, the sound reverberating throughout Mayhem.

ME:

Run

Madison screams, and it's beautiful. He takes off running toward the motel, which I find surprisingly lovely. I kind of figured he'd take off in the opposite direction, but no. He's coming toward me.

Like he actually wants this, too.

He rips open the door and disappears inside. I flip through the cameras on the other monitor until I find the hall he's running down, and then, I smile.

There he is.

I push out of the chair and grab my axe to start my hunt.

I fuckin' love some hide 'n seek.

MADISON'S TREMBLING, and it's so reminiscent of our first time together, I inhale deeply to see if I get that pleasure again, but unfortunately, not yet.

"Too slow, darlin'," I murmur in his ear as I replace his hand with my own, and the scream that rips from his throat is music to my bloody ears.

"O-oh, no..." Madison wails, and I cackle beside him.

"Oh, yes, my treat. Now, the real question is..." I taunt him as I drag my pointed glove around the slope of his neck around *my collar. Fuck, that's hot.* "Do I keep you now, or do I let you go, just so I can keep chasing you?"

"W-what?" he stutters, and it's so cute, I poke out my bottom lip.

"Awe," I brush his mouth with my thumb. "So cute."

"I'm not cute!" he snaps, jerking his head away from my touch with a snarl, and my eyes dance. Now *that's* more like it.

Feisty mouse.

"Yeah, treat. That's it. Bite me."

Through the flashing of the strobe lights, I can barely make out the way Madison's eyes narrow, but the next thing I know, he's jumping on me, sending my axe clattering to the ground as I fall backward. Madison is scrambling to sit on top of me, legs around my waist, as his own hands find my painted throat, and what does he do?

He fuckin' squeezes.

"*Ohhh,*" I groan low and slow, eyes rolling into the back of my head as my little mouse steals the very breath from my lungs. This is not what I was expecting, but *fuck,* this is good.

He never fails to surprise me.

"You think you have control, *Static?*" he sneers my name. "Look who's in control now!" he screams in my face, spittle flying and sounding a bit hysterical, but also so fuckin' hot, my dick is throbbin' where it rests against the crack of his ass.

"Goddamn, treat," I groan. "Yeah."

"Yeah?" he parrots, and I hum. I don't have anything else to say. I think right now, I'd be happy just to end it all right here, if he'd have me.

But no.

Of course, it's never that easy.

Madison readjusts on my lap—and that's when he feels it —the very thing that freaks him out.

"Oh!" he squeaks and scrambles off me. I lift a brow and watch as he backs away like I'm on fire, quickly making his way out of the large room and back the way we came from.

"Come back, treat," I warn him, low and slow. I reach down to grab myself to readjust, but just the simple pleasure of touching myself gives me the slightest relief.

"N-n-no." He's further away now, and I hate it.

"Yes."

I can barely see him now. The lights are too strong, the smoke too thick.

He's nothing but a whisp.

"Make me." And with the smallest grin, Madison whirls around and sprints to the left, leaving me alone in the motel lobby, jaw hanging wide and dick impossibly hard.

"What a fuckin' treat he is," I say to nobody but myself. He never ceases to amaze and confound me.

Just when I think I'm getting to know every bit of him, he turns around and surprises me, yet again.

I've never met someone more perfectly aligned to my crazy parts and my... less crazy parts.

Shaking that thought away, I narrow my eyes and stare down the way Madison just disappeared from.

It seems the strobes and the smoke have disoriented him, but not as much as last time.

I'll have to step up my game.

With a grin, I step back into the shadows with a low cackle.

"Ohhhh, darlin'... Where are you..." I'm dragging a length of rope behind me, along with my axe. The lights are still flickering, and the fog is still dispersed, but I'm able to blink through it because I do this shit every day, so it doesn't affect me the same as it does other people.

I almost can't hear anything over the chugging of my own heart, but then...

Ah, yes.

There it is.

Another creak of a door shutting—the thud of the wood against the frame.

I click my tongue. *Tsk. Tsk. Tsk.* Such a little rookie mistake.

Veering to the right, I let the tell-tale sound of my axe let Madison know of my presence as I near the room he has holed himself up in—and fuck *me,* if it's not the most perfect room for what I have planned.

I walk past, just to fool him, and then, I pick my axe and rope up off the floor and whirl around to swing my blade into the wood of the door.

Madison's scream reverberates around me, and I cackle as I hack my way through the door he's tried to lock me out of. Over and over, I swing my axe, chipping through wood until my arms are screaming from the burn and it's left hanging in pieces off the frame.

I step over the threshold, axe and rope swung over my shoulder, to find Madison cowering in the corner. "P-p-pl-please," he begs so prettily.

"Please what, darlin'?"

"Please... *don't.*"

With a smile, I crouch in front of him and drag the tip of my pointed finger down his cheekbone, pressing into the soft flesh until I'm sure I'm leaving a red mark in my wake. "But you want me to. You asked for this. I'm just giving that to you."

"C-ced—"

I reach forward and wrap my fingers around his throat, cutting the word off before he can finish spitting it out. "You wanna finish that word?" I spit in his face.

His eyes grow comically wide. "Uh, um. Erm."

"It's Static, treat. I think you know that by now."

"Y-yes."

"Good boy."

And when he shudders, I know he's gone for.

Madison stares into the glowing iridescent of my eyes, fat bottom lip quivering just how I remember it, and *damn*, it's even better than the memory.

"What am I gonna do to you, my little mouse?" I drawl as I push up on my feet to circle him where he cowers. "You've been running from me, hiding, like you didn't want me to find ya."

"B-but, but—"

I crouch once more, lips inches from his, and cock my head. "But, but, but what?"

"Y-you told-told me t-to."

"Did I?" I purr softly, unable to resist touching that

bottom lip. It's wet with saliva, and when my finger is free, I suck it into my mouth, just for the slightest taste of him. Madison's pupils widen, and I relish in the sight.

"Yes."

"So, you wanted to run from me?"

He whimpers. *Fuckin' whimpers.*

God, he's perfect.

"S-static, I'm con-confused." He's hiccupping between his sobs, tears and snot streaming down his face, and I let my eyes dance for him.

"Be confused, darlin'. There ain't nothin' about this that's gonna make any sense."

"What-what? What does that m-mean?"

I reach out and snatch his throat, causing the smallest squeak to escape as the last of his air puffs out. "It means, you're gonna go to sleep now."

He tries to shake his head, eyes scrunching when he hears my words, but he can't move out of my hold. He starts to panic when he realizes he can't breathe—that I'm taking the air from his lungs—and that's when it gets fun.

Madison is a sight of beauty as he flails in the flashing of the strobe lights, smoke curling around his soft frame, each pixelated flare a moment seared into my brain. The throbbing of his heartbeat against my fingers makes my cock twitch in response, and I want to touch myself—*no.* I want him to touch me—but this is good.

What comes next is even better.

"Sweet dreams, darlin'," I tell him when his eyelids start to flutter with the first signs of unconsciousness. "Dream of me." And when he's finally out and falling limp in my hold, I release him and gently lie him down on the ground in front of me.

His longer hair—which has grown out a bit in the months

since we started talking—splays around him like the angel he truly is. I brush it back from where it sticks to his tear-soaked cheek and tuck it behind his ear before I turn around and go about setting up the room how I want it.

This is gonna be so fuckin' fun.

Madison, unbeknownst to him, brought us right to the perfect spot for what I have planned... and what that is, is to completely take him apart.

Piece by piece, layer by layer, I want Madison Payne absolutely obliterated before me in this shitty motel.

Leaving him to lie where he's at, knowing I don't have much time, I turn to the bedframe that's to our right and grab the rope that I dropped to start tying pieces to each side. I use my axe to cut the pieces to the length I need, leaving more than enough for each side so that he's not tied too tight, but I've gotta make sure he's not goin' anywhere.

Securing the knots to the rusted metal frame, I jump up on the plywood that covers the bottom of the full-sized bed and jump on it a couple times to make sure it'll hold our combined weight. It bows a little bit, but it doesn't crack or make any noise, which satisfies me enough.

I jump down with a grin and turn back to my boy, taking in his drool-slackened face and long eyelashes brushing the highest points of his cheekbones. He looks utterly angelic, and I want nothing more than to *ruin him.*

Feeling satisfied I have what I need for the moment, I make my way to Madison and crouch to lift him into my arms. He's light as I lift him, and that brings a smile to my face. Everything about him just fits so perfectly with me.

Without taking my eyes off him, I move him to the middle of the bedframe and splay him out wide—and it's as I'm staring at his clothed body that I realize that just won't do.

No, no, no.

My treat is far too dressed for this.

I need to see him.

I need his body, his mind, his soul.

Every bit of him.

With gentle hands, I pull his shirt over his head and gently set his head back down onto the wood. Next, I undo the button on his jeans and pull them down his legs, discarding them onto the floor without a second thought because my eyes are stuck on the body displayed before me.

Soft and supple and as perfect as I remember.

The only thing that would make this better would be—*No.* I shake my head to disperse the thought of tasting Madison's fear again.

No. This is just as good.

Gritting my teeth, I grab the rope to my right and tie a knot around his right wrist, securing it tightly before moving onto his left, ensuring there's barely any room for him to move, but that they're not too tight. I shuffle down his body, trailing my gloved fingers down his soft skin as I do, nearly groaning in ecstasy when his body breaks out in gooseflesh from my touch alone.

"Fuck, treat. You're absolutely perfect," I tell him, even though he can't hear me. He needs to know it, and I will tell him every day forever, if he'll let me.

By the time I reach his ankles, he's starting to twitch, and my heart jumps into my throat. I work as quickly as I can to secure his right foot, but by the time I make it to his left, he's gained some sort of consciousness and starts to fight against the constraints.

"W-what the hell? What is this?" He's yanking and pulling against them, straining with all his might, and I grin up at him before I spin around and put my full weight down on his left leg to keep it still as I wrap the length of rope around his ankle and twist the knot into place.

He jerks at the sensation, but I keep him in place enough to tighten it and then...

He's all fuckin' mine.

I slowly pull away from him and stand to my full height just beside Madison's quivering frame.

"Welcome back, darlin'."

"S-Static?" he intones, voice raspy from where I choked him. "What?..." he trails off and pulls against his restraints, eyes darting down to them, before shooting back up to my gaze pleadingly.

"Welcome back to Mayhem," I cackle, tossing my head back as I'm wracked with the laugh, and Madison's scream accompanies the noise.

Perfect.

Chapter Twenty-Seven
Now Open Wide

Madison

Everything comes back to me in disorienting flashes.

Static.

The Motel.

Me.

Why I'm here.

Why the hell am I here?

Fear has overtaken every part of me, and I can't remember anything other than *escape*.

But Static has me trapped—literally tied to him in every way imaginable—and there's no running away any longer.

But this is what I wanted, isn't it? *Isn't it?*

He'll take care of me, right?

"There he is, my little treat. Back to the land of the living." Static's thick southern accent garners every ounce of my attention, and I strain my neck as I look every which way to find what direction it's coming from.

"Over here," he taunts, and I jerk my head but come up short.

"No, this way." I whip around and again find nothing.

And then, I scream.

Because Static's face is directly in front of mine, and all I see are ghostly white eyes and sharp white teeth splayed wide in front of me.

My heart shoots into my throat, and I can't breathe.

"That's more like it. I was beginning to worry I'd lost my touch..."

"Wh-what? Why?" I'm stuttering, and I don't even know what I'm saying, but whatever it is seems to please Static.

"Yes," is all he says, and tears leak from my eyes, confusion swirling. "I've been waiting for you... for this... God, it's been so long, my treat."

"Oh, God," I cry out when I feel the tip of his pointed glove glide down my *naked* body.

I'm naked. Again.

Do I really want this?

Do I trust him?

I force my eyes open to stare at the man in front of me. The one who looks so different compared to the one I danced with at the club. Two sides of the same whole. But is this side a sane side?

Can I trust this side not to hurt me?

I think I trust Cedrick.

I *like* Cedrick.

But Static...

Static scares me.

But I also met him first, and he brought out something in me I never thought I'd experience, and if it wasn't for him, I never would've been able to experience anything with Cedrick at all...

Shit.

What do they call this?

A leap of faith or whatever.

Except faith has nothing to do with this. Because right now, it's just me and Static in this creepy motel, back where we started, back to finish it.

Because this is it.

I feel the resolution settle in my bones, and I shudder with it.

Yes.

I'm going to give him every bit of me, and then, we'll be done.

Because that was the deal we made—that's all he wants from me.

And that's okay. I knew that going into this.

I swallow the lump in my throat and pull in a shaky breath before slowly opening my eyes—and when I do, it's to Static's bright white irises staring down at me.

"What was that, treat?"

I gulp. *There's no going back from this.* "My resolution."

That makes a smile break across his face. "Beautiful."

IT's easy to let the fear consume me. It's an innate part of me that I can't control. Even though I know this time around that Static won't actually hurt me, my body doesn't seem to care and is working in overdrive, pumping adrenaline at a million miles a minute, curdling my blood and the acid in my stomach, making me feel queasy and lightheaded as he circles me on the bed.

"What to do with such a treat... so many options... so much time..." He's talking to himself, tapping his finger on his bottom lip, and I follow every step he takes with wide, searching eyes, waiting for his next move, but he hasn't done a thing.

He hasn't even touched me since I last spoke, and I'm crawling out of my skin.

"Did you know you made me chase you for over two hours? Such a long time to hide from me. I bet your little heart was just beatin' so frantically. I wonder if it is now." His heavy boots clunk against the wood as he steps onto the frame and climbs on top of me. His ragged and torn outfit is rough against my skin as he slides against me, resting his ass against my groin.

I groan involuntarily at the contact, having never felt anything like it before, and Static chuckles darkly. He then lifts his arm and slowly pulls his glove off his hand. I watch his long fingers come into view, and my already pounding heart kicks up in speed as it slowly moves toward my throat.

"Ahh," he sighs heavily when he presses his fingers against my pulse point. "That's exactly what I want. Such a good boy."

I swallow thickly and turn my head to the side, baring my neck to him even more, giving him all the access he could need.

"Oh. Now, that's even better. What a sweet treat you are," he purrs as he drags his long fingers along the slope of my neck, before circling it and squeezing, but not tight enough to cut off air.

"Static," I wheeze, and his white eyes *dance.*

"Say it again."

"S-Static." My tongue flicks out to wet my bottom lip, and the next thing I know, sharp teeth are sinking into my flesh and a tongue is invading my mouth. I let out a surprised gasp at his taste, but then, I melt into it because he tastes and feels so good, and how can that be wrong when it feels so right?

"That's it, treat. *Mmm,* so good." His fake, sharp teeth nip at me, and I hiss at the pain. This kiss feels so different compared to the kiss at the club but no less consuming or powerful.

I sink into the bedframe as Static devours me, and I melt into him, fear only an inkling in the back of my mind. Only because I know this man has the power to hurt me—physically, emotionally. In every way.

And I think I'd let him if that's what he wanted.

And it's that power that's the most terrifying thing of all.

"So good, darlin'. Fuck," he rasps against my swollen, spit-soaked lips. I stick my tongue out and taste the faintest traces of copper, and my dick twitches in my boxers.

"I felt that," he murmurs before swiping his tongue along my face.

"Oh," I gasp, back arching against the frame.

"You're fuckin' perfect," he growls in my face, and then, the next thing I know, he's shoving off me, leaving me cold and bereft. I shiver against the stark change in temperature as Static moves across the room. I try to reach out to him, but when my arms don't move, I grunt in frustration.

Damn ropes.

The lights are still flashing, distorting his every step, and with each blink, he's in a different spot in the room.

A foot in front of me, three feet away.

At the foot of the bed, right beside me.

My breathing picks up speed because with each passing

second, I never know where he's going to be. And I want to close my eyes, but it's almost more terrifying to do that...

But maybe I should.

I let my eyelids fall closed just as the heavy thud of Static's boot creaks across the old flooring.

"Too scared to look at me, little mouse?"

"No," I breathe. I can feel his breath right next to me. He smells of something dark and citrusy. It makes me shiver.

"Then open your fuckin' eyes."

I do.

And wish I didn't.

Because I see his axe—and it's being held suspended above my head.

The very same axe that tore through the door keeping me hidden from him—proving that nothing will keep us separated.

"Shit," I murmur at the sight of it. The old blood stains on the wood, the glint of the blade. Sharp and rusty, but I know it's strong enough to do damage. I've witnessed it.

"Scared?" he taunts, and I swallow.

"Yes."

"Good."

And then, he swings it down right beside my head, and I let out a blood curdling scream, but my eyes are locked open wide as the blade lodges itself in the wood beside my head. I think even some of my hair is caught beneath it because I can't move.

"Oh, now that's a pretty sight," Static murmurs, dragging his ungloved finger over where his blade is wedged.

I feel like I'm about to spew vomit.

"Hope you weren't too fond of your hair," he adds as an afterthought before yanking his axe back up and slinging it over his shoulder. I blink rapidly a few times, trying to process his words, before I shake my head.

I don't really care about much of anything besides this, at the moment.

I'm sure I'll care *later*. But right now, I just don't have the capacity.

"Always such a good boy for me, Madison," he purrs gently, and I shiver. "I wonder how else you can be good for me..."

"Wh-what do you w-want?" I ask, stuttering over the words, surprised I'm even able to make out the words.

He seems to think about it, painted eyebrows scrunching together for a minute before a wide smile breaks across his face, sharp teeth flashing in the light.

"I want you... *mmm,* yeah. I want you to taste me like I tasted you."

"Oh," I squeal, face flaming at the thought. "I-I have, I've never..."

"Oh, treat. Most people haven't done *this.*"

This? What is he talking about? My mind starts swirling at a million miles a minute as Static stands in front of me. He glances to the right before tossing his axe to the floor, and then, he starts undoing his pants—which are one half black with the other half black and white striped. He drags them over his thick, black boots that are laced up tight and covered in chunky buckles. His shirt, which he starts to unbutton next, is striped like half of his pants. And the more he exposes his stomach, the drier my mouth becomes.

"Like what you see, my treat?" he taunts me, and I flush from head to toe at being called out. But Static looks absolutely incredible. I've never seen someone who looks so good.

He's slim with the lightest ridges of abs across his midsection. His chest is narrow with a few scattered tattoos, and his nipples are small, but he has two spiked hoops through each one, and I swallow thinking about the needle that would have gone through such a sensitive area—how badly it must've hurt.

But the piercings match the rest of Static's. From the two in his lip, the spiky one in his nose, the stretched black ones in his earlobes.

Every part of him fits.

It's like he knows exactly who he is, and he has no shame in being that person.

And I... I admire that about him.

Static's briefs are black and tight around his muscular tattooed thighs, and the moment he hooks his fingers into the waistband and starts dragging them down said thighs, I choke on my own saliva.

I don't know what he wants from me, but I have a feeling that in this moment, I'll give him whatever he wants.

It's... different this time.

I *want* to be here.

I want this—just as much as he does.

I crave the freedom it brings, the resolution that settles deep in my bones when all is said and done. The fear, the trepidation, the overwhelming desire that burns through me hotter than flames—it all culminates into something so great that only *he* can give me.

Freedom from who I thought I was. Freedom to be who I really am, as messed up as I may be.

Because Static—*Cedrick*—doesn't care about how damaged I am. Because he's just as ruined.

Static's briefs slip past his half-hard dick, and I gasp at the sight of him in front of me.

He's circumcised and a lot longer than me, and I marvel at the sight.

"Keep lookin' at me like that, and I'm not gonna be able to do what I'm tryin' to do, treat."

I slowly lick my lips. I think I want to taste him—like he tasted me.

Is that something I can do?

"Fuck yeah, you can do that," he groans and grabs his balls, pulling them down. "But I'm gonna need you to stop for a minute because you're getting' me a little too excited right now."

I gulp. "Too excited?"

"I said I wanted you to taste me, darlin'."

"Y-yes," I quiver as I stare up at him before me, like an angel of darkness.

A beautiful temptation.

"But I never said *what* I wanted you to taste."

I blink up at Static, confusion swirling as I register his words and think back to what he said. *Taste me like I tasted you. If that doesn't mean...*

Oh...

Oh.

OH.

My face flushes and burns hot.

"Ah, my mouse figured it out, did he?" Static says as he kneels before me, dick slowly softening before my eyes. I gulp because now I know what he has planned, and I don't know if I'm ready for this.

This is...

This is gross, right?

Right?

I clearly didn't mean to urinate last time when I did. I was scared out of my mind, and it just... well, it just *happened*. And now... now Static is just going to... do it? On purpose?

"Oh, God," I moan, eyelids fluttering as the realization settles into my bones and my face tingles from the burn.

"Scared, darlin'?" he taunts me, and I let out a breathless huff.

"Y-yeah."

"Good. Now open wide for me."

And like the masochist I am, I close my eyes and open my mouth for the devilish clown before me.

"Fuck, I've been dyin' to do this since the first time I smelled you, treat," he groans, and then, I feel warmth splashing against my face. I gasp in shock and turn my head to the side, which allows Static's piss to hit my cheek and the side of my neck as it sprays down and gets in my hair, soaking into it and pooling onto the wood below me.

The faint smell of urine wafts around us, and I pant heavily, arching against my restraints as my stomach burns hot with... with something I've never felt before.

Something that's eating me alive.

Is this what fear smells like?

But what could Static possibly be afraid of?

"You have no idea, my treat," he answers my thought out loud, and I choke as his weakening stream trickles just inside my mouth before it cuts off and I'm left gasping, covered in piss, and my cock is harder than I think it's ever been.

That thought makes me gulp, swallowing the bitter liquid that's in my mouth without thought.

"Did you just... *Oh, fuck, darlin'.* You're absolutely perfect. *Fuck.*" A weight settles against my stomach, and then, Static's mouth is against mine, utterly devouring me.

He doesn't seem to care that I'm covered in his urine—that

I just *swallowed* some of it. No, he shoves his tongue deep inside my mouth, exploring and devouring every inch of me he can reach. And I'm putty in his hands.

I fall limp against the bed frame as I let Static take me apart, little by little, piece by piece, until there is nothing left of me but what connects me to him... and that just so happens to be so much now.

There's so much of me that is his, the lines are blurred and crossed, and I can't tell which way is up, but for the first time, I don't care because it just *feels* right, and that's all that matters.

I breathe out and let the static in my brain take over. It buzzes and vibrates my bones, making my dick twitch against Static's body where he rests heavily against me.

"You're so fucked up. You're my perfect little treat," he rasps against my throat.

"Static," I whimper, unable to say anything else. Because he's all there is.

"I've got you, darlin'. Just let go for me." He drags his finger down the length of my jaw to encircle my collared neck, and I fall into the abyss.

Chapter Twenty-Eight
Perfect Little Angel

Static

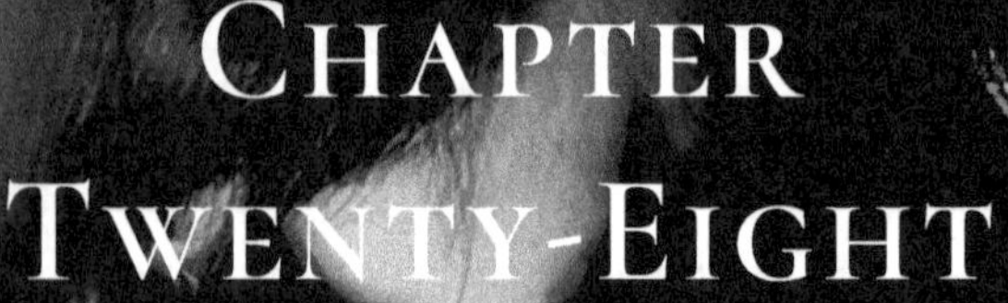

The sight of Madison taking my piss like a perfect boy instantly makes me harder than I've ever been in my life, and it makes me want so many more things with him, but I know we don't have all night.

We can't.

And some part of me fears this is the last night I'll have him—because we made a deal.

I tell him my truths, and I get Mayhem again.

We haven't talked about it, but I know this is the end of the line.

Madison won't want anything to do with me after this.

How could he?

I'm completely and utterly fucked up, and he sees all of me now.

He's handling me better than I ever could've imagined—even better than the first time—but I know this is a one-off.

How could anyone as perfect as him, as undamaged as him, ever want someone like me?

And don't get me wrong. I know Madison isn't *perfect.* I know he has his demons and a past, like the shit with his fuckin' parents and everythin' they put him through. But he's... he's *pure* in a way I never could be. In a way I don't deserve to experience.

And that's okay, I think.

As long as I have this, right now, I'll be okay.

"Static..." he breathes out, and I inhale deeply. He smells of me, and nothing has ever turned me on more.

"Darlin'," I purr. "You look absolutely delightful." And he does. His hair is soaked and disheveled, face bright red and glistening, eyes glassy and dazed.

Each distorted image brought forth makes my breathing a little harder.

"W-what..."

"I want to do so many things with you..." I tell him honestly as I tuck myself back in my briefs and stand from the bedframe. My heavy boots clunk on the wooden floor. "But what do you want?"

Madison's eyes drop downward, and I follow his gaze—to my boots. He licks his lips as he stares at them, and I raise a brow.

"You like my boots, darlin'?"

"*Mhm,*" he whines, and I let my head fall back with a groan. *Fuck, he's too good.*

I roll my head to the side, keeping my head cocked as I stare at Madison's limp form. "What do you want to do with them?"

"I-I don't... I don't kn-know..." he stutters, and it's so cute. He's still so pure and innocent, even after swallowing my piss.

What a prize.

I lift a brow as I rake my gaze over his body. I don't want to let him free, but if I did... I wonder if he'd run again or if his mind is too far gone.

"I'm gonna untie you now," I tell him as I reach for my axe and swing it down near his right arm. He screams at the impact of the blade against the wood, and then, the rope is severed. He doesn't move his arm for several seconds until I nudge him, then he jerks his arm to his chest and rubs where the rope is still attached at the wrist.

"Stay still," I warn him as I move down the bed and sever the ties to each ankle and his left arm. When he's finally free of his constraints, he slowly sits up, naked body glistening and dripping, and when I lick my lips, his flush spreads down his chest.

"You're free now, mouse."

"I—yes," he finally manages to say.

"What are you gonna do about it? You gonna run from me?"

I watch his throat roll with a distorted swallow. "I don't want to run anymore," he confesses softly, and I nearly swallow my tongue.

Does that mean...

"What do you want then?" My heart is beatin' frantically in my chest, the precipice of what comes next teetering on the edge.

He licks his lips, and his eyes drop down. I follow his gaze and smirk.

"What, treat?" And when he does nothing but swallow, I change tactics. "Come kiss my boots."

"W-what?" he balks, head jerking up with surprise.

"You heard me. Come. Kiss. My. Boots." I accentuate each

word as I point down at my feet, at the boots he keeps lookin' at.

They go half-way up my shin, laced tight with buckles secured down from top to bottom over the laces.

And I want to see Madison's mouth all fuckin' over 'em.

He shudders at the demand, but he slowly pulls himself up and crawls across the bedframe to where I have my foot up against the wood, so he doesn't have to get down onto the dirty floor—not that the bed is much better, but...

"What—" He clears his throat, and when he looks up at me through his lashes, I lose it. "What do I do?"

I reach into his wet hair and yank his head back, exposing his throat to my teeth as I lean down and sink them into his flesh. Madison lets out a yelp as I devour the skin of his throat, licking and tasting every inch of him that I can reach.

My collar gets in my way, and I'm most tempted to rip it off of him, but I barely manage to retrain myself with the memory of him touching it so reverently.

I settle for wrapping my fingers around until I can feel his pulse-point, and then, I pull back with a low growl and a final nip to his swollen bottom lip.

"I want you to do as I said."

He hesitates, but then, he slowly pulls away from my grip, eyes never straying from mine as he leans down before me and slowly puckers those fat lips to press them against the toe of my leather boot.

My jaw falls slack a bit. "Oh, fuck."

That seems to encourage Madison because he moves further up the leather, trailing a path of soft, featherlight kisses up the laces that travel my shin until he reaches the tie, and then, he stops and stares at me like he's waiting for more direction.

But fuck.

I just want him to let go.

I reach down and card my fingers through his hair. "Just do what feels right, darlin'. There are no rules."

"No rules?" he asks, brows twisting together in confusion.

"No rules," I parrot as I play with his wet hair, relishing in the fact that it's wet *with me.*

And that seems to confound him more than ever, but I just give him time.

He slowly wraps his arms around my legs and crawls a bit closer before lowering his head down to press a soft kiss against my bare knee cap.

I shiver at the soft, innocent touch, and then... then, I nearly black out because Madison crouches down and runs the flat of his tongue along the side of my boot and back up again —while never taking his eyes off mine.

My jaw falls open at the sight of the black of the leather glistening from his saliva.

The flashing of the lights makes every second glitch in the background, and I'm panting just from watching him.

"Madison," I groan as I tug on his hair. He pulls his head back slightly, tongue still sticking out, and I about come in my fuckin' pants. "Fuck, never mind. Don't do that."

"Why?" he asks innocently, and I huff a dry laugh.

"Darlin', you really are somethin' else, aren't ya?" I tuck a strand of hair behind his ear and trace the shell before cupping his jaw and tilting his head back. "You're fuckin' perfect."

He swallows. "I don't know what I'm doing," he confesses, and I smile.

"That's what makes you so perfect. You just *know.*"

His brows furrow. "I do?"

"You do," I confirm. "Keep going. Because if you keep

lookin' at me like that, I'm going to do unspeakable things to you."

Madison's mouth pops open slightly, and I notice the rise and fall of his chest. "W-what th-th-things?"

I narrow my eyes. "Don't tempt me, little mouse. You're not ready for that."

And that, for some reason, seems to piss him off. Madison drops low and... *oh, fuck. He's not...*

He is...

I stare with rapture as Madison *tongues* my boot, soaking it in his spit, laces, buckles and all, up and down, over and over, until the leather is glistening in the flashing of the lights.

I'm nothin' but a panting mess as he moves on to the other boot, his eyes either trained up on me or focused on his task at hand.

I've never been so hard in my fuckin' life. My cock is *burnin'*.

"Madison," I groan as I reach down to cup myself through my briefs. "You might wanna slow down—"

"No," he hisses as he continues his assault over my boots, and *fuck me. I never thought boot worship could turn me on like this.*

But here we are.

My little mouse is on his knees before me, utterly worshiping me, and I want nothing more than to do the same to him.

"Madison..."

"Shut *up, Static,*" he hisses, and I groan loudly, head tossed back in pleasure at his little feisty bite.

I love it when Madison strikes back, gives me that little edge of danger I know he's got in there somewhere.

It's fuckin' hot.

And I wanna devour him.

His tongue slides up from my boots to my shin, and I jolt at the sensation of his hot, wet tongue on my bare flesh.

"What—"

"Shh," he hums, and *fuck me, if this isn't a power switch.*

I'm not mad at it; I just didn't expect it.

I crack open an eyelid to watch my treat kiss his way up my legs, alternating between both as he works his way closer to my groin—and just as he reaches the edge of my briefs, I sense the trepidation there.

"You don't have to—"

"What happened to Static?" he snaps, and I blink with surprise at his tone. "You sound like Cedrick right now. And I don't want Cedrick. I want Static."

I blink a few times, and then, I reach down and wrap my fingers around the nape of his neck, digging deep into the muscle. "You want Static, treat? You've got it." And then, I yank his head forward into my groin until I know his nose is squished and all he can breathe is *me.*

"This what you want? I think the little brat in you just wants the control taken away. Is that it, darlin'? You don't wanna be in control anymore, do you?" I purr softly as I grind his face into me, softly humping against him. I pull him back and push my briefs down my legs to expose myself. My cock springs free, and Madison gasps when it smacks him in the face.

"Oh, don't act so surprised," I *tsk* him. "This is exactly what you wanted, my little brat. Now, lick it." I pull his head back and guide him toward the head of my cock, groaning when I feel the hot, wet slash of his tongue against my glans.

"That's it, darlin'. Now, open wide." And without waiting for him to get ready, I hook my thumb into the side of his mouth and stretch it wide before shoving myself inside him, into his hot, wet heat.

"Shit, that's it." I toss my head back with a groan the further I sink into his mouth. It doesn't take long for his gag reflex to kick in, but the tell-tale squeezing on my glans is euphoric, and I revel in it. "You're doin' so well," I praise him as I drag my thumb along his hollowed cheek, back and forth, before dragging it down to his stretched lips.

He garbles something, and I chuckle. "You know I can't understand you. But that's okay. You don't need to talk right now. You don't need to do anything except *feel*," I remind him as I graze his face and slowly thrust inside of him.

My cock is twitching the wetter his mouth gets. Saliva soaks my groin and drips between us, splashing onto my boots and the floor. "You're such a dirty boy, Madison, fuck. I didn't know you could suck cock like this." I stare down at him with rapture, utterly amazed at the way he's taking me.

He can only take half of me in his mouth without gagging, but that's better than I thought he'd be able to.

He just keeps surprising me at every turn, my sweet little prize.

"Perfect," I purr.

He moans, and the sound vibrates my cock, and I nearly spill down his throat.

I yank out of his mouth with a gasp. "Woah-oh, darlin'. Fuck."

He's on his knees, flushed and panting, and I've never seen a more perfect sight before me. "W-what..." He trips over his words, and I smirk.

"You're too good at that, darlin'. I was about to lose myself," I tell him honestly and earnestly.

"Oh," he squeaks, and I think if he wasn't already so flushed, he would be as red as he is now.

I drag my ungloved thumb down his hot, sweat-dampened cheek, smearing the wetness as I stare at him with a rapture that squeezes my heart in a way I've never felt before.

His vulnerability is shining through in a way I've never experienced. The way he's just on his knees before me, open-mouthed and willing to do something he's never done. Wanting and trying his hardest to make *me* feel good...

Turned on making me feel good...

My heart squeezes painfully in my chest at the thought of never having this again. Of this being *it*.

He's just fuckin' perfect.

"Where'd y-you go?" he asks, and I blink out of my reverie, disoriented as the room comes back into focus.

"Nowhere, treat. I'm right here," I tell him as I stare down at him, thumb rubbing the tears and sweat from the corner of his eye.

"Static..." he breathes, and I feel it. The shift in the room. The poignant moment of *this is it*.

And it hurts.

"Tell me, darlin'," I beg of him. I need him to say it because I can't take this from him. Anything but this.

"Please," is all he says, but for the first time, it's not good enough.

I squeeze my eyes shut as my cock twitches from the pleading sound. They roll back into my head. "I need more than that," I rasp, hating the desperation in my voice.

The tension in the room peaks.

And then, I feel movement against me.

Madison is standing on two shaky legs. His body slides against mine as he uses me to regain his balance. His clammy hands find respite on my biceps as he stands before me, but I can't bring myself to open my eyes. Not without knowing what's going to happen next.

He could reject me—which seems like the most probable option.

Who the fuck would want to fuck the psycho, obsessive clown?

Certainly not the perfect little angel...

"Static..." I feel his breath against my chest, and I shiver.

"Darlin'."

"I'm scared," he confesses, and I can't help but chuckle as his admission breaks some of the tension that has built between us. "What's funny?" he asks, sounding genuinely confused, and I shake my head, still laughing lightly.

"You, treat. You're just... perfect."

"I'm not," he argues, and I disagree, but I don't tell him that. I know he'll never agree, but that's okay. I'll tell him every day forever until it sticks in his skull that he is.

My lips brush the top of his head.

And then, I stop breathing.

Tell him...

Every day...

Forever...

Fuck...

Fuck.

I'm in deep. Way too deep.

This wasn't supposed to happen.

It wasn't supposed to be this way.

Madison was a release. The best release I'd ever had—but a release, nonetheless. And he's become so much more.

He fits with me like the sharpest jigsaw to my fucked-up edges, and I never thought someone like that could exist.

But there's only one problem.

He...

I don't think he feels the same way.

How could he when he's utterly terrified of someone—*something*—that's a part of me?

Static is who I am, partially. He's who I get to be when I need a release of everything that's going on in my life. He's the perfect outlet—and a healthy one at that.

I know I could've chosen a million different things because of the way Kase and I grew up, but when the carnival job fell into our hands, it kind of just played out this way. Fate or whatever you want to call it.

I have no regrets because I wouldn't be where I am. I wouldn't be as... *healthy....* As I am right now without Mayhem and the people that I work with, but Madison...

Fuck.

Madison has made me realize there's more to life than just scarin', partyin', and fuckin'.

I want more.

And I want him.

But not if he doesn't want me, too.

I can't take his free will from him.

Not this time.

"Madison," I breathe against him, nearly choking on the words. They burn as they come out, and I hate the sting in my eyes.

What the hell is wrong with me?

"What do you want?"

His bottom lip is trembling as he stares up at me, the white light flashing. "What do you mean?"

"Tell me," I demand, grabbing the hair at the back of his head to tilt it back. "Tell me what you want from me."

And in the span of ten seconds, I see it all flash before his eyes.

Worry, angst, fear. Indignation and resolve, before he finally settles on something close to determination if the hard set of his mouth is anything to go by.

I want to kiss it.

"I want you to take it all."

Chapter Twenty-Nine

Yes

Madison

I'm lost in the depth of Static's ghostly white eyes, and for the first time since I walked into Mayhem, I wish I was looking at Cedrick.

But this is good.

This is still him.

It's just... different.

"Madison..." he rasps, and I know in this moment, it's not Static speaking to me but Cedrick, and my heart squeezes in my chest.

Do I want this?

I pull back slightly to stare at the terrifying man before me, painted in black and white, teeth sharp and eyes white, and I think, *yeah. Yeah, why the hell not?*

"Static," I breathe in return because as much as I need this, I need the separation. I know Static and Cedrick are one in the same, but when we're here—at Mayhem Motel—it's easier to pretend they're not, and that I'm not giving all of myself away. Just... just this one part.

I swallow thickly and close my eyes to prepare myself for what's to come.

I want this.

I do.

"Do what you do best, *Static,*" I taunt him. I don't need or want control right now. I need Static to take it all, and I need him to make me mindless—just like last time.

He's given me too much choice—because too much has changed between us—and I need to go back to our roots.

He growls low in his chest, and then, his hands are on me.

I gasp as one gloved hand rakes down my back, surely leaving a red nail trail in its wake. I arch into the touch, eyes rolling back as my skin burns. Static's bare hand grabs the front of my throat and clamps tight, stealing nearly all my breath until I'm only able to wheeze in a slight whistle.

He tilts my head back, exposing my throat, making it even harder to breathe. I fight against the constriction, which just makes him laugh.

"That's right, little mouse. Keep struggling. Let's see how far you get." His voice is low and deep and sends goosebumps scattering across my whole body. I wrack with shivers down to my toes.

It's his words, those taunting words, that send my fight or flight into overdrive. I start struggling against his hold on me, using every ounce of strength I have to buck and throw my head back, swinging my body this way and that, but Static holds tight and simply *laughs.*

"You're so cute when you're trying," he teases, and that makes me flush with indignation.

"Fuck you," I snap, and then, I balk because I have never said that a day in my life.

"*Ohh, whooo.* Now, that's more like it, darlin'. Damn." He reaches down and adjusts himself in his briefs. "That just made my cock twitch."

"You've g-got issues." I swallow through the heat in my face that's burning its way down my throat.

"Oh, we already knew that, didn't we? But what we didn't know is that *you* have such a dirty little mouth for such a good boy. C'mon, *Madi*," he taunts, dropping his face low to mine and dragging the flat of his tongue along my cheek. "Let me hear more."

"What makes you think I want to?"

"Because it makes you feel powerful," he rasps into my ear, and I gasp.

He's right.

It does.

Shit.

Shitshitshit.

"I don't h-have to listen t-to you." I pull my bottom lip between my teeth and sink them into it. I regret the words as soon as I say them, but it's too late to take them back.

Static just smiles, like he was expecting that. "You're such a treat," is all he says, and then, he places a soft kiss to the tip of my nose that throws me off balance. And then, the next thing I know, I'm being shoved backward.

I fall onto the bedframe and land with a jarring thud against the wood. I let out a dull groan and try to roll to the side, but Static climbs on top of me and pins me in place with his body.

"Where do you think you're goin'?"

"Uh, um—" I stutter. I feel so hot all over, I'm burning *up*.

Static's on top of me. I can feel every inch of him pressed against every inch of me. His leather boots against my legs, the coolness of the buckles against my skin. It's dizzying.

"You're mine for the night, darlin', and you're stayin' right here," he drawls, and my body wracks with a shiver. Because, *yes*, I think I want that, too.

This is it.

I've gone insane.

But who better a person to lose my sanity with than Static the clown?

"Yes," I breathe my concession, and Static gasps.

"Fuck, you're too good for me." And then, his mouth is on mine and all I taste, breathe, smell is him as he attacks me with his tongue. It's hot and wet and persistent as it plunders my mouth, licking every inch it can reach.

I'm pliant against him, breath unsteady and shaky as his sharp teeth sink into the skin of my lip. I hiss, back arching, which makes more of our skin touch, and it's *electrifying*.

"Open for me, my treat. Give me more," he says against my mouth, and I don't know what he's asking for, but when his fingers enter my mouth, I open as wide as I can and suck the digits hard. "Fuck, darlin', that's it. Just like that. Get 'em nice and wet." I lave my tongue around his bare fingers, tasting the faintest traces of salt as I suck it off his fingers.

My mind lulls into a dull buzz that slowly gets louder the longer our eyes remain connected in the flashing darkness to light.

"Time to let go, treat, and see what comes next," he tells me softly, and I release his fingers with a wet *pop*.

His hand disappears from sight, but I feel the warmth as it moves down my body, and I know where it's going, but I don't tense.

I'm not scared.

I want this.

I want him and all his fucked-up craziness.

I want this before it's too late.

When wet fingers slip beneath the edge of my boxers, I can't help but gasp.

"Nervous, darlin'?" he asks, and it sounds like he's being sarcastic, but I know he's being serious. I stare into his eyes and note his pinched brows and curled in lips.

"No," I tell him honestly, not a single stutter in sight. I've never felt surer about a decision in my life.

Not even leaving my parents.

I need this—*him.*

"Good," he praises, and then, his wet fingers are between my cheeks and rubbing against my hole. I gasp at the sensation, having never been touched there before, and it's so foreign. I didn't know what to expect, but this...

"Oh..." I breathe out as I let the tension melt from my body while Static rubs softly but intently against me.

"You like that, darlin'?" he asks, and I nod as I bite my lip. "*Mhm.*"

His eyes are dancing, and it makes me feel hot. "What about this?" he asks softly, and one finger probes against my hole and slowly pushes inside. I gasp at the sensation. It's tight and weird, and I clench against it. "Relax. Just breathe, and let me in." He leans forward and kisses my forehead, but he doesn't pull his finger out as I twitch around it, and I'm thankful.

It stings just a bit, but the longer he waits, the easier it becomes to get used to.

This isn't so bad...

I breathe out, and when I do, his finger slides further

inside. I gasp wordlessly when I feel his knuckles bump against me, and Static drops his head against mine, panting himself.

"Fuck, you took my whole finger just like that, darlin'. Goddamn, you're perfect. Look at you."

I can't speak. All I can do is stare into the whites of his eyes, and while I love what I see, I also wish I could see green at the same time.

He starts to move his finger, and the feeling is incredible. He slowly pulls it in and out of me in small motions, just getting me used to it, I think, but whatever he's doing is making my face prickle with heat and my dick twitch against my belly where it's trapped in my boxers.

"Oh, you like that, don't you?" he teases me, and he starts to move a little faster, fucking me a little harder until soft little grunts are spilling from my lips and I'm arching my back to get as close to the sensation as I can.

"You think you can take more?" he asks, slowing his hand, and I blink through the daze.

"More?"

He chuckles. "Never mind. You just enjoy your bliss." He pulls his finger out of me, and I whine at the loss. I hate it. But then, he spits on his hand, and I flush hotly because that's... well, that's just...

But then, I feel the wetness back where I want it, and I suddenly don't care because I feel the tell-tale pressure, and I know what to do this time.

I breathe out like I did before, and my muscles just relax and let him inside, way easier than before. There's no sting, only a fullness that makes me groan. My back arches, and all I can hear is our mutual panting.

"You're so fuckin' tight, Madison, fuck. You've never let anyone in before, have you?"

It takes me a minute to register his words, but when I do, I shake my head.

"You're mine," he growls, fucking me harder with his hand, and I whimper when I feel the press of another finger against my full hole. "Mine."

"Yours," I gasp loudly as a third finger enters with a bit of a sting, but it feels so good, I don't mind a bit of pain. Static rotates his hand and spreads his fingers, and I can feel my muscles...

I flush hotly down my face and neck and throughout my chest.

I can feel my muscles *stretching*.

"You're beautiful when you blush," he tells me reverently, voice in a bit of a daze as he trails his mouth all over my face and my chest, and my heart stops beating in that moment as I stare up at him, full of shameful embarrassment, and he thinks I'm *beautiful*.

He stares down at me with glassy, dilated eyes, fixated on my face. Not my body or what he's doing to me, but on my face and how I'm looking at him.

Oh.

Oh, no.

My stomach flips just as my heart kickstarts all over again.

Is this...

Do I?...

Could this be?...

I love my stalker.

Holy shit.

I think I love my stalker.

And I think he might love me, too.

This...

This isn't good.

No.

This was not part of the deal.

The deal was no lies for one night at Mayhem.

Feelings weren't included...

I didn't anticipate this...

Tears sting my eyes as the realization sets in.

How could I let this happen? I didn't want to.

I don't think I want to, but how can I deny how good this feels... how good he makes me feel? Especially right now when he's taking care of me, being gentle and reverent and... and lovely.

Everything Static is not but possibly everything Cedrick is.

"Shit," I murmur by accident, and that pulls Cedrick back into the moment.

"What's wrong?" he asks, painted brows pulling together. "Did I hurt you?"

I swallow and shake my head to clear the thoughts. Realizations are for later. Right now, this is what I want. I want this with Cedrick—Static—at Mayhem. The beginning of the end and the end of the beginning all wrapped up together.

This is how it was always meant to be, and I want it this way.

"No."

"What's that look for?"

I swallow thickly as I stare into his white eyes. No painful truths right now. Just physical ones.

I slowly let out a breath as I let a calm wash over me. "I want you to fuck me."

"Oh, Jesus fuck, Madison." Cedrick groans loudly as he drops his face into my neck.

When I feel the wetness of his tongue, I decide to beg.

"Please."

And his answering intake of breath is how I know I've got him.

"Fuck, darlin'. You're killin' me."

I smirk against his shoulder, feeling a fresh wave of confidence I've never felt before. It's new and strange, but I revel in it because I don't know how long it will last.

I stick out my tongue and let the wetness slide across the salty slope of Cedrick's neck. He gasps and buries his face deeper, panting heavily before pulling back sharply, and I'm left cold as he moves his body off me.

I watch in fascination as he rips the sharp fake teeth from his real ones and tosses them to the side without a care in the world, and then, he's ripping my boxers down my legs and spreading them wide before him. I've only been so exposed once before, but it still makes me hotter than ever before—especially when he puts his face right into my groin.

"Oh!"

His mouth licks up my dick to suck it into his mouth for a few long, hard pulls, but then, he pulls off and moves down to my balls, licking at them and then moving further down to where he just had his fingers.

I tense from head to toe, every muscle locking tight. "Ced—"

"Shh, shh," he purrs, the sound vibrating against my skin. "Just relax. You'll love this." And then, he's shoving his face between my cheeks, and I feel his hot, wet tongue against my hole.

I gasp loudly, body bowing.

"*Mmm*," he moans, and the vibration is *insane*.

I'm lost in the sensation of hot and wet as Cedrick... oh... oh, God, he's... he's *eating me.*

I should feel embarrassed about that, and maybe I do, but right now, I don't care because it's so good.

This is so good, and I don't know why I've never done this before.

Heat curls at the base of my spine and my eyes roll back. I reach for my dick, but my hand gets smacked away. "Wha—"

"No," Cedrick says as he pulls away with a smack. "Not yet."

His denial makes me want to cry, and I feel the tears building until he says, "I want you to come on my cock, darlin'."

"Oh," I squeak, face turning red.

"You want that?" he smirks.

"Y-y-yes," I stutter, then gulp.

"Good. I want you to ride me, Madison. I wanna see what you can do with that body of yours."

I blink rapidly at him. I have no idea what that means, but when he flips us over so I'm on top of his cock—with it resting between my cheeks, my face gets even warmer, and I suddenly feel as shy as I've always been.

"Don't get nervous on me now, treat. C'mon." He wraps his large hands around my hips and moves my hips back and forth over his cock, rubbing it back and forth between my cheeks. The sensation is surreal, and I toss my head back with a groan.

"See, isn't that so good? Now, imagine that inside you, darlin'," he taunts me as he continues to work me over the length of his dick, and I get so worked up, my own cock is bouncing hard between us. I reach for it, mindless to the plea-sure, only to get denied once again.

"Ugh!"

"Put me inside you," he demands, and I'm so gone, I don't

think twice. I spit in my hand a couple times and swipe it through my crack to wet myself while Cedrick does the same to his dick.

By the time we're both dripping and slippery, I'm nearly blind from how hazy my vision has gotten.

"Lift up on your foot. Good boy, just like that." He tells me what to do as he holds the base of his cock straight so I can slowly sink down on it. I'm shaking from where I stay suspended above, but the second I feel the burning stretch, I groan so loud, I'm immediately glad there are no neighbors here.

"Holy shit," I pant.

"That's it, darlin'. You're doin' so well. Fuck."

I sink down another couple inches and hiss and roll my neck.

"C'mon, treat. You're almost there. Just a little further."

"So... full..." I groan, and with a final deep breath, I drop the rest of the way down, unable to hold myself suspended anymore. My body was screaming and aching for relief. Cedrick bows from the impact, and I shout.

His arms wrap around my waist, fingers finding the base of my spine as he holds on tight. "Shit, darlin'. That was fast."

"C-couldn't hold it." I clench my muscles, and my eyes shoot open wide. "*Oh.*"

Cedrick curls inward, clutching me tightly. "You're gonna make this over much sooner than you'd like, you keep doin' shit like that." He looks like he's in pain, face tense and sweaty. I run my finger down his cheek.

"Are you okay?" I ask.

He laughs. "Yeah, darlin'. Just tryin' not to come."

"Oh." I blink a few times. "Right."

"You're too good."

"Sorry..." I swallow sheepishly.

"Don't be. Just do what feels good," he tells me with a soft smile that, even with the face paint of Static, is so reminiscent of Cedrick, it makes me fall that much harder.

I close my eyes and let my head fall back as I roll my hips against him. I feel his dick move inside me, and it takes up so much room, I don't even know how it fits, but it does, like it belongs there, and it's so *good*.

I get lost in the rolling movement of our bodies. Sweat dripping and clinging, lingering kisses stolen between each panting breath shared in the hot, flashing space between us. Cedrick lifts up, and I wrap my arms around his neck, clinging to him.

Our sweaty bodies stick together as we ride one another closer to the edge.

"Oh, God, I-I'm—I'm close," I stutter, and Cedrick chuckles darkly.

"Me, too, darlin'. Let me feel you. Give me your cum, Madison."

"Holy s-shit!" I scream when the fire bursts through the dam, and I throw myself backward into Cedrick's awaiting arms. He catches me as my cock spurts my release between us, splattering it on our stomachs.

"Darlinnnn'," Cedrick groans as he holds me tight against him, and I feel his dick pulse as he floods me with warmth, and I flush from head to toe at the realization that he's *coming inside me.*

By the time we're finished, leaning against each other and panting, my thoughts come swirling back at a million miles a minute—in the sound of my mother's voice.

Abomination.

Sodimite.

Wrongwrongwrong.

I shake my head to try to clear them, but her voice echoes.

I just had sex.

With a man.

I nod. *And that's okay...*

I blink through the sting in my eyes.

But what if it's not?

Oh, God. Is it wrong? Am I going to go to hell? Do I even believe in this? I don't think so, but what if it's true, whether I believe in it or not?

Shit.

Shitshitshit.

I'm freaking out, and I know I'm freaking out, but I don't know what to do.

I feel the tears stinging my eyes and try as I might to keep them from escaping, I blink, and they fall. They splash, hot and wet and shameful, against Cedrick's shoulder.

He pulls back with a frown, his paint smeared from what we did. "Madison?..." he asks, sounding so concerned, it breaks my heart.

I swallow. I don't know how to explain this.

I... I can't.

"I've gotta go," I rasp and pull away from him with a wince. I feel the hot, wet trickle of cum escape from my body, but I don't allow myself to think about it as I scramble off Cedrick's lap.

The light is disorienting as I try to find my clothes, but I manage somehow and pull them on. All the while he sits there, naked, staring at me with wide, white eyes.

"Darlin', what's goin' on?"

"I—" I stop, unsure of what to say. I can't tell him I'm having an internal freak out that has nothing to do with him and everything to do with my shitty parents and my shitty past. I take one last look at him. "I'm sorry." And then, I turn on my heels and disappear out the door.

I stumble my way down the hall, trying to remember the way I came. Every damn hallway looks the same, especially with these lights flashing and disorienting me, but after what feels like forever, I eventually find a door that leads me to the outside.

I suck in a breath of fresh air for the first time in what feels like forever as I stumble toward my car and yank open the door. My hands are shaking as I drop into the seat and start it, shivering as the coolness of the night settles in over my sweat-dampened skin.

I pull my phone out to pull up a map to go home when I hear the creak of a door and when I look up, I see him.

Cedrick.

Static.

He's standing at the entrance of Mayhem Motel, just staring at me where I sit in my car. Arms at his side, eyes locked on me.

Swallowing thickly, I drop my phone into the seat and pull out of the gravel lot, leaving him behind without a backwards glance.

"I'm so sorry, Cedrick," I tell him with tears in my eyes as I drive away from him and everything we became tonight. "I don't know what's wrong with me, and I don't know how to fix it... If I even can." The distance between us grows as my heart pounds harder and harder. It hurts more than I thought it would, but I didn't know what else to do.

I can't be honest about this, but I couldn't lie to him because he hasn't lied to me...

Chapter Thirty

What Friends Are For

Madison

The drive home is a blur of trees and painted, glowing lines from my headlights.

I blink through the tears stinging my eyes, but it only causes more to fall, distorting my vision worse than the strobe lights.

What is wrong with me? Why am I thinking like this?

I don't believe in those things, and I know I don't, but I can't get my mother's voice out of my head, telling me I'm *wrong* for who I am. And I hate it.

I hate it all, and it's poisoning me.

This isn't how it was supposed to go.

Mayhem was supposed to be a final release.

And it was. It was full of revitalization and understandings.

I realized I love Cedrick... I mean, how could I not? The crazy man has been obsessed with me—*me*—since we met. He knows me. He's heard of my past and what I deal with, and it didn't scare him away...

But I ran. Because I scared myself.

These feelings are too big for me to bear alone, and I can't... I can't understand them.

I need help.

I need—*no.* I cut the thought off as soon as it comes. Pastor Laurence will not help me. He'll only confuse me more, and I know that.

No. What I need are people who understand. Someone to talk to.

Someone who cares.

And they don't—and never will.

By the time I'm pulling up to the house, it's just past eleven at night, and my body sags with exhaustion even worse than the first time I was at Mayhem. I put the car into park and drop my head against the steering wheel as I let the tears fall freely for the first time since I left.

The sobs wrack me as the thoughts swarm—and I let them.

I let myself feel it all because I have to.

There's no other way.

I've sinned. What I've done goes against God, and it's wrong. I'm a terrible person for loving a man. For wanting a man this way.

No, I'm not. There's nothing wrong with love. Love is the purest thing of all, and how could something like that be wrong?

You were told it's wrong. In the Bible, it says it's wrong.

In the Bible, it says you can't even eat certain foods, or if you steal something, you could get your damn hand cut off. It's not practical. This is the twenty-first century.

But why do so many people believe it if it's so strict and ridiculous? Do they just pick and choose what rules to follow? Because it seems to me, that's what they do.

They just choose to eat what they want. They choose to cheat on their spouses. They choose to hate queer people.

It's not fair.

Someone shouldn't be hated for who they are—for who they love.

How is that wrong?

A knock sounds against my window, and I jerk back with a gasp to find Kane standing out in the cold in only his pajama pants and a t-shirt.

I roll down the window. "What are you doing?" I croak.

"You've been out here for a while, and I thought something might be wrong," he says easily, but I see the tension in his eyes. "Looks like I was right."

I stare up at Kane, a denial on my tongue, but what's the point? I'm a damn mess, and I know it.

"Yeah," I breathe the truth, and Kane gives me a sad smile.

"C'mon, buddy. Let's get you inside so we can talk." He watches me roll up the window before I turn the car off and step out, shivering as the cool autumn air washes over my bare skin. I walk beside Kane to the house. The tension is thick between us, but I find I don't mind it much.

"Madison..." he trails off as we trudge up the stairs. He reaches for the door and holds it open for me.

"Thanks," I say as I walk through. "What?"

"Can I ask you something?" he says, and his nose is wrinkled slightly as he looks at me. I don't sense any judgement, but the moment I notice his facial expression—confusion and slight aversion, I remember. And my face burns hot because I know I smell of Cedrick's urine.

"Oh," I squeak, choking on spit as it flies into the back of my throat. "I'm sorry," I mutter, feeling shame—not for the first time.

"No. Madison, *no*," he reiterates with a hand on my shoulder. "You have nothing to be sorry for. I just want to make sure you're... well. Not okay, but okay, if you know what I mean."

I blink at him a few times, confused, before his words sink in. "Oh. T-thanks. I'm... fine."

He gives me a small smile with tired eyes. "Why don't you go get a nice, long, warm shower and meet me in my room. We'll hang out, watch a movie, talk, whatever you want to do. But I don't think you should be alone. How does that sound?" he asks, and I... yep.

I'm gonna cry.

I turn my back on him as the tears make their way back and splash down my face in hot streaks. I'm ashamed of my fear, of my own shame. Of the guilt I feel. For feeling any of this at all when I *know* it's not wrong.

"Okay," I finally manage. And then, I start the trek up the stairs, leaving Kane where he stands.

My shower is long and full of white noise as my ears ring and buzz with thoughts and voices warring with one another. Back and forth. And just when I think the logical side is winning, I turn, feel my ass twinge, and then, my mother's voice is back, screaming at me.

I hate that I hear her at all.

She doesn't deserve to have space in my mind, but it seems I don't have a choice in the matter.

By the time I'm stepping out of the shower, my body is heavy with fatigue, and I barely make it to Kane's room before I'm falling onto his bed in a pile of limbs.

"Tired?" he asks fondly, and I nod, wet hair dragging against the blanket as I do. "Get some sleep, Madi. We'll talk tomorrow."

"You sure?" I ask, blinking heavily through the grogginess,

and I feel him nod from behind me. His body heat is warm, and I lean back into it, grateful I'm not alone.

I don't think I could stand to be alone right now.

"Sweet dreams," he says, and my eyes snap open for a few minutes of swirling thoughts before eventually, sleep takes its plunge.

I blink through the grogginess, feeling heavy in more ways than one—and that's when I realize Kane's arm is wrapped around my waist, not holding me tight but just holding me. And it's... nice.

I've never slept with someone like this before.

"So, do you want to tell me what happened?"

Anddd, there goes that.

I tense from head to toe, and Kane feels it because he tightens his arm around my waist.

"Look, you don't have to, but I think it might be good for you. And I'm here for you, Madison. As a friend, of course," he clarifies, then clears his throat.

I stare at the wall in front of me, and for some reason, with his touch but not his eyes, I find it easy to let the words fall from my lips.

Every thought I had last night in the car, on the way home and when I parked, spills from my lips in a sinful confession. One I never thought I'd make but one that feels necessary.

Kane doesn't say a word. He just listens as I cry over the hate I've experienced, the conflicting emotions I have—that aren't really that conflicting because I don't believe the hate; I just keep fucking *hearing it in my head.*

By the time I've explained my parents and their bullshit and what happened with Cedrick the previous night, I feel just as exhausted as I did before I went to sleep.

"Can I tell you something?" he says after a long while of mutual silence. His arm is still wrapped around me—he hasn't moved this entire time—and it's been at least an hour or so, and I've never been more grateful.

"Of course," I croak through a hoarse throat.

"You already know who you are, Mads. You know what hate is. You know you don't stand for it. It makes you sick to even think about, right?"

I swallow as I process his words, unsure where this is going. "R-right."

"So, maybe you just need to tell them."

I stop breathing for a few heavy beats of my heart. "What?" I ask, unsure I heard him right.

"I think maybe what you're hearing in your head is what you imagine your mother saying to you if you ever told her. Am I right?"

I swallow thickly as the tears burn. "Y-y-y-es."

"Do you think if you told them and heard what they really had to say, it would shatter that illusion? Maybe they'd be more accepting. Maybe they wouldn't. But at least you'd know, and your mind wouldn't have to make up scenarios."

"Oh... I never..." I blink rapidly a few times as I think about it. "I never thought about that."

"Just an idea..." he trails off, squeezing my waist, and I flush hotly but gratefully as I lean into his touch.

"No..." I nod a few times, feeling a sense of resolve settle in my bones. "It's actually a really good idea, Kane. Seriously, thank you. I'll think about it. And thank you for listening to me. It's... it's helped me more than you know."

"Of course, Mads. That's what friends are for." Kane drops his head down to rest against mine, and I close my eyes to breathe softly, just enjoying this moment of peace I feel with my friend.

And that's when I hear someone shout, followed by a bang. Then, there's more shouting. A closer bang that makes me jerk.

"What the—" The door to Kane's room flies open to reveal an absolutely *flaming* Cedrick.

He stands before us, face bare, chest heaving, dark green eyes alight and dancing with...

Oh.

Oh, no...

Oh, nonono.

"Cedrick—no!" I shout just before I'm gently pulled to the side with a grace I don't deserve, and then, I watch in abject horror as Cedrick's fist lands directly against Kane's jaw. The crack resounds, and I wince, jerking back from the impact that was so close.

"No!" I scream, lunging for Cedrick just as he goes to swing again, but Kane's already pushing from the bed, shoving him back and swinging his arm out to clock him in the face.

"What's your fucking problem?" Kane spits as they go back and forth, and all I can do is watch in horror as my friend and my... whatever he is, throw punch after punch. And I don't even know why.

"C'mon, that's enough!" Collin shouts as he runs into the room and wraps his arms around Cedrick. He growls furiously, managing to escape easily, but Lenny has grabbed Kane and is keeping him contained.

I run in front of Cedrick and plant my hands on his

chest, feeling the rapid chug of his heart against my palms. "Cedrick, stop." His eyes are wide and crazed, but when he feels my touch, they dart down to look at me, and then, they soften.

"Madison," he says, and I can't help but to give him a soft smile.

"Cedrick," I repeat.

"You didn't come home," is all he says, eyes dancing back and forth between mine, and it takes me a minute to realize that's why he's here.

He showed up and barged into my house because he couldn't see me in my room.

He didn't know I made it home safe.

He had no idea, and he's been worried this whole time.

"Shit..." I wince. "I'm so sorry... I didn't... I wasn't..."

His eyes narrow as he glares over at Kane. "Clearly."

I reach up to grab his face to direct his thoughts back toward me and away from my friend. "No, it wasn't like that, I swear. He... he was helping me figure stuff out."

"Why couldn't I?" he asks pleadingly, finger tracing the line of my cheekbone now that he's been released, and it breaks my heart.

I swallow thickly, but I can't blink away the tears. "I don't know..."

"I was worried."

"I know."

"I couldn't see you."

"I know."

"And when I couldn't see you..." he trails off, and I nod. Because I get it. I messed up. In more ways than one. And we need to talk. *Finally.*

I don't know if I'm exactly ready for it, but it needs to

happen because something like this... this misunderstanding, can't happen again.

To any of us.

I'm...

I'm ready now.

Maybe.

With him, I could be.

"Well, this is all fine and dandy, but what the fuck is going on?" Lenny blurts, and Kane bursts into laughter even though *he's* the one that got punched in the face.

"Everyone, meet Mads's boyfriend. Boyfriend, meet Lenny and Collin. We've already had the pleasure of meeting," he says with a bloody grin, and I wince, eyes darting toward Cedrick.

His eyes are still glowing, but he sticks his hand out for both of them to shake. "Sorry 'bout the misunderstanding. Needed to see Madison."

"So, you just barged in here?"

"Yes," he deadpans, and I giggle. It's really not funny, but I mean... c'mon...

"Well, let's give them some space. They've got loads of shit to work out," Kane says, and I wince, but Cedrick just nods his thanks as they all leave the room and close the door behind them.

Cedrick turns toward me and crosses his long arms over his chest. "I don't like this room," he says after a moment of blandly perusing it.

"I know."

"You were in bed with him."

"I know."

"But it wasn't..." he trails off, and I watch his throat bob with a swallow, and my heart constricts. I rush toward him, not thinking twice before wrapping my arms around him.

"No, of course not. He's just a friend, and he was there for me last night when I needed him. It was just comfort. He helped a lot, actually. And helped me see a lot of clarity."

Cedrick's arms tighten around my waist as he speaks into my hair. "Clarity?" he asks.

"Yeah. About... everything."

Cedrick breathes me in, and I let my eyes fall closed as I fall into him, allowing myself, for the first time, to really *feel*.

"Care to shed some light on me?"

I swallow thickly, already feeling the inevitable tears building up. "I'll tell you everything. But..."

"But what?" he asks, pulling away with a frown.

"But first, I think I need your help with something."

"You sure you wanna do this, darlin'?" Cedrick asks as we round the driveway, and I nod.

"I need to. It's a chapter I need to close. And... and you'll stay, right?"

"Of course, I will." He reaches across the console and squeezes my hand, and I immediately feel better.

"You know this could get pretty ugly, right?" I tell him, just to make sure he knows.

"I know, treat. It's all right. I'll be fine," he reassures me for the tenth time in the last hour.

"Okay... just making sure."

"Madison Thomas!" I hear my name screeched from the top of the stairs, and I wince. *Well, that didn't take long.*

"Ready?" Cedrick asks, completely ignoring my mother as

he stares into my blue eyes. And while we haven't talked fully yet —we have plenty of time for that—I have given him a lot about what happened that night at Mayhem and what I discussed with Kane. I had to tell him, so what we were doing here made sense.

And he's been so good, so understanding. And I know I don't deserve it. But I'm grateful to him, nonetheless.

"As I'll ever be," I mutter before squeezing his hand one last time and stepping out of the car. The autumn air is frigid this morning, and I shiver as it soaks through my thin hoodie, but I welcome the sting because it keeps me alert—and I need to be sharp for this conversation.

"Mother," I nod my head as Cedrick and I make our way up the stairs. The butler, Roman, stands by the door, and when I meet his gaze, he gives me the warmest smile that makes my own break out across my face.

"What are you doing back here? And who is... *this?*" she hisses the word with disgust. I chance a glance at Cedrick, and all he does is lift a brow.

"Where's Father?" I ask instead, ignoring her.

Her eyes narrow, annoyed with my rudeness. "In his office. Why?"

"I wish to speak to you both." I choke down the nerves.

She looks between us, eyes bouncing for approximately fifteen seconds before she concedes, probably out of sheer curiosity. "Fine. We'll talk in there." And then, she turns her back on us and expects us to follow.

"Thank you, Roman." I smile at him when he holds the door open.

"Mr. Payne," he returns with a small twitch of his lips, and it makes my heart pang. He's the only good one here.

The walk through the spacious halls is honestly pretentious, and I wince, but Cedrick doesn't seem to give a shit about any of it as he walks beside me, head held straight, eyes looking forward, never glancing around.

He doesn't care where I came from.

He only cares who I am now.

Fuck... I love him.

It nearly steals my breath away.

"Guess who showed up," Mother says as she pushes open the door to Father's office. He glances up from his desk, eyes widening when he sees me.

"About time you came home," he starts, but I cut him off with a hand in the air.

"I'm not home," I clarify to both of them. "I want to make that clear. I only came by to tell you both something." And that's when the nerves really hit. Because this is it.

There's no going back after this.

Remember, you don't want to go back.

I hear Cedrick's voice in my head from what he told me earlier in the car on the way up here, and it steels my resolve. I walk further into the room, feeling Cedrick take matching steps, until we're directly in front of my father's desk.

"What's going on, son?" he asks, eyes imploring, and it takes everything in me to say the words. To know I'm disappointing them but needing to do it anyway—for my own sanity and survival.

For us.

And for me.

"Mother, Father," I address them both, and when both sets of eyes are on me, I glance down, grab Cedrick's hand in mine, and entwine our fingers. They're strong against mine, and they hold me steady as I tremble. "I'm gay. And I just wanted you to know." I speak the words to the wall, unable to meet their gazes, but I've said them. They're out there.

I fucking did it.

It's silent for the length of four heartbeats, and then, my mother screeches, "What?!"

I wince but try to push through. "If you—"

"This is *wrong,* Madison! I knew you leaving was going to corrupt you! I just never imagined this! *This!*"

All the while she's spitting her fury, my father's face gets redder and redder. And I know we need to leave—before it's too late.

I squeeze Cedrick's hand, and when he reaches over and grips my chin to bring our eyes together, I nod minutely. *Yes. Take me away from here.*

Take me home.

"Get your hands *off* him, you, you—"

"Don't say it," I turn toward Mother and bite softly back at her. "Don't you *dare.*" And with those final words, hand in hand with Cedrick, I walk out of the room, out of that house, out of that life—for good.

The seat I'm sitting in is a comfort as Cedrick reaches for my hand and takes it in his, holding me as tight as I need.

"I'm so proud of you, darlin'," Cedrick says as he starts the drive back to Grosse Pointe.

I'm shaking, and I can't help it. My adrenaline is pumping hard, but the words are a comfort. A necessity I didn't know I needed until I heard them from his lips. "T-thank y-y-you," I hiccup through my sobs.

"Darlin'."

"*Hmm?*" I swallow thickly as I stare out of the slightly fogged over window.

"I love you."

My jaw falls slack, and tears burst from my eyes before I can stop them. The sobs are ugly and wracking and horrendous, but Cedrick doesn't seem to care because all he does is let me feel them.

He simply grabs my hand, presses a kiss to the back of it, and lets me feel my feelings.

I don't say the words back yet.

I can't.

Not until he knows all the truth, just like he told me.

But I think he knows I feel the same.

How could I not when this is who he is?

My clown.

My stalker.

My...

Chapter Thirty-One

You're Mine

Cedrick

I was losing my mind without Madison.

I waited for him, my eyes locked on the screen of my phone for him to show up in his room. But he never did. He never fuckin' did.

And that's when I knew something wasn't right.

So, I got my ass to Grosse Pointe, only to find my boy in bed with another man—and I lost my fucking mind.

Turns out, it wasn't what I thought at first—which, granted, what I thought at first was pretty bad—but I still don't feel great about it.

I don't like Kane.

And I tell Madison as much.

"I know… and I get why. But he's my friend. He's helped me so much."

I just grunt, irritated. I don't want to talk anymore. I want to kiss, lick, suck, and fuck my little treat until neither one of us can breathe, but he won't let me until we *clear the air,* or whatever the hell that means.

I want to roll my eyes and groan.

But I'm trying—for him.

"*Mhm,*" I murmur as I watch the way his pulse throbs in his throat, steady and thick. I want to bite it.

"Cedrick."

"*Mmm.*" What would happen if I were to puncture his skin there? Not deep, but just for a little taste of his blood...

"You're not even listening to me!" he accuses, slapping my arm, and I startle.

"Nope. I wasn't," I admit, eyes still trained on his neck.

He flushes, and the rush of blood only makes my dick harder.

"You're making this conversation very hard."

I look him up and down, cocking my head. "Am I?"

He blooms the prettiest pink. "Oh... no! Not like that!"

I arch a brow before looking down at his tented crotch. "You sure about that?"

He shoves his hands in his lap and bites his bottom lip. "*Anyway...* we're supposed to be talking."

"I'm done talkin', darlin'. I wanna fuck." I reach for him, and he lets me grab him and pull him against me.

"Shit," he hisses as I drag my tongue up the front of his throat, over the ridges of his Adam's apple.

"*Mmm,* isn't this so much better?" I tease him with small nips.

"*Yessss,*" he hisses, arching against me. But the moment I reach down to grab his thighs, he pulls back. "No, no. Wait."

"Okay." I pull back with a breath, separating us.

"I really want to talk first, Cedrick. Please."

And I've never been able to deny my treat a damn thing.

"Fine," I concede. "But then, I fuck you," I agree.

He flushes hotly. "If you still want to after…"

"Darlin'… you're the crazy one if you think anything you say could ever change my mind."

At that, Madison bursts into tears.

"Ah, shit, I'm sorry, darlin'." I reach for him and pull him back into my arms. He buries his face into my neck, soaking my shirt with his tears as he sobs, his body releasing all the stress and tension of the last couple of days.

And that's exactly what he needs—that release—in more ways than one.

I press a kiss to the top of his head, breathing in the scent of his shampoo. "You better never fuckin' leave me again." I voice my own vulnerability for the first time, needing him to know how badly it hurt to watch him walk away.

I can understand why he did, but that doesn't mean it didn't hurt.

"I know you've got shit to work on and work through, but you do it with me. Just like I'll do it with you. Because I understand you, darlin', better than most. And I want the chance to really understand this, too." I drag my fingers through his long, tangled strands, enjoying the way they entwine with my fingers.

Madison gulps. "I don't know what's wrong with me or why I'm feeling this way. Or…" he trails off for a minute before continuing. "I do. But I don't understand why it's still affecting me."

"Trauma doesn't just go away, darlin'. It's somethin' you'll have forever. Trust me, that's somethin' I do understand." When he doesn't respond, I reach down and pull his chin toward me, to force him to look me in the eye.

"You want me, yes?" I swallow, hoping I'm not wrong. *Needing* to not be wrong. "You want this?"

Madison nods, bottom lip trembling.

"Then, we'll figure it out together, and that's all there is to it. It's not all going to be fixed in a day, or a week, or even a month. It's a process, I think. But you're not running from me again, Madison," I tell him as I pinch his chin tightly. "I won't let you." I draw closer until our lips are grazing. "You're mine."

Madison gasps against me, opening wide, but he nods his concession because that's what he wants, too, and then, he presses his mouth to mine in a hot, all-consuming connection that I need more than the breath my lungs are screaming for.

It's surprisingly soft but demanding and full of every bit of the need he feels, and it drives me up the wall.

I devour him, turning him over until I'm pressing him into the mattress with my body. Madison groans loudly, and I encourage the loudness. I want him to make all the noise.

I want everybody to hear whose he is.

That makes me grin as I kiss my way down his neck, nipping and sucking at his skin.

"Oh, God," he breathes when I pull his shirt over his head and expose his torso to the cool air of his bedroom. I suck his nipple into my mouth, making him arch beautifully off the bed and right into my awaiting mouth.

"Fuckin' perfect," I growl as I make my way down his stomach, following the line of hair until I reach the waistband of his blue pajama pants. I pull them down his legs, along with his boxers, tossing them both on the floor and exposing his cock to my sight.

"Oh, fuck yes. You're lovely," I praise him as I crawl up to place kisses all around his groin before nipping softly at his cock.

He yelps, and I chuckle. "You like that?"

"You bit me!" he shouts, eyes wide as he stares at me in shock.

"But you're still hard..." I remind him with a pointed lick. "*Nughhhh.*"

"That's what I thought." And then, I take him the rest of the way into my mouth, swirling my tongue around his cockhead, soaking the glans, and slurping with every bob of my head. Madison groans and pants, clutching my head and mewling pathetically, and it's the best sound I've ever heard.

"Come here..." I feel a tap against my thigh, and I pull my head up with a slurp, confused.

"What?" I ask. And when I see the redness of his cheeks, I know it's something he's embarrassed to say.

I smile softly. "It's okay, darlin'. We can do anything you want."

"I want..." He swallows, and then, he meets my eyes and seems to steel himself, and I feel a flash of pride for my boy. "I want you on top," he confesses, and my eyes widen.

"Like... while I'm suckin' you?" I ask, a grin spreading across my face.

Madison turns red as a tomato, and I brush my fingers over his cheek to feel the heat. "You don't have to say it like that..."

"Darlin', you wanna sixty-nine with me, is that it?"

"Oh, geez, never mind," he says, throwing his hands up. I reach for them, bring them together, and kiss 'em.

"No. I want to. It'll be hot as fuck to fuck your face." My eyes dance as I rip my clothes off and toss them across the room without shame. Madison eyes my body with a hungry gaze, and it makes me feel alive.

"Ready, treat?"

He gulps. "Yes."

"Oh, you're going to regret sayin' that," I tell him with a cackle as I tackle him to the bed to kiss him.

The kiss turns hungrier by the second, and before I know it, I'm climbing on top of Madison, legs spread around his head, cock bobbing in front of his face. His breath is hot against me, and I know he's nervous because I can feel the tension in his body.

"Relax, darlin'." I rub his thighs as I pepper kisses up each one. "Shh, just relax." And then, I slowly suck his length back into my mouth. I keep my suction soft and gentle, enough to drive him insane but not enough to send him over the edge.

He's mewling and panting all over again, and then—"Oh, fuck, yesssss," I hiss when I feel the wet flash of his tongue against my cock. It's a quick dart—just a taste—and then, it's back for more. Hungrier. More insistent.

Desperate.

And I'm burning alive.

Before long, I'm thrusting into Madison's mouth, and he's humping up into mine. His cock lodges in my throat, and I swallow around it.

"Oh!" he shouts, and then, I'm swallowing for an entirely different reason. His cum is hot and wet as it spurts into the back of my throat, and I nearly choke on it because Madison doesn't stop thrusting—it's like he can't.

And it's so fucking hot.

"I'm gonna come, darlin'," I warn him, my own cock twitching with impending release.

"*Mmm,*" he hums, and the vibration sends me over the edge. I thrust down into his mouth, and Madison splutters. Cum spews out from between his lips, but I don't care. I can't stop as I fuck into his mouth, reveling in the perfect warmth that is *him.*

By the time my release is over, I'm dazed and buzzed, and I roll over onto my back, flipping around and pulling Madison with me. I turn to face him and then grin as I swipe cum from around his mouth where it leaked out.

"You're a mess, darlin'."

"I thought you liked messes. You seem very messy."

"*Mmm,* I do." I lean over and swipe my tongue over his mouth, cleaning him up before kissing him deeply.

THE NEXT FEW days pass in a blur of sex whenever Madison isn't in class.

I can't seem to keep my hands off him, and thankfully, he seems to be in the same boat.

"I know we've kinda been holed up in here the last couple of days, but I wanted to ask..."

"What's that?" I kiss his bruised neck.

"Do you want to meet my roommates? Like... officially?" he seems shy asking, and my heart squeezes in my chest.

"Do *you* want me to?"

"...Yes."

"'Kay, let's go." I pull away to get dressed, and Madison balks.

"Right now?"

"Why not?" I ask as I pull on my jeans.

"I don't know. I'm not prepared!"

"You were prepared enough to ask," I remind him with a smirk, and Madison frowns at me.

"Cedrick..."

"C'mon, treat. Introduce me to your friends."

He frowns, and it's so cute, I can't help but kiss the little dimples before pushing him out the door and down the stairs.

"Well, well, welcome to the land of the living!" Collin barks when we step into the living room.

"Y'all reek of sex," Lenny adds, and I watch in fascination as Madison blooms in red from head to toe. I lean down and press a kiss to the top of his head and tighten my arm around his waist.

"Madison wanted me to introduce myself—officially. I'm Cedrick, his boyfriend."

A chorus of whoops and hollers ring out, and I didn't think Madison could get any redder, but here he is.

"Awe, darlin'," I tease him as I feel the heat for a moment.

"Shut up," he hisses at everybody, but it comes out choked, and we all chuckle light-heartedly because we know he doesn't mean it. He's grinning at all of us, and when his eyes meet mine, I know this is good.

This is the way it's supposed to be.

We're almost there.

"WHAT IF THEY don't like me?"

"Kase will like you just fine, darlin'."

"But..."

"But nothin'," I reassure him as we walk inside the apartment.

This moment feels pivotal.

My best friend meeting... my boyfriend.

Oh, fuck.

"So, this is the elusive Madison," Kaser says as we walk into the living room, and Madison, of course, flushes from head to toe.

"H-h-hi," he stutters, and I smile softly at him.

"It's okay, darlin'. It's just Kase."

"Yeah, it's just Kase," they say as they push to their feet. They hold out their hand to Madison.

"It's nice to finally meet the boy that captured Ricky."

"Ricky?" he parrots, glancing up at me as he shakes Kase's hand. I glare at them, but they just grin right back.

"Oh, yeah. He didn't tell you about the nickname?"

"No..." Madison drawls, and Kase pulls him closer as he walks toward the couch.

"Oh, I've got stories for you, Madi. So, you know that Ricky and I grew up together, right? Well, you see, he's always been this fuckin' crazy, believe it or not..."

And as I watch my best friend make a spot for Madison on the couch right beside them like he's always belonged there, something inside me shifts. Something big.

Something painful.

Something that causes my breath to hitch and my hand to fly to my chest to press against the ache.

"Cedrick?" Madison calls out, and I open my eyes to find him staring at me with his wide-eyed, blue gaze, and I smile through the pain.

Pain I've never known before but looking at Madison... I now know what it means.

It's fear.

Of losing him. This. Us.

"I'm good, darlin'. Enjoy Kase's embarrassing stories of me," I tell him with a smile. "You want a drink?"

"Sure!" he chirps. "Thanks." And then, he turns back to Kaser like they've known each other forever, and I walk into the kitchen with this new ache I have to learn to live with.

I pull three pops out of the fridge and set them on the counter. I rub against my sternum as I blink away the sting in my eyes.

I never knew love and fear could be so deeply entwined.

EPILOGUE
I LOVE YOU

"**F**uck, darlin' that's it." I pant against him.

Madison rotates his hips faster, pressing harder against my painted face, and I know he's gonna be covered in it, and that makes me feel all the fuckin' hotter.

I press my tongue into his hole, breaching the tight ring, and he squeals, bucking his hips. I pin him in place, keeping him exactly where I want him as I fuck my tongue inside his tight little channel over and over, soaking him in my spit. It's smeared across my face, leaving traces of paint behind on Madison's skin, and I revel in the sight every time I pull away to catch my breath.

"Oh, God!" he screams out when I press two fingers inside and stretch them, readying him for my cock.

"Fuck, treat, you taste so fuckin' good," I growl against his skin before sneaking a quick bite of the supple flesh.

"*Nngh!*" His back bows, pushing his ass closer to my face, and I can't resist another taste.

I need more of him.

Always.

I slurp my tongue all over his hole until it's sloppy and dripping and Madison is crying pathetically above me.

"Perfect," I breathe as I drag him down my body to watch him ride my cock. I reach for the lube and lather my dick and watch in awe as he lines himself up. He slowly sinks down with a breathy moan, head rolling to the side as he slowly breathes in and out, taking me inch by fucking inch.

"So good," he moans, and I nearly come right then and there.

"Watch it, treat," I snap, tightening my hands on his waist as he finally seats himself against me.

He turns around and smirks at me before lifting his hips and smacking them back down. "Why?"

My back arches with a groan at the tight, hot slide of him. "Oh, you fuckin' brat."

He giggles, face flushed and beautiful, and I've never loved him more.

"Come here," I pull him off to place him under me, and I slowly enter him again. Madison spreads his legs wide to accommodate me, head tossed back on a moan as I roll my hips, searching for that spot inside him.

When I hit it, he arches, and his eyes fly open on a pant.

"There it is." I grin.

"Fuck."

"Oh, I love it when you talk dirty, darlin'." I squeeze his ass and thrust again. Madison moans and reaches for me. I let him yank me down and devour my mouth. His kiss is wet and sloppy and desperate, and I love every second of it.

"I fucking love you, Cedrick. I love you, okay? I love you." Tears leak from his eyes as he buries his face into my neck, and I stop the movement of my hips at his confession.

I mean... I thought he felt the same, but I didn't know for sure...

Fuck.

Fuck.

"I love you, darlin'," I return the sentiment with a soft kiss to his neck. "So fuckin' much."

He pulls back to stare up into my eyes, his glassy but shining with a love I always wanted to see reflected back at me.

"This means we're crazy right... 'cause this is pretty crazy. A stalker and his victim... in love..." But he smiles, and my heart fuckin' soars.

I kiss his chin. "We're pretty fuckin' crazy, treat."

The End.

Afterword

Ahh!!

I can't believe it's over!

These boys mean so much to me and their story was one that brought me so much joy to write. Cedrick was just so surprisingly sweet and loving, and he cares so much for Madi. He's been through some shit, but he only let it fuel him in the end. And Madi... he came so far from the family he grew up in, surrounded by hate and disgust.

If you've never known that, I love that for you so much.

But if you have, if you get it, I am sorry. I hope you made it out. I hope you've healed from it the best you can—just as Madison has. And while he has people to help him do it, just know, it's possible to do it alone. You are strong and beautiful just the way you are.

This story, while kind of a passionate horror stalker romance? Is that a thing? I don't know, but anyhoo, this story is something I never thought I would write. Not because of the content, or the characters, but because I didn't believe I was capable of writing this kind of love.

This crazy, obsessive, stalker-y, deeply passionate and sweet kinda love. But boy, was I wrong. Cedrick—and let's be real, Madison, too, definitely took over my brain and consumed me. I wrote this book so fast. They had so much to say and I loved every minute of it—as I hope you did, as well.

You might notice Phantom's book listed under Mayhem's Series for upcoming books—and yes, that is Kaser's book. I don't have a release date yet but just know it's coming soon!

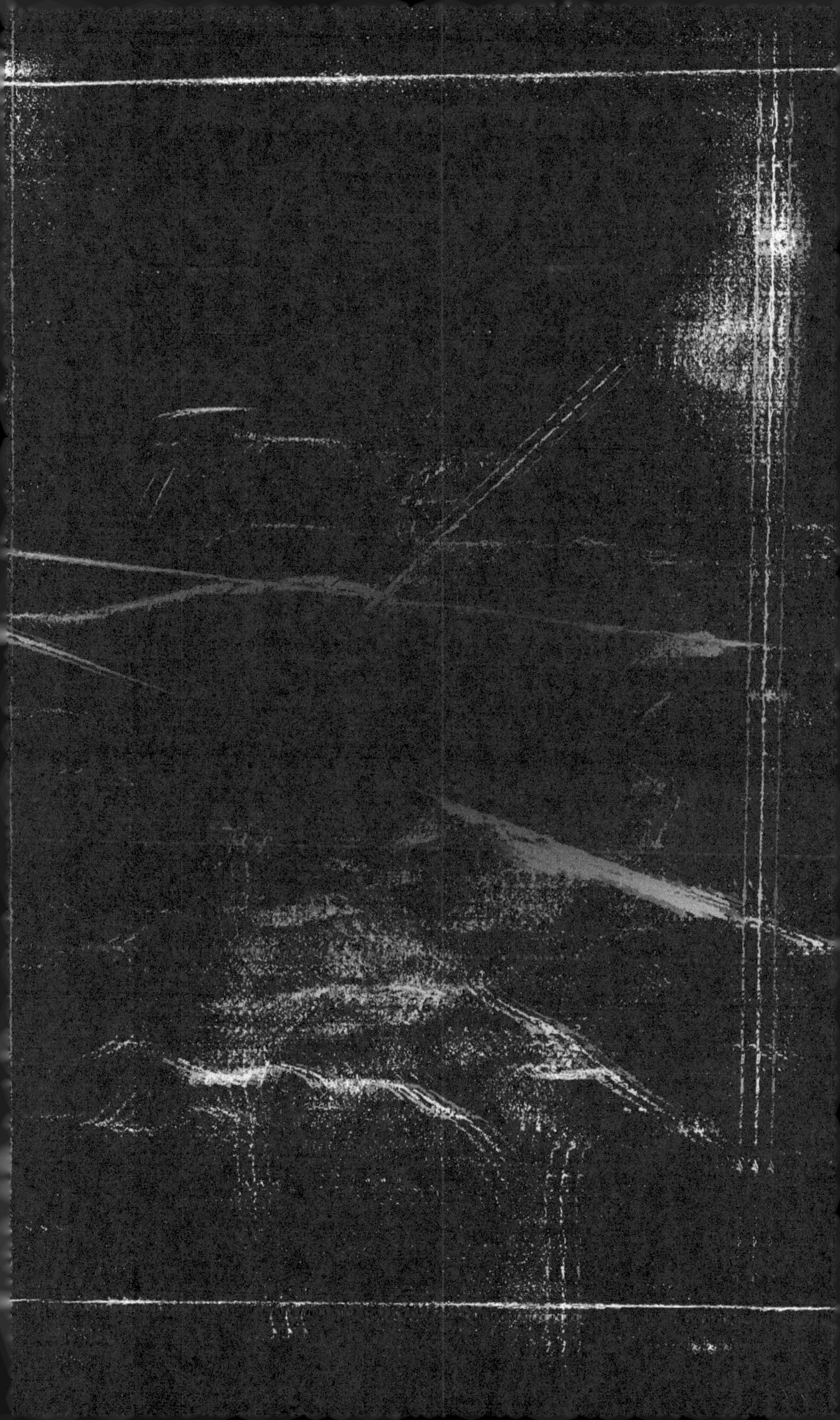

Acknowledgments

My husband for being my lifeline, always.

My son for being my biggest supporter.

Rae, I cannot thank you enough for not only reading my raw words and loving them, but for making this perfect fucking cover. You made it two years ago, back when I first wrote Static into existence. You took a chance on me, and I am so grateful you never gave up on me. Thank you for believing in me and working with me on this project. It's been a dream. I love you, endlessly.

Cait. Ugh. Fucking thank you. You saved my ass and I am so grateful for you. You are a bright light in my life, and I don't know what I would do without you. And thank you so much for this special edition hardcover. I couldn't love it more. You took my vision—and your own—and created something so perfectly beautiful for the boys and I'm just so grateful.

Bailey, always.

My betas for being the best, ever.

My street team because they fucking rock and are the best supporters. Seriously, I'm so lucky.

My editor, Tiff, who is such a badass. I adore you!

My lovely readers who I couldn't do this without! Thank you for supporting me always and loving the *literal* crazy shit that I write. It means so much. I hope you stick around for some more.

Books by Marie Ann

Standalones:

My Lovely Tragedy

Inevitable Destruction

Quiet Is the Night Now

Strangled

Abysmal

Fragmented Illusions

Capitulate (Coming Soon)

Amaranthine (Coming Soon)

Visceral Series:

Make Me Pretty: Visceral Vol One

Make Me Scream: Visceral Vol Two

Make Me Bleed: Visceral Vol Three

Mayhem Motel:

Static

Phantom (Coming Soon)

Poetry:

Skin&Bone

Mea Culpa

About the Author

Marie Ann is a writer of the weird and unorthodox who loves spending their free time reading fanfic and bingeing their favorite shows and movies.

If you liked what you read, stalk them!ツ

www.authormarieann.com

subscribepage.io/V53eQE

www.ingramcontent.com/pod-product-compliance
Lightning Source LLC
Chambersburg PA
CBHW071448140726
47997CB00005B/1634